LAST LIGHT OVER CAROLINA

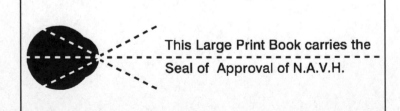

This Large Print Book carries the
Seal of Approval of N.A.V.H.

LAST LIGHT
OVER CAROLINA

MARY ALICE MONROE

THORNDIKE PRESS

A part of Gale, Cengage Learning

GALE
CENGAGE Learning·

Detroit • New York • San Francisco • New Haven, Conn • Waterville, Maine • London

GALE
CENGAGE Learning®

Copyright © 2009 by Mary Alice Kruesi.
Thorndike Press, a part of Gale, Cengage Learning.

Thorndike Press® Large Print Famous Authors.
The text of this Large Print edition is unabridged.
Other aspects of the book may vary from the original edition.
Set in 16 pt. Plantin.

LIBRARY OF CONGRESS CATALOGING-IN-PUBLICATION DATA

Monroe, Mary Alice.
 Last light over Carolina / by Mary Alice Monroe.
  p. cm. — (Thorndike Press large print famous authors)
 ISBN-13: 978-1-4104-4394-6 (hardcover)
 ISBN-10: 1-4104-4394-9 (hardcover)
 1. Shrimpers (Persons)—Fiction. 2. Shrimp fisheries—Fiction. 3. South Carolina—Fiction. 4. Large type books. I. Title.
 PS3563.O529L37 2012
 813'.54—dc23   2011039180

Published in 2012 by arrangement with Gallery Books, a division of Simon & Schuster, Inc.

Printed in the United States o
1 2 3 4 5 6 7 16 15 14 13 12

This book is dedicated to my brothers:
James, Gregory, Brendan, Vincent, John

ACKNOWLEDGMENTS

Thank you, Clay and Martha Cable, for inspiring me to enter the world of shrimping, for sharing stories, checking my facts, and introducing me to others in the field. Most of all, thanks for being the best neighbors and friends.

I can't thank James Cryns enough for his ideas, brainstorming, editing, and insights during the writing of this book.

There are shrimping communities all along the southeastern coast. Many people were helpful and I thank you all. I have made changes in the geography of these towns to fit the needs of my story and beg the towns' understanding. In particular:

In McClellanville, I owe a great debt to Georgia Tisdale. Her family history with the *Miss Georgia* was an inspiration for my heroine. Thanks also to her daughter, JoAnn, and to Captain Gardner McClellan (the *Miss Georgia*). Also in McClellanville, I want to thank Lucia Jaycocks, Billy Baldwin, Selden "Bud" Hill and his book *McClellanville and the St. James, Santee Parish,* and Rutledge Leland.

In Shem Creek, I'm eternally grateful to Tressy Magwood Mellinchamp and her book *East Cooper: A Maritime Heritage.* Tressy answered countless questions and opened the doors to Shem Creek, introducing me to her father, Captain Wayne Magwood (*Winds of Fortune*). Thanks also to Captain Rocky Magwood (the *Carolina*), Captain Donnie Brown (the *Miss Karen*), Captain Robert Schirmer, Jr. (aka the Hagg), Captain Warren "Bubba" Rector, Frank Blum, and Eddie Gordon.

In Beaufort, thanks to Hilda Gay Upton and the Gay shrimping family.

In Wadmalaw Island, thanks to Micah and Daniel LaRoche of Cherry Point Seafood.

I'm grateful to Jason Zwiker for sharing his valuable research on the shrimping industry and discussing the story in the early stages. Thanks also to Sally Murphy, Anton "Trey" Sedalik, Nina Bruhns, and Terri Ehlinger.

Every character and situation in this book is strictly fiction. However, I have given the names of John Dunnan and Judith Baker to two of my characters with their permission.

I also honored a few of the many captains I've met by dropping their names or their boats' names into the pages.

A heartfelt thanks to my editor, Lauren McKenna, for her continued faith in my work, and to Louise Burke. And to my agents, Kim Whalen and Robert Gottlieb, for their constant support. A special thanks to Jean Anne Rose in publicity and Marjory Wentworth for behind-the-scenes magic. My love and gratitude also go to Eileen and Bob Hutton and all at Brilliance Audio.

As always, I end with those who come first — my family. Thank you, Markus, Claire, John, Gretta, Zack, and our own jumbo shrimp, Jack.

What greater thing is there
for two human souls,
than to feel that they are joined for life —
to strengthen each other in all labor,
to rest on each other in all sorrow,
to minister to each other in all pain,
to be one with each other
in silent unspeakable memories. . . .
— George Eliot
Adam Bede

1

September 21, 2008, 4:00 a.m.
McClellanville, South Carolina

For three generations, the pull of the tides drew Morrison men to the sea. Attuned to the moon, they rose before first light to board wooden shrimp boats and head slowly out across black water, the heavy green nets poised like folded wings. Tales of the sea were whispered to them in their mothers' laps, they earned their sea legs as they learned to walk, and they labored on the boats soon after. Shrimping was all they knew or ever wanted to know. It was in their blood.

Bud Morrison opened his eyes and pushed back the thin cotton blanket. Shafts of gray light through the shutters cast a ragged pattern against the wall. He groaned and shifted his weight in an awkward swing to sit at the edge of his bed, head bent, feet on the floor. His was a seaman's body — hard-

13

weathered and scarred. He scratched his jaw, his head, his belly, a morning ritual, waking slowly in the leaden light. Then, with another sigh, he stiffly rose. His knees creaked louder than the bedsprings, and he winced at aches and pains so old he'd made peace with them. Standing, he could turn his bad knee to let it slip back into place with a small *pop*.

A salty wind whistled through the open window, fluttering the pale curtains. Bud walked across the wood floor to peer out at the sky. He scowled when he saw shadowy, fingerlike clouds clutching the moon in a hazy grip.

"Wind's blowin'."

Bud turned toward the voice. Carolina lay on her belly on their bed, her head to the side facing an open palm. Her eyes were still closed.

"Not too bad," he replied in a gravelly voice.

She stirred, raising her hand to swipe a lock of hair from her face. "I'll make your breakfast." She raised herself on her elbows, her voice resigned.

"Nah, you sleep."

His stomach rumbled, and he wondered if he was some kind of fool for not nudging his wife to get up and make him his usual breakfast of pork sausage and biscuits. Lord knew his father never gave his mother a day off from work. Or his kids, for that matter. Not during shrimping season. But he was not his father, and Carolina had a bad tooth that had kept her tossing and turning half the night. She didn't want to spend money they didn't have to see the dentist, but the pain was making her hell on wheels to live with, and in the end, she'd have to go anyway.

He'd urged her to go but she'd refused. It infuriated Bud that she wouldn't, because it pointed to his inability to provide basic services for his family. This tore him up inside, a feeling only another man would understand.

They'd had words about it the night before. He shook his head and let the curtain drop. Man, that woman could be stubborn. No, he thought, he'd rather have a little peace than prickly words this morning.

"I'm only going out for one haul," he told her. "Back by noon, latest."

"Be careful out there," she replied with a muffled yawn as she buried her face back into the pillows.

He stole a moment to stare at the ample curves of her body under the crumpled sheet. There was a time he'd crawl back into the scented warmth of the bed he'd shared with Carolina for more than thirty years. Even after all that time, there was something about the turn of her chin, the roundness of her shoulders, and the earthy, fulsome quality of her beauty that still caused his body to stir. Carolina's red hair was splayed out across the pillow, and in the darkness he couldn't see the slender streaks of gray that he knew distressed her. Carolina was not one for hair color or makeup, and Bud liked her natural, so the gray stayed. Lord knew his own hair was turning gray, he thought, running his hand over his scalp as he headed for the bathroom.

Bud took pride in being a clean man. His hands might be scraped, his fingernails broken and discolored, but they were scrubbed. Nothing fancy or scented. He tugged the gold band from his ring finger, then slipped it on a gold chain and fastened it around his neck. He didn't wear his ring on his hand on the boat, afraid it would get caught in the machinery. The cotton pants and shirt he slipped on were scrupulously laundered, but no matter what Carolina tried, she couldn't get rid of the stains. Or the stink of fish. This was the life they'd chosen.

16

As he brushed his teeth, he thought the face that stared back at him looked older than his fifty-seven years. A lifetime of salt and sea had navigated a deep course across his weathered face. Long lines from the eyes down to his jaw told tales of hard hours under a brutal sun. A quick smile brightened his eyes like sunshine on blue water. Carolina always told him she loved the sweet smell of shrimp on his body. It had taken her years to get used to it, but in time she'd said it made her feel safe. He spat out the toothpaste and wiped his smile with the towel. What a woman his Carolina was. God help him, he still loved her, he thought, tossing the towel in the hamper and cutting off the light.

Carolina's face was dusky in the moonlight. He walked to the bedside and bent to kiss her cheek good-bye, then paused, held in check by the stirring of an old resentment. The distance to her cheek felt too far. Sighing, he drew back. Instead, he lifted the sheet higher over her shoulders. Soundlessly, he closed the door.

He rubbed his aching knee as he made his way down the ancient stairs. The old house was dark, but he didn't need a light to navigate his way through the narrow halls. White Gables had been in Carolina's family since 1897 in a town founded by her ancestors. When they weren't working on the boat, they were working to infuse new life into the aged frame house, repairing costly old woodwork and heart pine floors, fighting an interminable battle against salt, moisture, and termites. His father often chided him about it, telling him it was like throwing more sand on a beach eaten away by a strong current. In his heart, Bud knew the old man was right, but Carolina loved the house and the subject of leaving it was moot. Even in the dim light, he saw evidence of it in the shine of the brass doorknobs, the sparkle of the windows, and the neat arrangement of the inherited threadbare sofa and chairs. Every morning when he walked through the silent old house, he was haunted by the worry that he'd cause Carolina to be the last of her family to live here.

Bud went straight to the kitchen and opened the fridge. He leaned against the cool metal, staring in, searching for whatever might spark his appetite. With a sigh he grabbed a six-pack and shut the door. The breakfast of champions, he thought as he popped open a can of beer. The cool brew slaked his thirst, waking him further. Then he grabbed a few ingredients from the pantry and tossed them in a brown bag:

onions, garlic, potatoes, grits, coffee. Pee Dee would cook up a seaman's breakfast later, after the haul. He added the rest of the beer.

At the door he stuck his feet into a pair of white rubber boots, stuffing his pants tightly inside the high rims. The Red Ball boots with their deep-grooved soles and high tops were uniform for shrimpers. They did the job of keeping him sure-footed on a rolling deck and prevented small crabs from creeping in. He rose stiffly, rubbing the small of his back. Working on the water took its toll on a man's body with all the falls, twists, and heavy lifting.

"Stop complaining, old woman," he scolded himself. "The sun won't wait." He scooped up the brown bag from the table, flipped a cap onto his head, and headed out of the house.

The moon was a sliver in the dark sky and his heels crunched loudly along the gravel walkway. Several ancient oaks, older than the house, lined their property along Pinckney Street. Their low-hanging branches lent a note of melancholy.

The air was soft this early in the morning. Cooler. The rise and fall of insects singing in the thick summer foliage sounded like a jungle chorus. He got in his car and drove a few blocks along narrow streets. McClellanville was a small, quaint village along the coast of South Carolina between Charleston and Myrtle Beach. There had once been many similar coastal towns from North Carolina to Florida, back when shrimping was king and a man could make a good living for his family. In his own lifetime, Bud had seen shrimping villages disappear as the value of coastal land skyrocketed and the cost of local shrimp plummeted. Docks were sold and the weathered shrimp boats were replaced by glossy pleasure boats. Local families who'd fished these waters for generations moved on. Bud wondered how much longer McClellanville could hold on.

His headlights carved a swath through the inky darkness, revealing the few cars and pickup trucks of captains and crews parked in the lot. He didn't see Pee Dee's dilapidated Ford. Bud sighed and checked the clock on his dashboard. It was 4:30 a.m. Where the hell was that sorry excuse for a deckhand?

He followed the sound of water slapping against the shore and the pungent smell of diesel fuel, salt, and rotting fish toward the dock. Drawing close, he breathed deep and felt the stirring of his fisherman's blood. He felt more at home here on the ramshackle docks than in his sweet-smelling house on Pinckney Street. Gone were the tourists, the folks coming to buy local shrimp, and the old sailors who hung around retelling stories. In the wee hours of morning, the docks were quiet save for the fishermen working with fevered intensity against the dawn. Lights on the trawlers shone down on the rigging, colored flags, and bright trim, lending the docks an eerie carnival appearance.

His heels reverberated on the long avenue of rotting wood and tilting pilings that ran over mudflats spiked with countless oysters. Bud passed two trawlers — the *Village Lady* and the *Miss Georgia,* their engines already churning the water. He quickened his step. The early bird catches the worm, he thought, lifting his hand in a wave. Buster Gay, a venerable captain and an old mate, returned the wave with his free hand, eyes intent on his work.

There were fewer boats docked every year, dwindling from fifteen to seven in as many years. Of these, only five would be heading out today. Roller-coaster fuel prices and the dumping of foreign shrimp on the market made it hardly worth taking out the boat anymore. Captains were selling their boats.

Bud continued down the dock, sidestepping bales of rope, holes in the planks, and hard white droppings from gulls. As he passed, he took note of one boat's chipping paint, another's thick layer of rust. Every boat had a distinctive look. Each had a story.

"Hey, Bud," called out LeRoy Simmons as he passed. "Looks like rain coming."

"Yep," Bud replied, looking up to the deck of the big sixty-five-foot *Queen Betty,* where LeRoy was hunched over his nets. "Wind, too."

LeRoy grunted in agreement. "We oughta get a day's work in."

"A half day, at least."

"At least. I'm hopin' the rain flushes the shrimp down." Bud waved and walked on. There wasn't time for small talk. Bud had known LeRoy all his life. LeRoy was second generation of a McClellanville family of African American shrimpers. Captain Simmons could bring in more shrimp on a blustery day than most other boats on a good day. Bud knew it took a lot more than luck.

Time was, a captain with the reputation of bringing home the shrimp had his pick of top crew because the strikers got a percentage of the day's catch instead of salary. Now the catch was unpredictable, if not downright pitiful. Too often, the crew got little money and drifted off to higher-paying jobs on land. It was damn near impossible for a captain to hire on decent crew.

In this, LeRoy was more than lucky, too. Bud glanced back at the *Queen Betty* to see LeRoy and his two brothers nimbly moving their fingers over the nets, searching for tears. The Simmons brothers worked together like a well-oiled machine. He grimaced, remembering the days when he and his brother had worked together. Poor Bobby. . . . Then he scowled, thinking of his own nets and the work that needed to be done before he could shove off. Where the hell was Pee Dee?

Peter Deery had been born to a dirt-poor farming family on the Pee Dee River, and the nickname stuck. For all the damage booze and drugs had done to his brain, Pee Dee was clean and sober on deck and as nimble as a monkey on the rigging. And he worked harder than two men. He was Bud's cousin once removed. Sometimes Bud wished he were more removed. A man couldn't pick his family, but a captain could pick his crew — and Pee Dee was somewhere in the middle.

Bud's frown lifted when, through the mist and dim light, he spied the *Miss Carolina* waiting for him at the end of the dock. His chest expanded.

The *Miss Carolina* was a graceful craft, sleek and strong like the woman she was named for. He'd built the fiberglass and wood trawler with his own hands and knew each nook and cranny of her fifty-foot frame. He spent more time with this boat than with any woman alive, and his wife often complained that the *Miss Carolina* was more his mistress than his boat. He'd shake his head and laugh, inclined to agree.

Every spring he gave the *Miss Carolina* a fresh coat of glistening white paint and the berry-red trim that marked all the Morrison boats. Yes, she was a mighty pretty boat. His eyes softened just looking at her. All captains had their families and loved them dearly. Yet there was a special love reserved for their boats.

The morning's quiet was shattered by the roar of an engine coming alive. Bud swung his head around to see the *Queen Betty* drawing away from the dock and making her way out to sea, her green and white mast lights flashing in the dark. Ol' LeRoy would have his nets dropped by sunup, he thought with a scowl. Damn, he'd get the best spot, too.

Fifteen minutes later, the *Miss Carolina*'s diesel engine was growling and Bud had a mug of hot coffee in his hand. He sat in the pilothouse, breathing in the scent of diesel fuel mingled with coffee, and listened to the marine radio for weather reports. The boat rocked beneath him, warming up and churning the water like a boiling pot. After finishing his coffee, he began his chores. There was always one more job that needed doing, one last repair he had to see to before he could break away from the dock. He needed to get ice in, fuel up, and get some rope. . . . Bud sighed and shook his head. He couldn't wait for Pee Dee to show up. He might as well get rolling. Bud climbed down from the boat to the dock.

A weathered warehouse with a green-and-red-painted sign that read COASTAL SEA-FOOD dominated the waterfront. The warehouse was the heart of the dock where fishermen could get fuel, ice, and gear, then unload shrimp at the end of the day. Under its rusted awning a few men in stained pants and white boots stood smoking cigarettes, drinking coffee from Styrofoam cups, and bantering while waiting to load ice. They grunted greetings as Bud moved past them. Inside, the big room was sparsely filled with a few metal chairs and tables and a rough plywood counter.

A young, broad-shouldered man with

unruly dark hair leaned against the counter. He wore a denim jacket against the morning chill and white rubber boots high over his worn and stained jeans. He looked both boyish and edgy, with the congenial air of a man who is well liked. He turned when Bud approached and broke into a lazy grin.

"Hey, Bud," he called out.

"Hey, Josh," he replied, hearing the resignation in his own voice. He hadn't expected to see Josh Truesdale this morning.

"I was hoping I'd run into you," Josh said, straightening.

"Yeah?" Bud replied, stepping up beside him at the counter. Josh met Bud eye to eye. Bud narrowed his. "And why's that?"

Josh shook his head with a wry grin. "Don't look so worried, Cap'n. I ain't gonna launch into Lizzy now."

Bud barely suppressed his grin — the kid had hit the nail on the head. His daughter was exactly the subject he was hoping to avoid. "You know I don't have nothin' more to say to you on that subject. You and Lizzy — that's your problem. Not mine."

"I hear you," he replied. "But I got this other problem I was hoping you'd take a look at. My winch. Not my wench." He chuckled at his joke.

Bud's eyes flashed in warning. He didn't

care for jokes about his daughter.

Josh's smile fell hard. "Sorry," he blurted. "You know I didn't mean no disrespect."

Bud liked Joshua Truesdale, always had. There weren't many young men going into shrimping these days. He could count the ones he knew on one hand. Most of the captains in these parts were too old and too stubborn to change their ways. Josh was one of a new breed of shrimpers. Though he came from an old line of fishermen in the Shem Creek area, Josh had ideas on how he could make the business pay. While Bud liked his enthusiasm, sometimes those new ideas made the kid a bit cocky. Still, Josh Truesdale was the best deckhand he'd ever had.

Even if he was the worst son-in-law.

"Well," Bud drawled, lifting his hand to signal to Tom Wiggins behind the counter, "I sure don't got the time to help you now."

Tom was a small, wiry man who looked to Bud like a gray squirrel, with his gray stained clothes, a wreath of gray, frizzy curls, and a beard that was as bushy as a squirrel's tail. Ol' Tom had worked this counter for as long as Bud could remember, and the thing of it was, he'd looked the same when Bud was a kid as he did now.

"Tommy, you got a couple hundred feet

of three-quarter-inch rope back there?"

"Yeah, hold on and I'll get you some."

"What's the matter with your winch?" Bud asked, turning again to Josh.

"Keeps slipping. Has no tension."

"And what can I do?"

"I remembered how you jerry-rigged your winch."

Bud rubbed his jaw. Adjustments on equipment were common enough among captains. Especially among those who'd built their own boats to their own specifications, as he had. Bud didn't always have the money to buy a new part, or maybe he didn't even know what part could do the job he had in mind, so it called on him to be inventive. Most every boat had been rigged by its captain one way or another. It was a point of pride and gave a boat its personality.

"I'm always tinkering with that old winch," he replied. "But I don't rightly know that I can recall what I did to it."

"Come on, Bud. Everyone knows you're the best damn mechanic in these parts."

"That's for true," added Tom.

Bud scratched behind his ear with a self-conscious smile, not immune to flattery.

"Will this do?" asked Tom, handing over the rope.

Bud made a cursory inspection. "Yeah, it'll do. Put it on my tab."

Tom blanched and rubbed his neck. "Sorry, Bud. Can't do that. Everything's on a cash basis now."

Bud's head jerked up. "Since when?"

"Since nobody can pay their bills and they're falling behind. I don't mean you," he stammered. "But, hell, Bud, you know how the times are. I got no choice and I can't be making exceptions. That's the word I got direct from Lee, and I got to do it. Or I'd make one for you. You know that."

Bud's ears colored and he tightened his lips as a surge of anger shot through him. Lee Edwards had once been like a brother to him, but he'd proved to be more Cain than Abel, and there'd been bad blood ever since. It still burned that Lee had done so well over the years. He owned Coastal Seafood and just about all the preferred real estate along the docks. Bud hated to admit it, but Lee was a good businessman. If the shrimp boats failed, Lee would still be sitting pretty.

Bud silently cursed. His haul was hardly worth a day's wage, and that was before taxes. Hell, Lee and his pals probably spent more on lunch than Bud earned in a day. Running a tab at the fish house was how most fishermen made it through a rough patch. Most every shrimper in town was in hock to Lee, and it gnawed at Bud that he was one of them.

"Well, shit, Tom," he said, struggling to keep his anger in check. "I didn't plan on buying rope this morning and I don't have enough cash on me."

"Here, let me," Josh said, pulling a worn black leather wallet from his back pocket.

"No way," Bud said gruffly. "I don't need your money. I can pay my own bills."

"I ain't saying you can't. I'm just lending it to you. No big deal. Besides, I owe you."

"You don't owe me nothing, son."

"I think you know I do." Josh's emotion was too strong and he cleared his throat. "You can take it as a down payment for working on my winch."

Bud struggled with a reply. He'd never take a handout, but this seemed fair — and he needed that rope now.

"I reckon I could come by and take a look at that winch later today or tomorrow, weather depending."

"Yes, sir. Anytime."

Bud nodded, grateful for Josh's respectful tone. And the kid had a winning smile. It must've been the dark tan that made his teeth shine so white. He wasn't blind to the fact that his daughter still thought so, too.

Josh laid out bills on the plywood counter.

Tom gingerly handed the rope into Bud's hands, relieved to have the transaction settled amicably. "Sorry about that. Nothin' personal."

"Yeah, sure," Bud murmured. "You tell Lee Edwards he can stick his policy where the sun don't shine. Nothin' personal." Bud hoisted the rope and turned to leave.

"Where's your boy?" Josh asked, tucking his wallet back into his pocket. "Don't you usually send Pee Dee on these errands?"

"Ain't seen him," Bud replied, walking out.

"He's probably on some bender again," Josh remarked. "What a loser."

Bud turned fast and walked back toward Josh. No matter what Bud might think or say about his own, he wouldn't allow anyone else to slander them, not even Josh.

Josh took a step back as Bud leaned close. In a low voice, he said, "Pee Dee and the *Miss Carolina* aren't your concern anymore. Nor, for that matter, is my daughter. Got that?"

Josh straightened his spine and locked eyes with Bud. "Lizzy *is* my concern. But I'm sorry for what I said about Pee Dee."

Bud considered Josh's words, impressed

by his unflinching gaze. He remembered the boy, but this depth of feeling reflected a man. Maybe the kid grew up some in the five years since Lizzy dumped him. Bud acknowledged Josh's apology with a curt nod and stepped back.

"I'll come by your boat later."

He adjusted the rope, then walked out, but not before he heard Tom mutter to Josh, "Boy, ain't you learned your lesson yet?"

By force of will, Bud shoved the roiling thoughts about Pee Dee, Lizzy, and Josh into a far corner of his mind to deal with later when the nets were dragging and he had time on his hands. Thinking about all that was like dredging the mud. Right now he had to clear his head and focus. Without Pee Dee here, it'd take twice as long. He still had to load the ice and more work to get done than time to do it.

Bud put his back to it. As each minute passed, with each chore he ticked off his list, Bud's anger was stoked till it fired a burn in his belly. He knew in his heart that Josh was right and that Pee Dee was likely on some bender. He ground his teeth, feeling the betrayal of the no-show.

A short while later, the roar of engines sounded and he jerked up to look out over the bow. The final two boats slowly cruised

32

along the narrow creek toward the Atlantic. Josh's small but sturdy forty-five-footer, the *Hope,* followed in the bigger boat's wake. Clever boy, he thought with grudging respect. With his smaller boat and his ideas for niche markets, he might do all right.

Bud cleared his throat and spat into the ocean. But there was a lot of life left in this salty old dog, he thought, rolling his shoulders. He'd match his experience against some young Turk any day. Bud pressed the small of his back while his brows gathered. At times the pain was so severe it felt like a hot iron was being jammed into his lower lumbar.

Time was wasting. It was already late. Bud crossed his arms while he mulled over the pros and cons of the decision that faced him. The dawn was fast approaching. He couldn't wait for Pee Dee any longer. Could he go it alone?

It'd be tough to take a boat this size out alone. But he'd done it before, hadn't he? Bud cast a wary glance at the drifting clouds. He wasn't fooled by the seeming serenity. His experienced eye knew they were the tips of a rain front likely to hit sometime later that afternoon. At least, he hoped the rain would hold off till then. God knew, he desperately needed a good haul today, and it would be easier to get in and unload before the first drops fell.

No doubt about it. It would be a risk out there alone if the wind picked up. But he'd only be out for one haul. He'd be back in dock before things got rough.

Bud brought his arms tight around his chest and narrowed his eyes. To his mind, a man worked hard to take care of his family. He did whatever he could, whatever toll it took. With or without a crew, he was the captain of this vessel, and it was his duty to bring home the shrimp. He leaned forward, gripping the railing tight, and stared out at the dock. He only needed to bring in one good haul to pay the diesel fuel bill. One good haul, he repeated to himself, and he could keep his boat on the water.

What choice did he have? Failure would mean the loss of everything he'd worked so hard for.

Bud tugged down the rim of his cap, his decision made.

"Well, all right then."

2

September 21, 2008, 6:50 a.m.
White Gables, McClellanville

Carolina awoke with a start. Her arm shot across the bed, instinctively reaching for Bud. She patted the mattress to find his side of the bed empty and the sheets cold. Turning to her side, she lifted herself slightly on one elbow. The dull gray light of early morning filtered through the curtains. Knowing it was late, she looked at the clock. Bud was gone.

She fell back against her pillow and let her forearm rest over her eyes. He's always gone, she thought.

She had a vague memory of waking earlier, in the dark predawn hours. A shadowy image of Bud standing at the window came back to her. His words sounded like an echo in her brain. *You sleep. Back by noon, latest.* That was hours ago. He'd be on the water by now. The thought that she hadn't made him breakfast brought a twinge of guilt.

The house was quiet. She sighed and let her mind drift to that velvety, drowsy state where, if she lay very still with her eyes closed, she could slide back into her dream. She didn't often have the luxury of time to lie in bed in the early morning. And her dream had been so vivid it lingered in her subconscious, calling her back. It was one of those dreams that felt so real. She could recognize the voices, smell familiar scents, even feel the satiny coolness of skin.

In the dream, she and Bud were together aboard the *Miss Carolina.* She was standing aft, her chin slanted into a cool, crisp wind that tossed her hair. She was young — in her twenties — and Bud's arms encircled her, strong and secure. Ardent. They watched the sun rise — or set, she couldn't tell. She remembered it was a blinding, breathtaking panorama of lavender, rose, and yellow that spread out over the ocean into infinity. They were engulfed in color. Most of all, she remembered being happy — filled with a heady, tingling, deeply abiding joy at just being on the boat in her man's arms.

Then, with a sudden cruelty, a dark storm had risen up, swift and violent. In an instant Bud was wrenched from her arms, and though she reached out for him, cried out for him, she felt only a savage emptiness. In the darkness, she could hear his voice calling her name in the wind, over and over. She clawed out into the mist, crying. But he was gone.

That's when she'd awoken, reaching for him.

Carolina shuddered and moved her arm to stare up at the ceiling. Her heart was beating hard. Waking hadn't taken the edge off the fear and panic or the sense that something was wrong. She brought her hand up to her tender jaw. Could it have been her bad tooth that caused the nightmare?

Or maybe it was the cross words that she and Bud had exchanged the night before.

Carolina felt an old sadness well up at that thought. When they'd first married and were in the throes of love, they'd sworn never to go to bed angry. That promise, like so many others, had been broken over the years. Now they both could fall asleep before an argument was settled. She sometimes came into their darkened bedroom to find him already in bed, lights out, the blanket high around his shoulders, his back to her, rigid with resentment. In fairness, there were nights she was as cold. Too often the argument never was settled. It hung like a dark cloud over them for days, making them snip at one another, before it dissipated into indifference.

Carolina grimaced. It hadn't always been this way. She remembered again the intensity of emotion she'd felt in Bud's arms in her dream. Where had that youthful exuberance gone? That passion? Was the slow slide from passion to companionship the inevitable fate of a long marriage? she wondered. She wanted to feel that way about him again. She wanted to be loved like that again. How much longer could she pretend she was happy?

She curled on her side and stared at the pale linen curtain flapping at the open window, remembering the shadowed strength of Bud's body standing there, the curve of his muscled shoulders. Carolina closed her eyes and lay in bed until she could no longer ignore the dull pain that pulsed from her rear molar. That tooth had taken her to hell and back and it wasn't going to get better by itself. She'd hoped that somehow the problem would magically go away if she could settle the pain down with over-the-counter pain relievers. That only worked so many times. She would have to call the dentist.

The resonant chimes of the grandfather clock sounded from the front room downstairs. What kind of seaman's wife was she to be such a lazybones? She rose, stretched, and slipped into her robe, thinking it was kind of Bud to give her a few more hours of sleep. He could be thoughtful that way.

Carolina caught the scent of coffee and followed the delicious aroma down the narrow stairwell. The walls were adorned with black-framed photographs of the Morrison family. She passed a photograph of the Morrison brothers in happier times: Bud, the elder, and Bobby. In the center was Lee Edwards, Bud's best friend growing up. The photograph had been taken about the time Carolina had met them, back when they were in their twenties. The boys were aboard Bud's boat, the *Miss Ann* — muscled arms around each other, cocky grins spread across tanned faces, salt-spiked hair. They were so handsome in their youthful confidence.

Beside this was a picture of Bud's father, William Osgood Morrison II — the Great and Mighty Oz. Captain Oz was the stuff of which legends were made. He had a frame like an ocean freighter and biceps like ham hocks from his early years of hauling nets without benefit of a winch. In this photograph, his teeth were clamped down on a pipe in a crooked smile under his ever-present cap. The boys used to call him Pop-eye behind his back.

Moving down the stairs, she paused at a photograph of herself and Bud aboard the *Miss Carolina* on the day he brought their shiny new trawler to Jeremy Creek. Oh, what a gloriously happy day that was! The mayor had made a short speech. She reached out to touch the glass, remembering again her dream.

Beside this was a photograph of their only child. Lizzy was smiling brightly in her third-grade school photo. Lizzy hated the picture because she thought she looked dorky in her uniform, her pale freckles, and her crooked ponytail. Carolina loved it because she saw shining in Lizzy's eyes an innocence and an unshakable belief that she was special and could be anything she wanted when she grew up.

"Mama, are you all right?"

Carolina started and her eyes darted over to see Lizzy standing at the bottom of the stairs.

"Girl, you scared me!"

The child had grown into an attractive woman. Once again in a makeshift uniform, Lizzy wore a black T-shirt and jeans for her job as a waitress at a local restaurant. Her strawberry blond hair was pulled back into a ponytail. Searching her face, Carolina wondered what had happened to that light in her little girl's eyes.

"Mama?"

"I'm fine," Carolina replied with a wave of her hand.

"You don't look fine," Lizzy said, her brows knit in concern. "You look kind of pale and you're still in your pajamas. It's not like you to dawdle in the morning."

"Daddy didn't wake me because this tooth's been bothering me. I didn't sleep well last night."

"You haven't slept well in weeks. Mama, go to the dentist!"

"I know, and I will," Carolina replied, walking down the stairs. "Though how we'll pay for it, I don't know."

"We'll manage. We always do." Lizzy wrapped her arm around her mother. "Come on," she said gently. "I made coffee."

"Mmm . . . I can smell it." Carolina searched her daughter's face, interpreting her mood. At twenty-seven, Lizzy was still young, but she had an aura of worn-out resignation that was beyond her years. That came, Carolina knew, from having her girl-

41

ish dreams stripped away by a failed marriage and the responsibilities of having to work and raise a child on her own. She placed a kiss on her daughter's cheek.

"What was that for?" Lizzy asked with a surprised smile.

"Can't a mother kiss her daughter for no reason?"

Lizzy cast her a puzzled look, then, shaking her head, hurried back into the kitchen to the oven. The heavy iron door creaked as it fell open, releasing a steamy waft of cinnamon into the air. Carolina thought of how Bud liked to call the kitchen the pilothouse of the home.

Lizzy had moved in with them soon after her divorce from Josh Truesdale. Will had been a toddler and Lizzy needed support. That was a sad, roller-coaster time of tears, recrimination, and blame for all of them. Carolina still felt that the words flung and sins committed then remained unforgiven. But they'd survived.

The one joy from all that pain was William Morrison Truesdale. Her eight-year-old grandson was sitting at the table, dressed in his school uniform and shoveling eggs into his mouth.

"Morning, Will," she said, planting a kiss on her grandson's cheek. In the nook of his neck he smelled of soap and something that she could only call ambrosia.

"Morning, Nana," he said, then squirmed when she kissed his neck.

"Cupcakes are done," Lizzy called out.

"I want one!" Will waved his hand.

"Just one. They're for school. Mama, would you frost them for me after they cool?"

"Sure." Carolina stepped back to go straight for the coffee, opening the wood cabinet and pulling out a thick pottery mug.

"Want one?" Lizzy asked her mother.

"They smell great. Maybe later," she replied, pouring coffee.

"Be sure to eat something before you take one of those pain pills."

"I know." Carolina rolled her eyes.

"I'm just saying —"

"Okay, okay. . . ." Carolina nodded, then took a sip of coffee. Almost instantly she could feel her woozy mind sharpen as caffeine flowed through her veins. Fishing families liked their coffee strong. Carolina's devotion to her morning brew was a family joke. Once Lizzy had tried to fool her and served her decaffeinated coffee in the morning. An hour later, when Carolina complained of feeling sluggish and headachy, Lizzy had confessed to the ruse. Carolina wasn't sure if her addiction to coffee could be called a vice or not, but if it was, it was one she could live with.

Will lifted his empty glass. "I want some milk."

"Be polite if you expect anyone to help you," Carolina admonished.

"Please!" he shouted in an exaggerated tone.

Pulling out the gallon jug, she noticed that the sandwich lunch she'd packed for Bud was still on the shelf. And the beer was gone.

"Your father left without breakfast, and now he'll miss lunch," she said to no one in particular.

"Pee Dee will cook him up something," Lizzy replied from the oven.

"He did say he was coming back early today," Carolina acknowledged.

Lizzy looked out the window. "Good. They say a storm's coming."

Carolina felt a shudder run down her spine. She shook it off as a remnant of her dream and muttered, "He knows what he's doing. He'll be fine." She turned to her grandson. "Will, sit your bottom down in your chair and stop jumping around or you'll spill your milk."

"I wish I could go out on the boat with Papa Bud instead of going to school," Will groaned, slipping down into the wooden chair.

"You can get that idea right out of your head. You're going to school, and that's that," Lizzy said, bringing a cupcake and setting it down on the plate in front of Will beside the remnants of scrambled eggs. "For a long time, too, so get used to it."

"Aw, Mama, I don't want to."

"That's too bad, because you're going all the way through college."

Will slumped in his chair and set his chin into his palm like he'd been handed a death sentence. "I don't want to go to no college. I'm going to be a shrimper when I grow up, just like Papa Bud and my daddy."

"Over my dead body," Lizzy shot back, flipping the rest of the cupcakes out. She tossed the cupcake tin into the big farmer's sink.

"Lizzy, let the boy have his dreams."

"I do let him dream," she said defensively. "He can dream about being a doctor or a lawyer or an Indian chief. But not about *that*. I want more for my son than working on a boat."

Will frowned. "Aren't you happy, Mama?"

Lizzy exchanged a loaded glance with Carolina.

"Sure, I'm happy." She bent down closer

45

to Will. "I'm happy I have you! And Nana and Papa."

"And Daddy?"

Lizzy's brows furrowed, and she rose and went to the sink. With a twist of her wrist, she turned on the faucet.

"Daddy said he'd take me out on the boat."

"No. It's too dangerous out there for a boy your age. You could be knocked overboard and I'd lose you forever."

"Papa Bud takes Skipper out all the time."

"Skipper is two years older than you. But if you ask me, he still shouldn't go out."

"But, Mama —"

Lizzy stiffened. "I said no!"

"Will, honey," said Carolina. "Why don't you go on upstairs with your cupcake and find your shoes. You're going to be late for school."

Will cast his grandmother a look that told her he knew when he was being shuffled out of the room. "Yes, ma'am." Grabbing his cupcake, he dragged himself from his chair. Carolina waited till she heard his footsteps climb the stairs.

"He's a smart little boy," she told Lizzy.

"Too smart. Please tell Daddy to stop offering to take him out on the boat. He knows I don't like it."

"I will. But, honey, he's a Morrison. You can't keep him off the water. Or from his daddy."

Lizzy lowered her shoulders.

"Smart as he is," Carolina continued, "he's got to be confused. You've been seeing a lot of Josh since he came back to town. Going out to dinner, taking walks. If I didn't know better, I'd say you were courting."

"I'm only trying to be nice. After all, he is the father of my child."

"Uh-huh," Carolina said, carrying Will's dirty dishes to the sink and dumping them into the hot water. "And that's all?"

Lizzy began scrubbing the tin.

"If I'm wondering," Carolina said, "you've got to know your son is, too. And what's more, he's hopeful."

Lizzy stopped scrubbing and turned to face her mother, her face forlorn. "I know. I can see it in his eyes and it near kills me. His face lights up when Josh walks into the room. And he's always asking if we're going to be a family again. Pleading is more like it." She tossed the sponge into the sink. It landed with a noisy splash. "I don't see why he cares. I mean, he doesn't hardly know Josh."

"He knows he's his daddy. That's enough for a boy."

"It's not enough for me to marry him again."

"Of course not." Carolina grabbed a towel from the counter, picked up the tin, and began drying it. "Why? Is Josh asking you to get married again?"

"Not in so many words. But he wants us to spend more time together, and I can see where it's all heading."

Finished with the tin, Carolina folded the towel neatly into thirds, forming her words. "And what do you want?"

"I don't know what I want," Lizzy replied soberly. "But I know what I *don't* want."

Carolina looked up, narrowing her eyes so as not to miss any innuendo.

"I don't want to be a shrimper's wife. I'm done with that life."

"It's the life I chose."

"That was your decision," she snapped back. "I'm never getting up at four in the morning to cook grits for a man again."

Carolina suddenly felt so much older, so much wiser than Lizzy. Calmly, she asked, "What if you love the man and he's a shrimper?"

"Then I'll just have to find myself another man to love."

That sounded so naïve. As if one could direct the heart, Carolina thought. "Lizzy, honey, the heart doesn't work that way. First, there's the matter of commitment. Second, you can't pick who you're going to love."

Lizzy's face fell, and she said softly, "Maybe not. But I can pick who I'm going to marry. Burn me once, shame on you. Burn me twice, shame on me."

"Is that why you're dating Ben Mitchell?"

"Ben's a good man. Smart. From a good family. And he has a steady job with a good salary. I'm looking at my future. Will's future. I want a man who can provide for Will, give him a nice life. What's wrong with wanting security?"

"I suppose there's nothing wrong with that."

"You say that but you don't mean it. Mama, I have to decide what's going to make me happy."

"Are you thinking of marrying Ben?"

Lizzy threw up her hands with an exasperated sigh. "Why do you always have to see things in terms of my getting married!"

"I was just wondering, is all."

"Well, don't. It makes me mad."

"I don't see why. I'm your mother. It's my job to wonder. After all, Lizzy, you *have* been dating Ben for a while now."

"One year."

"I was engaged to your father before six months was up."

Lizzy rolled her eyes. "Please spare me the story of how you took one look at him and knew he was the one."

"But I did. It was Cupid's arrow, straight to the heart."

"Mama," Lizzy said, turning around.

Carolina's smile fell at her daughter's change in tone. Lizzy's eyes moistened and her lower lip trembled.

"Don't you know it's hurtful to me to hear you tell that story? It makes me worry that if I don't feel that, then I haven't found the right one. Maybe it's not like that for everyone. Did you ever think of that? Maybe the rest of us have to settle for good enough."

"Never settle," Carolina said. "Not with love. It's hard enough to make a go of it."

Lizzy turned away.

Carolina pursed her lips. She'd never meant to be hurtful. She'd always thought her story would shine like a beacon for her daughter, so she'd know such things could happen. So she'd not sell herself short. At some point since her divorce, the light in Lizzy's eyes had dimmed. Carolina only wanted her daughter to be happy.

"I seem to recall you telling me you felt

that way about Josh when you first met him."

"I was eighteen. I got married right out of high school. You should've stopped me."

"Darlin', there was no stopping you. Your mind was made up."

"I was a fool."

"Oh, Lizzy," she sighed. "You were in love. You just were so young. Both of you."

"What did I know about love? About life? I should've gone to college."

Carolina bit her tongue. Oh, the fights they'd had back then over that very subject. Carolina had begged Lizzy to wait, to go to college, but she wouldn't. Lizzy could be strong-willed, like her. She was hell-bent on marrying Josh. Bud often said that the apple didn't fall far from the tree.

"Lizzy, you still can go to college, if you want."

"Oh, yeah? How, Mama? How can I afford to go to college?" Her voice grew strident. "I haven't one dime to rub against another. And I've got Will to take care of. Josh is struggling to make his child-support payments, and you know this summer's shrimping is bad. He can barely keep the boat afloat, and I can't afford to get my own place on what I make waiting tables. I'm twenty-seven years old and I'm still living

51

with my parents. So tell me, how can I go to college?"

Carolina looked into her daughter's eyes and saw the desperation of a trapped animal. Once Bud had caught a raccoon in the attic with a Havahart trap. He'd carried that critter out to the back, intending to kill it. Lizzy was nearly hysterical begging her daddy to let it go somewhere far off, and in the end, Bud had relented.

Lizzy's plight was common enough in their community. Folks were hanging on to their jobs and houses by their nails. Shrimp boat captains were juggling days at sea with "off-boat" jobs. Wives worked, too. Often two jobs to make ends meet.

Carolina had always worked. She'd been a deckhand for Bud, then the office manager for the Coastal Seafood Company, and when that ended she went back to teaching at the local primary school. On the side she did the books for Bud's business and babysat for Will so Lizzy could work. In a stroke of bad timing, right before this school year began she'd been laid off from her job as a teacher. She was on the list of substitutes and she'd been looking for work elsewhere, but jobs were scarce.

Her face flushed as she absentmindedly rubbed her aching jaw. "Things will be all right, don't worry. I've got an interview tomorrow. There's a new housecleaning service in Pawleys Island."

"I'm sorry, Mama," Lizzy said softly. "I didn't mean —"

"No, of course not."

The words they were exchanging sounded false in her ears, just meaningless platitudes to avoid hurt feelings. Carolina was confident she'd find a job. Hard work never frightened her. Her worry was that at some fundamental level, she'd failed as a wife and mother.

"What I mean to say is," Carolina said, looking at her daughter with deliberation, "we'll find a way if you want to go to college. I could sell the house."

Lizzy's eyes widened slightly. Everyone knew what White Gables meant to Carolina. "No. It's too late for me. But my boy is going to college, that's for sure. He's not going to grow up to be a shrimper like his daddy."

Carolina wanted to scream at her that she was still young, with so many possibilities, that she had to stop thinking her life was over. She wished she could tell her daughter that a day would come when her son was grown and she'd feel old and worn-out and wish she were twenty-seven again. But she didn't, knowing that was a wisdom earned only through experience.

"Ah, Lizzy, as long as Will grows up to be a good man, that's all I care about."

"Like I said —"

"Josh has changed. He's going to church regular, and I hear he doesn't drink anymore."

"Oh, yes, he's a God-fearing man now," Lizzy added with sarcasm.

Carolina cringed at the harshness in Lizzy's tone. "It can happen. We prayed it would."

"Maybe." Lizzy shrugged, then said more sincerely, "I hope so. For his sake. I care about him . . . loved him once. But he's still a shrimper, and I'm not going back to that life."

"Here we go again."

"Mama, don't pretend you don't know how hard it is to live with a man who's gone from before the sun rises till after the sun sets. Then when he's home again, he's too tired from working like a slave under the hot sun all day to talk. Josh would just sit there like a zombie and his eyes would be all red and he'd barely have enough strength to shovel food into his mouth. Most nights he'd fall asleep in front of the TV. He'd never even say good night."

Carolina knew Lizzy was blending the histories of both Bud and Josh. "He'd have to be up again before four," Carolina said in both men's defense.

"Oh, I know that. But it doesn't change anything. It didn't get any better when the season was finally over. What did they do? They packed up the boat and followed the shrimp to Florida. We wouldn't see them for months at a time, and we both know they were up to no good down there."

"Lizzy," Carolina said tersely. "Don't go back there."

"You asked me, so I'm just telling you. We both did it — stayed home, keeping house, minding a child, working our jobs, looking out the window, waiting on them to return. Some life." She dried her hands with the towel, then tossed it back onto the counter. "Thanks, but no thanks."

"I know Josh did wrong and you have a right to be mad at him, but your daddy worked hard all his life and he did it for us. Don't you forget that."

"I haven't forgotten. He's my daddy. That's why I love him. And why I could forgive him." She walked to the hall, pausing to turn and add, "But Josh was my husband. He cheated on me and I don't have to forgive him. Not ever."

Carolina swallowed hard, and her hand shook as she brushed some crumbs from the table. "Girl, you've got a lot of growing up to do."

"It's not like you and Daddy are so happy."

Carolina felt that comment to her bones. She leaned on the back of a chair and spoke slowly. "Every marriage has its hard times. We're working it out. The point is, we stayed together."

Lizzy tightened her lips, holding in a retort. She turned on her heel and walked out of the room, calling, "Will! Hurry on down. We're going to be late!"

Carolina sighed and moved to lean against the doorframe and watch the commotion of her daughter and grandson as they gathered Will's homework, his lunch box, Lizzy's pocketbook, and tumbled out the door amidst a flurry of complaints, orders, and good-byes. When the door closed and peace was restored, Carolina closed her eyes and felt the dull throbbing of her back molar. Sometimes being a mother and a grand-mother caused her more pain than this bad tooth.

The hardest part about being a mother was realizing she couldn't save her daughter from her own decisions. When Lizzy was a little girl, Carolina could give an order and Lizzy did as she was told. But since she'd become a woman — since her decision to leave Carolina and Bud's home and become another man's wife — Lizzy's life was her own.

The lethargy of the morning hung about her like a shroud. The start of a new school season without her teaching had thrown her rhythm off. She slumped into a kitchen chair and wrapped her hand around a mug of coffee, feeling its warmth in her fingers. The pale yellow kitchen with the bright green trim had been inspired by photographs she'd seen in a book about Monet's house. Clay pots of herbs sat in a row at the mullioned windows, and on the lower cupboards were brightly colored paintings of trees and birds and boats and the sea, all done by Lizzy when she was young. What colors that child had seen in the world! The paintings had faded and chipped over the past twenty years, and Carolina didn't want to think of the obvious analogies.

Poor Lizzy, she thought, worried about the anger bubbling in her daughter. Lizzy's words played again in her ears. *I don't want to be a shrimper's wife.*

Carolina felt again the strong emotions stirred by her dream. She rested her chin in her palm and thought how being a shrimper's wife was all she'd ever wanted to be.

3

September 21, 2008, 5:30 a.m.
On board the Miss Carolina

The engine rumbled beneath him as Bud maneuvered the *Miss Carolina* away from the dock. He looked back. Under the dull light over the warehouse, he saw Old Tom step outside and wave. Bud lifted his hand. The *Miss Carolina* was the last of the shrimp boats to leave McClellanville that morning, but she was on her way at last. He knew the murky water of the creek as well as he knew the narrow stairwell of his home. Overhead, a guard of gulls flew in sloppy formation around the *Miss Carolina* like tugboats.

He motored through Jeremy Creek. Lights from houses shone like stars through the fog. He crossed the Intracoastal Waterway and moved into Five Fathom Creek in the dim light, past barrier islands with their maze of winding creeks and lush acres of marshes. Then, suddenly, the vista opened, and in a breath, he was on the Atlantic. The pitch of the engine rose and the diesel fumes filled his nostrils as he throttled up. The wheel vibrated with the power and the water churned into whitecaps and froth in the wake. Above, the gulls began their raucous screaming.

At long last, Bud released the ear-to-ear grin he'd held in check throughout the early-morning hours. This was the moment he lived for. This was what he rose early each morning in search of.

Freedom!

Out here, all the problems with his house, all the worries about money owed, the fights with his wife, the struggles with Lee, his father, Pee Dee — all that was behind him on shore. All that lay ahead was the majesty of a dawn breaking across a horizon that went on forever. Out here, he was his own man. Bud wasn't looking back. He was rushing forward, standing wide-legged with his chin up and his hands firmly clasped on the wheel. Bud took a long, deep breath, then laughed out loud, feeling the wind flow over his skin like water.

Bud passed other boats with their nets already in the ocean. He pushed the *Miss Carolina* hard, racing against the pink rays of dawn already breaking through the periwinkle sky. At dawn, shrimpers all along the coastline could drop their nets.

"They'll be catching everything around here," he muttered in frustration, pushing the throttle up. No use hanging around. He had a place in mind, farther out than he usually liked to go. It was his secret spot. A treasure trove to which he was pinning his last hope.

Bud pushed the *Miss Carolina* faster and harder than he should have across the rolling water — and the wind pushed back. The boat was hitting the chop hard. The nets swung violently on the outriggers, spitting out bits of entangled dead fish and creaking almost loud enough to drown out the gulls. Bud locked his jaw and cut his course through the black water, leaving a wide, ruffled wake behind. Overhead, the sky grew lighter by the minute.

An hour later, there were no other boats in sight. The gulls above and the occasional dolphins racing at his side were his only company. Bud slowed and flicked on the marine band radio. Instantly he heard the crackle, then chatter among the captains. He smiled, recognizing Wayne's twang, then LeRoy's gravelly voice. It was comforting to hear friendly voices out in the middle of nowhere. Usually Bud joined in to exchange jokes and trash talk as much as important information. Most of the time, they were lying about their catch, same as him.

He sat back in his chair and steered with one foot, stealing a precious moment to sip hot coffee and chuckle at one of Buster's off-color jokes. They might be friends, but when it came to making a living, each man was on his own. He didn't want anyone to know where he was headed this morning. Friends were friends, but family was family. Blood was thicker than water. That's what his father had drummed into his and Bobby's heads.

Morrison pride ran as thick as saltwater in their veins. Bud chuckled low and thought how he and Bobby sure had some good times together back in the day. Back when money was running as plentiful as the shrimp. Back when their credit was good. He and his brother didn't have a care in the world besides getting cash in their pockets. Their bodies were lean, their hopes fat, and their heads lush with thick hair.

Bud leaned farther into his ratty old cushion and brought to mind one of the last times the Morrison men had fished together. Twenty, thirty years ago? Could it be that long? Damn, where did the time go? He remembered it now, all of them on one boat, the *Miss Ann,* a fine wood-frame vessel named for his mother. It was a great day with a record haul.

Yes, those were the days, he thought. It was a golden time when he'd learned what it meant to be a son, a mate, a man.

December 1973

On board the Miss Ann

The north wind was wet and bit through Bud's slicker, sending shudders down his spine. It was colder than a sea hag's teat, and the flaming sun on the horizon didn't do much to warm up the day. With the engine off, the *Miss Ann* was rolling and pitching like a watermelon in the waves. His father stood firmly at the winch, wearing a yellow slicker and thick gloves on his big hands. Oz was undeniably the captain of the ship. Beneath his cap his sideburns were long and slivered with gray, his chin stuck forward like a masthead, and his eyes glittered as he guided the thick iron cable evenly across the drum.

The *Miss Ann* grumbled as the winch revolved, raising the big nets. Bud watched and waited, his gaze trained on the water, his hands tucked into his armpits to keep them warm. His breath was a plume of steely steam. When the great wood doors broke the surface, his anticipation shot skyward. He swung his head toward Bobby and Pee Dee standing across the deck. Nearing twenty, both men stood rooted to the rocking deck, ready in their yellow slickers, their deeply tanned faces alert under knit caps. All eyes were now on the prize.

The *Miss Ann* listed under the weight of the rising nets. The men held their breath, leaning forward. Oz shouted curses at the machinery as he maneuvered the outriggers up and over the deck. The moment the nets emerged from the water, they knew what they had.

The cone-shaped mesh nets were bursting with the translucent gray bodies of shrimp. Water cascaded from the nets in sheets, and icy droplets caught the sun like shards of diamonds. The outriggers groaned with the weight of the booty. Below the nets Bud saw two, maybe three sharks circling.

"Whooeee!" Pee Dee punched his gloved fist into the air.

"Fellahs, looks like we hit pay dirt!" Bud called out, grinning ear to ear.

"That's my car payment in that net," Bobby shouted, slapping his brother's back.

"Hell, that's beer for a month!" Pee Dee added.

"Let's go, boys!" Oz hollered, his impatience ringing clear. He had to get the nets out of the water and lowered onto the work deck — fast. With one eye on the nets and the other on the winch, he guided them with a master's precision.

Bud vaulted toward the nets, throwing his full weight into untying the rope at the bottom of the net. In a tremendous *whoosh*, the webbed bag exploded like a popped balloon, flooding the culling table with untold pounds of commercial shrimp.

There were good hauls and there were bad hauls. And then there was a haul like this. Bud had never seen so many shrimp before. He dropped to his knees in the payload and scooped up two fistfuls of shrimp by their whiskers and with a jubilant whoop lifted them for his father to see. These were big shrimp, jumbo and prime, in time for Christmas feasts. A bonanza crop.

Father and son shared a glance of victory, their eyes gleaming. They were all laughing out loud for the joy of it. This was a day for the books.

"Stop goggling and move your asses!" Oz barked.

Bobby gave a war howl and scrambled to obey. Pee Dee grinned from ear to ear as he shook the empty nets. Small fish and stray shrimp were flung loose to join the squirming mass on deck. Oz was itching to drop the nets again, lifting them almost before Pee Dee removed his hands.

Oz headed for the pilothouse. "I'm bringing her around. I want to hit the exact spot."

Bobby retied the nets, then jumped back before they dragged across the deck to slink over the side back to the ocean like some green sea creature. Bud felt the jerk and heard the low throb of the engine as the big nets began to tow. Bobby and Pee Dee joined Bud at culling through the squirming pink, gray, brown, red, and silver sea creatures.

Their teeth chattered and their fingers felt numb, but the men didn't slow down. When a catch like this came around, adrenaline raced through the system and they were immune to cold. They moved swiftly through the pile, separating crustaceans from fish. They tossed the big shrimp into one set of baskets and the medium into another. Pee Dee worked with a cigarette dangling from his lips. Bobby wiped his brow, stretched his back, and then went back to work. Bud was almost giddy, a grin plastered on his face.

After they finished culling, Bobby and Bud swept the bycatch through the scupper holes. Immediately, hungry dolphins, pelicans, and screaming gulls swarmed and swooped to feast.

A few hours later, the excitement built again. The *Miss Ann* shuddered, the winch rattled, and once more Oz brought up a bloated net. In another great *whoosh,* the deck was filled with shrimp.

"This is just too much!" Bobby bellowed. "Merry Christmas!"

"Happy damn New Year!" shouted Bud.

"Damn," was all Pee Dee could come up with. What he lacked in eloquence he more than made up for in sincerity.

Bobby and Bud punched each other's shoulder. The season was almost over and they'd caught a run.

"It seems we're finally getting the hang of this job, eh?" Bud joked.

Pee Dee laughed so hard he started to cough, a deep smoker's cough.

"Don't die, fool!" Bobby roared. "You ain't been paid yet!"

"No way. I got a date with these here shrimp." Pee Dee jumped into the enormous pile of life released by the net.

The sky was dark when they finished sorting the catch and loading the shrimp on ice. The decks were scrubbed till they gleamed and the holding bays were crammed full with more than three tons of shrimp. They couldn't take on another shrimp. The ice was maxed out. It was a record day, and they knew it.

The *Miss Ann* lazily cut through the water, following the blur of faint white lights along the creek toward home. In the warmth of the pilothouse, the men drank beer and smoked the special cigars Bud kept in his sleeping quarters. Fatigue set in, but they continued to tell and retell memories of the great catch that day. Bobby's and Pee Dee's eyes were glazed, and Bud knew they'd been smoking something else below deck.

His father was in rare form, feeling magnanimous. In such a mood, he often liked to regale them with stories of what it was like growing up near Bulls Bay when life was simple and he and his brothers ran barefoot and wild with the creeks as their playground. They'd had the adventures of Tom Sawyer and remembered building forts on hammocks and seeing devilfish as big as cars leaping from the water and slapping down like thunder. Those were the old days before boats had modern conveniences like winches and depth finders, and shrimpers relied on their memory and skill.

Bud leaned back and closed his eyes, enjoying the cadence of his father's voice against the omnipresent rumble of the engine. He'd heard the stories before. He couldn't imagine what it was like to pull up a net with the brute strength of his arms.

Bud pried open an eye and glanced at the irascible old coot. Oz's shoulders and arms still strained the checked flannel shirt, though his belly had grown paunchy. He loved his father something fierce. And he respected him — even if he was a tyrant and hell to work for. Everyone knew there wasn't a better captain along the South Carolina coast.

A good captain knew the uncharted bottom of the sea like the back of his hand. Where the rocks hid that could snag and tear his nets, where the sunken vessels lay like dangerous skeletons, and where the tall grass could swamp his engine. The captain knew, better than any fancy high-tech equipment, where the shrimp were. His tools were experience and instinct.

But this catch was a record even for this stoic old fisherman.

"Boys, I'm right proud of you," Oz said, dragging deep on his cigar. In the dim light, his hair was silvered and his weathered face looked like shoe leather. He released a long plume of smoke.

"You taught us all we know, Daddy," Bobby said. He patted his father's shoulder with affection.

Oz ruffled the thick curls atop his younger son's head. Anyone could see the old man doted on the boy.

"You learned it from your daddy," Oz told him. "I learned it from mine. And he learned it from some Portuguese fishermen. They knew the old ways." He sighed and leaned back, the chair squeaking under the weight.

"Times are changing, boys. There are lots of fancy new things for boats, and they're all good. But a captain worth his salt knows how to pick out his markers, and I hope I learned you that. The spot we fished today is a honey hole. It's our secret spot, eh?" He narrowed his eyes and cast a warning glance at each of the three young men. "We ain't gonna tell nobody about it. That's our ace in the hole when times are tough. Right?"

"Yes, sir," they mumbled.

Oz nodded, satisfied, then puffed again on his cigar. "The way I figure it," he continued, "this haul is the mother lode. I been waiting for this one. Setting store on it." He paused. "Bud!"

Bud blinked, opened his eyes, and grew alert at his father's tone.

"You're my eldest boy, and you've proven you're ready to captain your own vessel. I'm of a mind to settle the *Miss Ann* on you."

70

Bud straightened, stunned by the unexpected gift. "Thank you," he said with disbelief but a boatload of pleasure. It felt so little a reply for so much, but Oz knew what it meant to his son without words. Bud's pride at receiving such a boon was written all over his face.

"Bobby," Oz continued, turning to his youngest, "I guess that means I need a new boat. With my take on this haul, I'm able at long last to build my own. I've been planning this trawler for years, down to the tiniest detail. It's going to be my pride and joy." His face softened. "As you are. That's why I'm gonna call it the *Cap'n and Bobby,* 'cause it'll be your boat someday."

Bud grinned with pleasure at the startled expression on his brother's face. With his untamed curls and sleepy, handsome face, Bobby still looked like the sweet kid Bud used to carry on his back through deep water. They'd all known that one day Bud would take over the *Miss Ann.* But it was a surprise that Oz would build a second boat for his second son. It was a good thing, too, since Bobby liked to party and money flowed like water through his fingers. He'd never afford his own boat.

Bud looked over at Pee Dee sitting against the wall. He was as skinny as a pole and his blond hair fell over blue eyes so wide with expectation it was painful to witness. Bud glanced at Oz, and he felt sucker-punched. He saw in his father's face that there'd be no announcement for his cousin.

Oz caught his expression. "What?"

Bud shrugged.

"What about Pee Dee?" Bobby asked. He was close in age to Pee Dee and had always stood up for his cousin. While the boys saw their cousin as a brother, Oz had never regarded Pee Dee as his son.

Oz looked somewhat surprised by the question and rubbed his grizzled jaw, stalling. "Yeah, Pee Dee . . ." he said slowly. "Tell you what. I know a guy who knows a guy in the Coast Guard. Seems this fellah is looking to *lose* one of their boats, if you catch my meaning. I might could set it up that you'd know where to look on the particular day that boat gets lost. Sure, it'd need some fixing up to make it right for shrimping, but it'd be a nice boat once you were finished with it."

Bud lowered his gaze to pick at the label on his beer bottle. It was a lame offering, and they all knew it.

Pee Dee wagged his head and smiled amiably. Born of a father who'd deserted him, raised by an indifferent mother and her harsh boyfriend, Pee Dee was eager to please.

"Aw, no, Cap. That's not for me. I like being a striker on a Morrison boat. But thanks anyway." He brushed a hank of hair from his eyes as he brightened. "Anyways, I got my eye on a sweet li'l bateau. I can get her fixed up for oystering right quick."

"Oh, yeah? Cool," Bobby exclaimed. He loved to get oysters, maybe more than shrimp. "Can I go out with you?"

"Sure thing," Pee Dee exclaimed, head bobbing.

"You're not talking about Charlie Pickett's old bateau, are you?" Oz said, his eyes squinting. "Hell, boy, that thing's older than I am!"

Bud saw Pee Dee's face fall, and he could've kicked his father.

"No, that's a good little boat," he exclaimed.

Bobby nodded in agreement. "You'll do great."

"Yeah," Pee Dee exclaimed, gaining heart. "We'll do great."

Bud tilted his chair on its hind legs to lean against the wall of the pilothouse. The men fell into a complacent silence as they motored through the dark maze of creek and marsh toward McClellanville and home.

Bud blinked as he looked out over the sea. It was bright now with morning sun. He'd remember that December day for the rest of his life. He'd been surrounded by the three men he loved most in the world — his father, his brother, and his cousin. None of them went to church with any regularity — weddings and funerals mostly. A night like that was as close to a service as they came.

Oz was right that time changed things. Thirty years ago he'd been a lion. Today, Oz was too infirm to captain a boat and spent his afternoons sitting on the dock with the other old captains, retelling stories of the sea. Pee Dee was the same aimless, sweet-natured, hardworking guy, but he had no future. And Bobby . . .

Lord, he missed his brother, Bud thought. After all this time, his stomach still grew tight in pain remembering him. The day Bobby died, he'd taken a good part of Bud's soul along with him. He'd lost more than his brother. He'd lost his best friend. There were days when he was alone out on the sea, like now, that he felt Bobby's spirit on the deck with him. It was said a dead seaman returned to haunt the sea where he'd died.

Bud shook his head. Fishermen were a suspicious lot. They needed — and took — all the good luck they could get and were careful to ward off the bad. Oz had passed on secrets to Bud that his father had shared with him, and likewise Bud had passed them on to Josh and Will: That shrimping was best under the light of a full moon. That a fisherman never washed his hands before going to sea. And that a fisherman never, not ever, whistled on deck because it scared the fish away. Bud's favorite was that a naked woman was lucky on board a ship. He liked to remind Carolina of this one.

One thing he knew for sure, though, was that sitting on board the *Miss Ann* that day with the best damn captain on the southeastern sea and the boat's belly full of booty, the men had felt proud. They were the hunters returning with their kill. Thousands of little critters were nestled on ice. Back then, they'd felt like kings of their world. And for a shining moment, they were.

Today they were paupers. No matter how hard he worked, no matter how many hours, he couldn't make it. He was sick of the boat, sick of the shrimp, and sick of scraping by. This morning's order from Lee Edwards canceling his credit was a new low, and it still burned in his craw. What would Bobby have made of this turn in the business? Would he have quit it and turned to oystering? Taken a land job like so many of his friends? Or would he still have been as drawn to the open sea with her salty scent, the cries of gulls overhead, and the feel of her swells beneath his feet as Bud was?

"Hey, Bobby," he called out. "If you're out there today, I need your help. I'm heading back to the honey hole. Our secret spot. Help me get one good haul so I can pull myself out of debt. I'm gonna pay back every damn penny I owe. Then" — he gritted his teeth — "I dunno, brother. I might sell this boat and get out of this godforsaken business for good."

A short while later, the water changed to a murky green. Bud sat up and tossed the empty coffee cup in the trash. Dead ahead, a series of hammocks clustered in a semicircle resembling an island. A brisk wind was rustling the palm fronds. He recognized his markers. Bud looked at the screen of the depth recorder and checked his radar, then slowed his engines. This was the spot he was looking for.

Alone, Bud had to work twice as fast. He tied the wheel in place and hurried out on deck to the winch that rolled cable around a steel drum. Slowly, he lowered the try net into the water. The net blossomed like a flower, bellowing out in the slow drag.

Now he had nothing to do but wait. Bud walked across the deck, checking the ropes, cables, chains, and nets that were neatly stacked. A gust of wind rocked the boat and he grabbed for a rail. Bud grimaced as his knee twisted and the old injury flared up. He cursed his luck and, ignoring the pain, limped back to the winch.

When the try net rose dripping water from the sea, he hurried to reach out with a long metal pole to retrieve the bag and pull it to the deck. Bud untied the knot at the bottom, and with a *whoosh,* the catch spilled out into a squirming mess on the deck. He quickly bent and sorted through the pulsing mess of jellyfish, bottom fish, sea slugs, a small shark — and the precious shrimp.

Bud kicked the bycatch to the side with his rubber boot and anxiously counted the shrimp. He sat back on his haunches and whooped. Ninety-two! He pumped the air with his fist as his face broke into a grin. The honey hole had come through for him! This could be one of his best hauls of the season. Bud rose and, looking out over the sea, laughed out loud, congratulating himself on his decision to go it alone this morning.

Now it was time to lower the big nets.

He moved quickly, eager to begin trawling. The sun was getting higher in the sky. More clouds were moving in. Every minute counted. He shoveled the bycatch over the edge of the boat. Instantly the gulls' screams crescendoed and they began diving and vying with the dolphins and each other for the free meal.

Bud moved to the main winch, and his thick, calloused hands gripped the lever and shifted. He smelled the pungent grease and heard the whine as the cable rolled around the drum. The great steel outriggers slowly lowered. He smiled, thinking how Carolina always said they looked like folded butterfly wings opening up over the water.

Maybe it was his eagerness, or perhaps it was because lowering the big nets was usually a two-person job. And just maybe it was because his mind had drifted for that instant to Carolina. But when the wind suddenly gusted, Bud's gimp knee gave in and he lost his balance. His hand slipped into the drum.

Bud instinctively jerked his hand back, but it was too late. His world became a crushing vortex of pain, shattering his thoughts, shooting up his arm to his brain where it exploded — white, blinding, incomprehensible, hot. He threw back his head, stretched his mouth wide, and bellowed like a gored bull, a horrendous, gut-wrenching, primeval howl ripped from his lungs. It echoed over the ocean, scattering the gulls, then vanished into the vast loneliness.

4

September 21, 2008, 7:45 a.m.
White Gables

Carolina stood in her garden resting against her shovel. The early morning was the best time to work outdoors, before the sun rose high. It was also the best time to catch the small white worms that fed on her kale. Three clay pots sat one on each step of the porch, each filled with a red geranium. The green, ruffled leaves held fat droplets from her watering. She reached to pluck the dead heads and the brown, curled leaves, releasing the distinctive peppery scent.

She had tomatoes in her garden and a few vegetables. Herbs, of course. But she came outdoors each morning to see the flowers. Perennials mostly, and of these she was partial to the common but cheerful echinacea that called the bees into her garden and came back, year after year, like an old friend. She patrolled the garden every morning, checking leaves, pulling weeds, watering. Like most things, a good garden took consistent tending rather than fits and starts.

In the south the summer sun beat down mercilessly, turning the ground hard and the grass brittle. The rains weren't regular, either. It took a commitment to each plant to see it through the season. Yet no matter how much mulch she spread or how much water she offered, the summer garden always seemed spindly. It limped along without vigor or showy blossoms like it was just hanging on till fall.

She wiped the sweat from her brow with her sleeve. Maybe that's what was going on in her marriage, she thought with a short laugh. She and Bud were just in a dry season. She just had to hang on and hope for better times.

Wasn't that the way with a long marriage? she wondered. After thirty-three years, she could look back and say they'd gone through their seasons. There were good times and bad times, like the Bible said. Days of blessings. Days of sin. She felt a shadow cross her face as she remembered those bitter cold days of winter.

She had to keep the good memories close, to remember spring during winter. The fall garden always seemed like a second spring. At some point in September, right about the time the ducks and hawks came migrating through, the flowers in her garden sprang back to life. The cooler weather and the rain brought such promise it set her heart to blooming.

Carolina looked out over her lawn. The brittle, brown grass was parched, more weed than grass. The rain barrel was dry. Please, God, let there be rain today, she prayed, shading her eyes with her hand as she checked the sky.

The dull blue overhead was laced with wispy cirrus clouds. Lizzy had said rain was coming. She turned toward the sea. Even after all these years, she felt uneasy whenever Bud was at sea in stormy weather. She couldn't shake the nagging feeling that something was wrong. She didn't believe in fortunetellers or horoscopes, but she absolutely believed in a woman's intuition. Ask any wife or mother and she'd tell you she had a sixth sense about her loved ones.

And she loved Bud. God help her, for better or for worse, he was the love of her life. She'd told Lizzy that it was love at first sight. A slight smile spread across her face as she remembered in a flash that zing of attraction she'd felt the minute Bud Morrison turned his head and locked gazes with her.

Though a distant memory, some days it still felt so fresh.

September 1974
McClellanville
The first time Carolina saw Bud Morrison, she fell in love.

On that fateful September day, Miss Carolina Brailsford was sitting on a bench overlooking Jeremy Creek with Judith Baker and Odelle Williams, fellow schoolteachers who boarded at White Gables. Carolina's great-uncle, Archibald Brailsford, had passed on ten years earlier, and to make ends meet her great-aunt, Lucille Brailsford, had opened her home on Pinckney Street to unmarried, respectable schoolteachers.

Carolina was sharing histories with the two women who were fast becoming her friends. She and Judith were doing most of the talking. An instant friendship had sparked the moment Judith had willingly relinquished the front bedroom and moved to the small corner bedroom at the rear of the house. The front bedroom of White Gables with the black iron bed and the white lace curtains had always been Carolina's when she'd visited White Gables as a child.

Odelle was reserved compared to Carolina and Judith. Not that she was shy. Odelle could be very firm and free with her opinions. Rather, Carolina had the impression that Odelle preferred to listen carefully rather than join in conversation. "Collecting ammo," Judith had succinctly summed up when Carolina had mentioned this to her.

It was Labor Day, the first holiday the three young women had enjoyed since beginning their duties at the local elementary school. Within a few weeks, the fresh, dewy-eyed college graduates had been smacked with the realities of being elementary teachers in the South in August, when the sun mercilessly blistered the earth and the enormous ceiling fans twirled noisily in a losing battle against a haze of humidity and an army of mosquitoes.

"Tell me we're still in McClellanville," said Judith, wiping her brow. "After last week, I'd swear we were in the Belgian Congo and I was teaching a bunch of savages. Rotten little pygmies who shoot spitballs like poison darts."

Judith Baker had graduated from the University of South Carolina with a degree in physical education. Of average height and weight, she wore her thick brown hair short with shaggy bangs that fell over blue eyes so bright Carolina always thought she had a joke to share. But as Carolina and the fifth-grade class had quickly learned, her sweet face masked the heart of a drill sergeant. In the two weeks since school had opened, she'd marched an army of children to the principal's office, and two boys caught in a fistfight were made to drop and do twenty push-ups.

Carolina lifted her thick shank of hair from her neck to savor the breeze. She was proud of her hair, its fiery color and shine. She'd been the first at Clemson to wear the Farrah Fawcett hairstyle. "Lord, it *was* hot in those classrooms!"

"The little monsters," said Odelle, fanning herself with a copy of *Glamour* magazine. "I was a breath away from throwing my books into the air and walking out. I'm not even kidding!"

"They've got your number," Judith pointed out. "You let them get away with murder. You should be more like Carolina. I didn't hear a peep from her room."

Odelle bristled at the comparison. "I'll have you know I didn't become a teacher to be a warden."

Carolina turned her head to look at

Odelle. While teaching, Odelle pulled her long brown hair back in a ponytail; with her horn-rimmed glasses, she was the very picture of a prim martinet. But on weekends, she let her hair flow long and straight to her shoulders and wore miniskirts so short Aunt Lucille didn't think it was decent.

"I tell you," Odelle added, "the first decent proposal I get, I'm accepting and giving up teaching forever. What was I thinking?"

"Don't you dare," Judith warned. "If you quit, Carolina and I will have to divide your class."

"If you hate it so much, why did you become a teacher?" asked Carolina.

Odelle shrugged. "It's a respectable profession. And to be perfectly honest, I'd hoped to get a job at Ashley Hall in Charleston, teaching proper young ladies Shakespeare and Blake and Byron." She sniffed and shifted in her seat. "I need to have more experience before they let me through those illustrious gates. So here I am, teaching first-graders how to spell their names." She turned to Carolina. "What about you?"

"It was the only way I could think of to come back to McClellanville."

Judith scrunched up her face. "Why would

you want to do that?"

"I always knew I'd come back here to live someday. The happiest, most treasured moments of my childhood were spent right here."

"But I thought your family was from Mc-Clellanville," said Odelle. "Didn't they practically found this village?" It both irritated and fascinated Odelle that Carolina's family could trace its lineage to a plantation family along the Santee River and that her forebears had helped establish McClellanville.

"Yes and no. My ancestors were here early, but my daddy grew up in Mount Pleasant. He spent summers here with Aunt Lucille and Uncle Archibald. Then he went north to study at Clemson, and after he graduated, he married my mother and stayed in Greenville. That's where I was born. Now he loves banking, and shrimping is just some distant memory. But every year he'd bring us back here to spend two glorious weeks at White Gables.

"We had such good times! My parents would be so stuffed with shrimp and groggy from gin and tonics they'd hardly know or care where we kids were. My brother and I ran wild through the village from sunup to sundown. Aunt Lucille used to call us her own Sewee Indians. I'll never forget this little jon boat we had — the *Moby Dick.* We went everywhere in it. It's a miracle we didn't get lost in the marsh."

She paused, lost in a vision of the winding creeks that spread out like arteries through the thick green marsh. They were never afraid of the funny, darting fiddler crabs that scurried across the pluff mud, each with its oversize claw raised in a threatening stance. She'd point out the serene white ibis resting among tall green fronds and the proud blue heron with a fish in its beak. They'd lie on their backs and search the sky for the soaring ospreys that, from time to time, tucked in their wings and dove into the water, shattering its stillness to emerge victorious with dripping fish in their talons.

"I knew I belonged here, and I cried every time we had to go back to Greenville. I counted the days until I could return. So when I graduated from Clemson, the first thing I did was look for a job teaching in McClellanville."

"You haven't had much time to go swimming or to gorge on shrimp since you got here," Odelle said ruefully.

"No," Carolina groaned. "More's the pity."

"I've got a jon boat," Judith interjected.

"You do?" Carolina sat up. "Where?"

"Right over there." Judith pointed to the marina at the end of the park. "While you two were arguing over closet space at White Gables, I was finding myself a slip to dock my boat at. We all have our priorities."

"Can we go see it?" Carolina asked.

"I don't see why not."

"We're not going out on the boat now, are we?" Odelle asked, adjusting her straw hat as she rose from the bench. She looked down at her Bermuda shorts and Villager print blouse. "I'm not dressed for it, and I'm not going out in those creeks without lots of bug spray. I'll get eaten alive."

Carolina was already walking toward the docks with Judith. She couldn't wait to see the boat, and if Judith was willing, she'd go right out into the creeks today. So what if her clothes got wet? She'd been dying to get back out on the water since she'd come back. Her eyes were shining with excitement as she and Judith walked at a fast clip across the sunburned grass to the brittle gray wood of the dock.

It was late afternoon and the docks were lined two deep with dozens of shrimp boats returned from a day's work, each with its riggings up, creating a blur of nets. Odelle hurried to catch up, linking arms with

Carolina. Ahead on the narrow dock, three young men were walking toward them, their T-shirts stretched over lean, muscled bodies. They wore torn shorts over deeply tanned legs and the white rubber boots that marked them as shrimpers. Their carefree laughter and the swagger of their walk told the world that the docks, the boats, and the sea made up their empire.

They looked to be about the same general age and build. She knew they'd spotted the three women walking toward them because the one on the right leaned over to mutter a few words that caused the other two men to smile and chuckle. She glanced at Judith. Her face had scrunched into a frown. Then she turned to Odelle, who held her shoulders back and lifted her hand to smooth her hair, a sure sign she was cocked and ready.

As the three men drew closer, Carolina stole a furtive glance at them. Her stomach clenched and she could feel a blush creep up her neck to her cheeks. Then, without warning, the man in the center lifted his head and their eyes met.

Carolina sucked in her breath. It felt as if time stood still. She was aware only of him; the rest of the world disappeared. His eyes drew her in like a blue laser; she couldn't look away. It was a handsome face — well-formed lips, chiseled features, brown hair brushed back from his forehead. She memorized each detail even as the zing of attraction melted her spine. Her mind, her body, every cell screamed that this man was the one she would love forever.

He felt it, too. She knew it instinctively.

She was vaguely aware that she was walking, heard mumbled hellos echo as they awkwardly passed each other. It all happened in a blur. When she could breathe again, she realized that, unbelievably, they were walking away. She stopped abruptly to look over her shoulder. He'd looked back, too, as though to make sure he'd seen what he thought he'd seen.

He saw her looking at him. She was sure of it because the ghost of a smile crossed his lips. Then he turned away and kept walking down the dock.

"Oh, my, my, my," Odelle said, squeezing her arm. "Weren't they dreamy? I call dibs on the tall one in the middle. Did you see him look back? I waved at him. Nothing showy, just a brief . . ." She waggled her fingers. "I'm sure he saw it. Did you see him smile?"

Carolina couldn't answer. She was in a daze, not sure that what had just transpired was real.

"Are you coming or what?" Judith called from a few yards ahead. Her hand was over her eyes, shielding them from the western sun, but Carolina could see she was still frowning.

Carolina had forgotten all about the jon boat. "We're coming," she called back. When they caught up with Judith, she asked, "Isn't there a dance in town tonight?"

The Labor Day dance was held at a converted warehouse in town. It was an event the town anticipated eagerly. The Mercantile had been decorated with colorful paper lanterns and was packed with young and old alike. Carolina waved at Aunt Lucille chatting with friends near the punch table.

She stood against the side wall of the dance hall, shoulder to shoulder with Odelle and Judith. The three were a united front, aware that everyone in the room was eyeing the pretty new teachers in town. Carolina nervously fingered her strand of pearls. She wore her favorite green paisley print dress and had spent hours getting her hair to flip back like Farrah Fawcett's. Even though the big, barnlike doors were open wide to the night air, she could feel her curls drooping in the intense humidity of the packed room.

Odelle leaned close to whisper, "I don't

see them."

Odelle's brown hair fell like a waterfall down her shoulders. Carolina bit her lip as she glanced at the cherry-red halter top that accentuated Odelle's slim shoulders and waist. Carolina knew they were both looking for the same guy, and her own dress with the puffed sleeves, while pretty, seemed tame in comparison. Flirting was a competitive sport.

Carolina's gaze swept the dance floor, but she didn't see him anywhere.

"Which one are you looking for?" Odelle asked.

"No one in particular."

"Uh-huh," she replied in a tease.

Carolina released a reluctant smile. "Okay, I know this sounds weird. But when they walked past us on the dock, the guy in the middle looked up all of a sudden and we locked gazes. It was only for a second, but it was like time stood still. I had this mule-kick feeling and thought, *Oh, Lord, he's the one.*"

Odelle's slim brows gathered in doubt. "So, you're trying to tell me it was love at first sight?"

"Something like that."

Odelle sniffed. "I don't believe in it. And I never pegged you for a romantic."

Carolina crossed her arms and gazed out over the dance floor. She prided herself on being sensible and modern. She had been president of her sorority and had "Most Likely to Succeed" written under her yearbook photograph. The two marriage proposals she'd received during college had been delivered by men so young and foolish that she'd never considered either one seriously. Until today, she would have laughed and agreed with Odelle.

Judith smoothed her navy skirt. "I don't believe in it either. My mother's friends like to talk about how they met their husbands. Every once in a while you get the one who tells about the day she just looked across a crowded room, saw this guy standing there, and *bam* — she knew he was the one." She chuckled. "What a load of crap. It was the wine talking."

Odelle giggled and leaned over to face Judith. "Those poor, socially inhibited women weren't in love, just *in lust,*" she said in a tone of authority. "They didn't have the freedom that girls today have to experiment a little before settling down."

"So now I'm socially inhibited?" Carolina asked. Odelle's teasing was beginning to annoy her.

"I wouldn't know about that," Odelle said

sweetly. She winked and leaned back against the wall. "Let's just see what happens tonight."

"I'm thirsty," Judith said. "Want to get some punch?"

"Is it spiked?" asked Odelle.

Carolina was about to reply when she saw a young man approaching. She recognized him as one of the three men she'd seen on the dock earlier. He smiled at all three girls, but his gaze landed on Carolina.

"Hi, Red."

Carolina narrowed her eyes. "Didn't I see you on the dock today?"

"Yep. And I sure saw you. I'm Lee Edwards."

Carolina was struck by his cool confidence. She found him attractive, with his pale blue eyes and shaggy blond hair. "I'm Carolina Brailsford, and this is Odelle Williams and Judith Baker."

Her friends muttered polite hellos, aware that Carolina had his attention.

"Carolina's a pretty name," Lee said, returning his gaze to her. "Would you like to dance?"

He wasn't the one she'd come for, but to refuse would be rude, so she smiled and extended her hand. "Sure."

He took her hand and guided her to the

middle of the floor. The song had a slow, steady beat, and their feet shuffled in a smooth shag. He was an exceptionally good dancer, twirling her lightly back and forth. On any other night, she might have been attracted to him, but she couldn't forget the pull of the gaze she'd felt earlier on the dock.

"Who were those other boys you were with today?" she asked, trying not to sound overly interested.

"The Morrison brothers. They're water rats, like me."

Carolina smiled. "Really?"

"Yeah. We're more brothers than friends. Oz says I'm more a Morrison than an Edwards." He chuckled, and Carolina heard the pride in it. "We all work on Oz's boats. Did you see the *Miss Ann*? And the *Cap'n and Bobby*?" When she nodded, he said smugly, "Those are Morrison boats."

"So, are your friends here?"

"Bobby is." He craned his neck, searching the room. His face broke into a grin. "That's him over there, dancing with your friend."

She turned her head, squinting in the colored lights to see a broad-shouldered boy with wavy brown hair dancing with Judith. Bobby wasn't the brother she was looking for.

Her gaze swept the room. "What about the other brother?"

"Bud? He might come later. You never know with him."

Bud. She mentally repeated the name, liking it. "He doesn't like dances?"

"He likes them fine. But he just broke up with his girlfriend. He might not be in the mood."

Carolina cataloged every bit of information she learned about Bud and tucked it away. She knew he was handsome enough to have just about any girl he wanted, but was he the kind of guy who dumped girls on a whim?

They danced another two dances before Bobby cut in and Lee traded places to dance with Odelle. Bobby was a charmer, with a deep dimpled smile and eyes that sparkled with the devil. The Morrison boys were obviously the big catches in town, and aware of that fact. Carolina caught the slanted glances she was getting from the local girls, and when she stood in line for punch, she heard a girl behind her say in a loud whisper, "What do you expect? The teachers who stay at White Gables only come to town to find husbands."

She danced past the time the older couples left for home and a new band stepped up to play rock and roll. The beer was flowing, and Lee seemed glued to her side as the hours passed. She grew weary of his hot fingers around her waist, so when Odelle came up and playfully asked him to dance, Carolina almost pushed Lee toward her. Heading outdoors, she walked around the side of the warehouse to lean against the mighty trunk of an ancient oak. The scent of night jasmine filled the air. Her cheeks were flushed and she lifted her collapsed curls high on her head, relishing the evening breeze on her neck.

"Hot night."

She dropped her hair and spun around. He stood in the shadows a few feet away from her, the tip of his cigarette glowing in the dark.

"I didn't see you here."

"I came out for a smoke." He dipped into the pocket of his white button-down shirt and pulled out a pack of cigarettes. Stepping forward, he asked, "Want one?"

She took a cigarette, even though she didn't smoke.

He reached into the rear pocket of his jeans and withdrew a pack of matches. The match hissed and sparked; then he stepped closer, cupping it with hands that were tan and crisscrossed with scratches. As she leaned toward the flame, she felt the air grow thick in the few inches that separated them. She looked up and their eyes met. She felt again the attraction, undeniable this time.

She took a drag on the cigarette. The tobacco tasted hot and foreign in her mouth, and she puffed it out without inhaling.

He shook the match and flicked it into the air. "I'm Bud."

She smiled, liking the smooth cadence of his voice. "I'm Carolina."

His eyes kindled, and she knew he'd already learned her name.

"You're one of the new teachers," he said.

"And you're one of the Morrison brothers."

He half-smiled. "Guilty. I guess you met Bobby?"

She nodded. "And Lee. It's a small town. I've met most everyone."

"Where are you from?"

"Greenville. South Carolina," she added.

"Nice town."

"You've been there?" she asked, a little surprised.

He shook his head and chuckled softly. "No."

She took another puff of her cigarette and coughed lightly.

"You don't smoke much, do you?"

She shook her head, embarrassed.

Bud reached out and she handed him her cigarette. She watched him bring it to his mouth. It felt unbearably sensual for his lips to be where hers had been. She inhaled as he did.

Footsteps sounded behind her, and she heard Lee's voice call out, "There you are!"

She groaned inwardly and turned to see Lee walking toward them, two beer bottles dangling from his hands. When he reached her side, he handed her one.

"I've been looking everywhere for you."

"I'm fine," she said, hoping her tone would discourage him and let Bud know at the same time that there was nothing between her and his friend. "It was hot inside and I came out here to cool down. I'm a big girl. You don't have to worry about me."

Lee slipped his arm around her shoulders. "I see you met Bud."

Bud took a step back and put his hands in his back pockets. "We met."

"I didn't think you were going to make it," Lee said to Bud. "Did you see Nancy? She's inside looking for you," he added pointedly.

"I saw her."

A heavy awkwardness gripped them. Bud

tossed his cigarette on the gravel and crushed it with his heel. "I'll be shoving off. Nice meeting you, Carolina."

Carolina felt her heart fall from her chest as she watched Bud turn and walk off down Pinckney Street. Lee's arm slipped down to her waist.

There were times in her life when Carolina, like most people, could be persuaded to take the polite course and go along, even against her wishes. And there were times when something snapped and she reared up, bucking. This was one of those moments. Carolina knew what she wanted and saw him walking away from her. She slipped out of Lee's grip.

"Bud!" she called out.

He stopped and turned, a questioning look on his face.

"Wait up!" She began trotting down the road, turning to wave back at Lee. "Thanks for the dance!"

Lee's face reddened. "Carolina, wait!"

But she kept running, cursing her ridiculous platform shoes, till she reached Bud. "You're going my way," she said breathlessly. "Do you mind walking me home?"

Bud's brows furrowed, and he looked over at Lee still standing under the light by the warehouse, hands on his hips, watching

101

them, and then back at Carolina. "I thought you were with Lee."

Carolina shook her head, not breaking eye contact. This was, she knew, a defining moment. "No. I'm with you."

He looked at her a moment longer, putting things right in his mind. Then he released a slow smile. "Well, then, I'd be pleased to walk you home."

He put out his arm and she slipped hers through it, holding tight, never looking back.

September 21, 2008
White Gables

That night seemed a lifetime ago, Carolina thought as she leaned her elbows against her knees and plucked off her garden gloves. She slapped the gloves against her leg, bits of dirt flung from them. A wry smile curved her lips. It *was* a lifetime ago. By the end of that year, she and Bud were engaged to be married, and at their wedding the following June, Odelle and Lee had announced their engagement.

The school bell from down the road began tolling. Eight o'clock already! Carolina thought, jolting upright. The morning was flying by, and here she was, daydreaming. She rose and brushed the soil from her jeans, then went indoors to the phone. She had to call the dentist. She didn't think she could bear any more pain today.

5

September 21, 2008, 10:00 a.m.
McClellanville

The breakfast shift was over at T. W. Graham's Restaurant. An elderly couple made their way out the front door. Toomer pulled off his chef's hat and went out back for a smoke. Only Mr. Hill remained at his usual table, drinking coffee from a heavy white mug and reading the newspaper. Lizzy was wiping the tables. Behind the counter, Nancy was putting fresh pastries on the glass-covered tiered stand, muttering under her breath. It had been another slow morning.

T. W. Graham's was an institution in McClellanville — the real deal. Converted from a grocery store to a restaurant back in the 1950s, it had wood tables painted with a local map, vinyl-covered chairs and booths, and wood shelving filled with old books — all original, lending an old-fashioned air that reproductions could not imitate. The colorful history of the town literally hung from the walls in the form of shrimp nets, photographs, and paintings by local artists. One had created an enormous wooden mechanical shrimp that hung from the ceiling. Outside on Pinckney Street, a chalkboard advertised daily specials beneath a big arrow pointing inside, emblazoned with the word EAT.

Unfortunately, these days, few people were following the arrow.

"Hardly needs nothing," Nancy said as she stared at the tower of pastries. A cake doughnut was clutched in her metal tongs. Nancy was about the same age as Lizzy's mother and, like Carolina, lean and fit. Her hair, though white, was cut in a youthful, spiky style.

"Such a waste. . . . Want one? You might as well. They'll go stale."

Lizzy shook her head. "No, thanks." She saw the worry etched on Nancy's face. "Maybe we'll get a good lunch crowd."

Nancy sighed as she replaced the glass bell over the stand. "I sure hope so."

Her sentence was punctuated by the ringing of the small bell over the front door. A man in an olive green uniform entered the restaurant.

"Here comes the pickle guy," Nancy said, using her derogatory name for a conservation officer.

"Shhh," Lizzy hissed, then looked up with a smile on her face. "Hey, Ben!" she greeted him as he came to the counter. He was about her height but so slender she always felt bigger standing next to him. "What brings you in so early today?"

Ben Mitchell's face eased into a grin. "You, pretty lady."

Lizzy blushed, aware of how carelessly she'd tied back her hair and how her pale Scottish-English skin could look washed-out with lack of sleep. Her hand darted up to smooth her hair.

"No, really," she replied demurely, walking to one of the small tables and setting down a menu.

Ben slid onto a chair, then brought his hands up to rub his eyes. His heavy-framed glasses bobbed as they bumped against his knuckles. He opened his eyes and smiled, folding his hands on the table. "I was nearby, working on a case."

Closer now, Lizzy could see on his face the kind of deep fatigue that could turn a tan chalky. His eyes, usually the color of a morning sky, were rimmed with red.

"How about a cup of coffee?"

"Sounds great."

"Want a pastry with that? They're right fresh," Nancy said, lifting the glass off the tiered stand with a flourish. "Made them myself."

"Uh, thank you, ma'am. Sure, why not?"

Lizzy could tell he really didn't want one but was being polite. What southern gentleman could refuse to taste a woman's home-baked goods? Nancy smiled smugly and picked out an iced doughnut, set it on a plate, and carried it to Ben, offering a napkin beside it. She stepped back, crossing her arms. Lizzy knew she would roost there and watch him eat the whole thing.

"I'll get us some coffee," she said, tugging at Nancy's arm as she retreated behind the counter. Lizzy pulled two mugs from the shelf and filled them with hot coffee. "I'm going to take my break now, okay?"

"Sure, honey. It's deader than a church on a Friday night. I'll be in back making my crab cakes." Before she left she gave Lizzy a hooded glance warning her that, for all his buying her doughnut, Ben Mitchell was still from the South Carolina Department of Natural Resources and wasn't one of "them."

Lizzy carried the coffee to the table by the windows. She slid into a chair opposite Ben.

107

With two fingers, she pushed the heavy white mug toward him.

She watched his long fingers encircle the mug. Ben had delicate hands for a man. His job as a conservation officer kept him outdoors, but his hands, though deeply tanned and chapped, were unscarred and his fingernails clean. Lizzy always noted a man's hands. Her eyes followed the mug as he lifted it past the insignia of the DNR with its images of a shrimp boat, a deer head, and a fish.

She'd met Ben years earlier when he'd come to McClellanville to make sure the local trawlers were using the newly mandated turtle excluder devices on their nets. Back then she was newly divorced and cast her fiery anger over all shrimpers and the industry collectively. The captains were steaming mad back then, at war with wildlife officials and claiming that TEDs, with their escape openings to prevent sea turtles from drowning in the nets, cost them their catch and would drive them out of business. At that point in her life, any attribute a man had that bore no relation to shrimping was appealing.

Right from the start, she knew Ben was different. Soft-spoken and well-mannered, he seemed more at home alone on his boat or in a library than confronting a dock full of angry, fist-clenching men. When he climbed aboard the *Miss Carolina* that first time, he'd looked like a kid in his brand-new uniform next to her towering, broad-shouldered father. Bud knew he was an intimidating figure and never hesitated to use that clout. Derogatory remarks from local shrimpers were spat out with chewing tobacco, slurs like "turtle kisser" and "tree hugger."

She'd learned a lot about the power of a calm head and a respectful tone that morning. Ben had stood his ground with her father, something not many men could do. Years later, her daddy would say Ben Mitchell was as thin and strong as tensile steel. Once her father started using the TEDs in his nets, the other shrimpers along Jeremy Creek followed suit.

Of course, the name Ben Mitchell was mud at their dinner table for years afterward. Whenever it was spoken, it was in heat and accompanied by words that had her mother sputtering, "Your language, Bud! I'll not have such words at my table."

In the ensuing years, however, both the TEDs and Ben Mitchell were found to provide a useful service, and though her father would never admit it, Ben had earned a grudging respect in McClellanville. Ben covered the coast from Sullivan's Island to Winyah Bay, and he spent a lot of time on the surrounding creeks, shallow flats, and docks. It was natural that he and Lizzy would cross paths. Last year when Ben had asked Lizzy out on a date, her first thought was how it would make her daddy mad. After all, no matter how well Ben got along with the locals, he was still DNR. To her surprise and disappointment, all her father mustered when he found out was raised brows and a weary shake of his head. Over the past six months, however, she'd found she liked Ben Mitchell — liked his gentleness, his intelligence, his honesty. A lot more than she'd ever imagined.

"You look tired," Lizzy said to Ben. He sat leaning heavily on his elbows. His shirtsleeves were rolled up, revealing tanned arms covered with bug bites. "Like you've slept in your clothes."

Ben released a weary chuckle. "As a matter of fact, I did. What a night."

"What happened?"

"I had to stake out some guys trying to sell shrimp they caught over bait."

"Hope you got them," she replied, indignant. "My daddy always told me that he didn't begrudge a fellah going out and catching his limit to fill his freezer. But he says some folks get greedy and go out every night, fixing to sell it. That kind of bait shrimper is no better than a thief, as far as I'm concerned."

No professional shrimper liked shrimp baiting, open to anyone who had a boat, a cast net, and a twenty-five-dollar license. But it was supposed to be strictly recreational. A person could catch forty-eight quarts of shrimp — with heads on — per trip for personal use, no more. To sell shrimp caught over bait was a crime, and one that shrimpers took personally.

"Yep, they're in the wrong, and that makes it my job to catch them. I had a tip about these two guys. I dogged them for forty-eight of the longest hours of my life." He took a loud sip of his coffee, then chuckled as he put the mug down. "They were something else. It was so dark I couldn't see my hand in front of my face, but with the light at the front of their boat, I could see them clear as day casting along their line of poles. So I followed them from the boat landing all the way over to their garage. I could see the coolers sitting there. I had the shrimp in my view the whole time." He lazily reached over to scratch the bites on his arm.

"So what did you do?"

"I hid in the bushes a ways off and waited all night. Mosquitoes the size of bats near drained the blood from me. It was boring as hell. Finally, around dawn, a truck pulls up with two more guys, all rested and clean-shaven. What I wouldn't have given for a cup of coffee and a shower at that point! I was dirty, thirsty, hungry, and blood-drained and I wanted to bust them all right then and there, but I waited till money passed hands. Then I stepped out and wrote up tickets."

Lizzy smiled wickedly. "I'll bet you surprised them."

His lips twitched. "Yes, I did."

There was a quiet moment between them, long enough for her to wonder what it would be like to have the kind of passion that kept you sitting like a human pincushion, prey to hordes of mosquitoes in bushes all night. It was his dedication that she found attractive in Ben.

Ben's job was steady, but he'd never get rich at it. When she'd asked him about that, he said being able to work outdoors at a job he loved made him the richest man in the world. She guessed it was her lot in life to be attracted to poor men who loved their jobs.

"Let me freshen your coffee."

He put his hand on her arm to restrain her. "I'm fine. I've got a thermos in the truck."

"You hungry, then? I could make you up some eggs and grits. Or do you want lunch? Nancy is making crab cakes."

"I'm too tired to eat. Thanks just the same."

She looked at him, so thin his bones protruded, and thought how he needed to sit down and eat three square meals a day for the next six months. "What's the matter? You seem kind of down."

He looked across the room, the angles of his face sharp in the shadow. "Oh, I don't know," he said wearily, scratching his neck. "Sometimes I just feel . . ."

"Feel what?"

"It's all so . . . futile," he said, his hand falling to the table. "I mean, I spend forty-eight hours — all frigging night — chasing down four guys. Not necessarily bad men, just guys doing something bad, trying to make some cash, trying to get by."

"You did the right thing. They're poachers."

"Sure. But it's not why I went into this. To confiscate some nets and a few measly shrimp? Write a few tickets? You ought to come with me sometime when I'm flying over the trawlers. I see mud wakes following the boats that crisscross nearly the whole coast."

"Ben, you know the shrimp live in the muddy bottoms." Lizzy held back from adding, *What do you expect them to do, just quit shrimping?* She didn't ask, because she didn't want to hear his answer.

"To be honest, in these waters the bottom is mostly mud anyway. But in other places, like the North Atlantic, those huge deep-sea trawlers are ripping up coral and destroying entire ecosystems. Some of those reefs are over four thousand years old. Think about it. It's in that coral that the fish we eat spawn. It's in those ancient beds that the fry and juveniles are protected from predators. What happens when it's destroyed? It's not going to bounce back. When it's gone, it's gone. And so are the fish." He picked up his coffee mug. "Someday, we're all going to be mighty hungry."

Ben sipped, then leaned back against the chair. "That's what I'd like to stop. Or at least try." He released a defeated chuckle. "Maybe it won't make a rat's ass bit of difference."

His weariness affected her deeply, because he'd put in the hours that earned him an opinion. She'd lived in this town all of her life. She'd rarely left the county. Generations of Morrisons and Brailsfords had made their living from these waters. She'd spent the first several years of her life aboard a boat and knew the names of many local fish, birds, and plants. But it was Ben who'd helped her appreciate that the landscape that had nurtured and sustained her and her family was fragile and needed tending. He'd challenged her to see that she couldn't just take, take, take. That she had to give back, too.

"Then why don't you?" she asked. "You're young. Unmarried. Free. You can pick up and go anywhere. What's keeping you here?"

He raised his head. "I'm asking myself the same question."

His eyes searched hers and she knew that Ben — the man, not the officer — was trawling for her answer. Her mother's words from that morning sprang to mind — *it was Cupid's arrow, straight to the heart* — and Lizzy realized with bone-deep certainty that she did not feel that pang of love for Ben. The realization saddened her.

She reached up to sweep a lock of hair from her face, breaking his gaze. "You have a calling, Ben. A passion. Not everyone has that."

"Why do you always do that?"

"Do what?"

"Sell yourself short."

"I — I wasn't."

He shrugged. "If you say so. But what I heard was you telling me you don't have a passion. Am I wrong?"

This arrow struck true. She sat back. "We were talking about *your* goals."

"And I'm talking about yours. What is your passion, Lizzy?"

She clamped her lips tightly and glared.

Ben spread open his hands, as though to concede the point. After a pause, he said softly, "You're smart, you know."

She looked at her hands, seeing in her mind's eye the many books he'd given her to read: Matthiessen, Bartram, Carson, Pilkey. She'd held them in these hands, devouring each word. He'd been her tutor, her friend. So when he complimented her, his words fell sweet on her ears.

Lizzy looked at the clock above the cash register. "Listen, I've got to get back to work." She started to rise.

"Lizzy, wait." He seemed suddenly shy, unable to meet her gaze. "I really stopped by to see you and invite you to dinner. I have to drive over to Fort Johnson to get some paperwork finished, then crash for a while." He glanced up, squinting. "I could come by later, say five o'clock?"

"Sure. That'd be nice."

He rose, then leaned slightly over the table to say, "I'd like to talk more about what's holding me back."

Her breath held as he straightened; then he added, "You smell real nice. Lavender, right?"

Lizzy nodded with a shaky smile, then watched him walk away, waving once before he closed the door behind him. She stared at the door, hearing his words again, understanding full well their import and wondering if she could learn to love a good friend like that in time.

"Lizzy, got a minute?"

Nancy had emerged from the back room, drying her hands on a towel. It occurred to Lizzy that she'd been waiting for Ben to leave. The restaurant was empty. Lizzy groaned inwardly, expecting another lecture about how she shouldn't be dating the "pickle guy."

Nancy slid into Ben's chair across from Lizzy. She narrowed her eyes and said, "Looks like things are getting tight between you and *him*." The way she said *him* spoke volumes of her disapproval.

"We're just friends."

"Uh-huh. What's that phrase you kids use

117

now? Friends with benefits."

Lizzy barked out a laugh, surprised Nancy would know it. "Isn't there some phrase about harassment at work?"

"Come on, girl, I'm just worried about you. You know he's never going to be accepted by your daddy."

"You're making too much out of this, really. Like I said, we're just friends. End of story."

Nancy picked a bit of flour from her nail and said cagily, "I thought you and Josh were friendly again."

Lizzy puffed out a plume of air, thinking, Is my whole life up for public scrutiny? "We are."

"He's a good boy. He might've got himself into a bit of trouble before, but he was young. It's to his credit that he cleaned up his act. I've seen it for myself down at the Crab Shack. Josh is there sometimes with his friends, and the most I ever seen him drink was a beer or two. He's never rowdy. Always polite. I'm telling you, the boy has changed." She nodded her head in affirmation. "The Truesdales are a good family."

Lizzy fixed her smile and wondered if her mother and Nancy hadn't plotted out this PR campaign for Josh.

"Take some advice from an old married lady."

Lizzy sighed. Here came that old chestnut about how men might be the captains of the ship but women were the navigators.

"Even the best marriages have bad patches. All those talk shows have folks airing their dirty laundry in public — and some of it is damn stained, if you know what I mean. I'm not whispering out of house when I tell you there were days Toomer and I didn't think we'd make it. The difference comes in whether or not you can forgive and move on. No matter if it's his fault or yours. Because at the root of forgiveness is love. Pure and simple. You either love him or you don't. And if you do, you make it work."

Nancy was fiddling with the slim gold band on her ring finger. It was common knowledge that back in the day when Toomer was a shrimper, he'd fooled around with loose women up and down the Florida coast. One day Nancy had had enough, packed up, and left him. When Toomer fell from the rigging and almost died, she'd come back to his house to care for him and never left again. Toomer never went back to shrimping, and instead they'd taken over the restaurant from his parents.

At least Nancy didn't bring up the notorious exploits of Lizzy's grandfather, Oz Morrison, with his three mistresses and two wives. And nobody ever talked about the separation between Bud and Carolina.

"It's our way," Nancy added, bringing home again the point that there was a code of solidarity in the shrimping community.

Lizzy looked up at the nets that hung from the ceiling, feeling trapped in them. "I'll try to remember that. Thank you," she said, beginning to lift herself from her chair.

"Lizzy, honey . . . that's not what I meant to talk to you about."

Lizzy relaxed back into her seat, surprised. "Oh?"

Nancy took a deep breath and heaved a ragged sigh. "Well, Lizzy, there's no easy way to say this, so I'll just speak plainly."

Lizzy's gaze sharpened, noticing again Nancy fiddling nervously with her ring.

"You know things have been slow. The summer crowd wasn't what it should have been, and with the local economy . . ." She shrugged. "We held on as long as we could but, well, I'm afraid we have to close the restaurant."

Lizzy sucked in her breath. "Close Graham's? You've got to be joking! It's been here forever."

"Don't you think we know that, honey? And don't you think knowing that made this decision the hardest one we've ever made? Toomer is sick about it. We been over and over this, and there really isn't any decision we can make except to close."

"But . . . business might pick up."

"We can't afford to keep our doors open. It's as simple as that."

"Maybe someone else wants to buy it. To keep it going."

"If you know someone who does, send them our way." Her face softened in sadness. "Oh, Lizzy, I know this puts you out of a job, and I'm sorry. You've been with us for so long you're like family to me and Toomer. I always said, if we'd of had a son, I'd of wanted him to marry you. As it is, you're the daughter we'd like to have had. So it pains us to let you go."

Feeling shell-shocked, Lizzy looked at her hands clenched on the table.

"Don't look so down in the mouth. We'll advertise to sell the place, and just maybe someone *will* come up and buy it and keep it going. Wouldn't that be nice?" She wiped an imaginary spot off the table with her towel. "Anyway, I just wanted you to know from me."

Lizzy was floundering. Her one security

— her job — had just slipped out from under her. But it was more. There had been signs all over town for years that the shrimping industry was in trouble. Boats were being docked. A walk down the block showed one house for sale after another. Now it affected her, and she knew fear.

"I never thought I'd see this day."

"Me neither, honey."

"Everything is changing," Lizzy said mournfully.

Nancy reached out to pat Lizzy's hand. "Why don't you get some fresh air? I'll hold the fort for a while."

6

On board the Miss Carolina

It was the pain that brought Bud back to consciousness. A constant throbbing of intense hurt. He blinked heavily, his eyes stinging from a salty crust of sweat and tears. His left arm ached like someone had tried to rip it from its socket. Turning his head, he saw that he was hanging from his left arm, half slumped on the winch and half lying on the deck. He'd pulled muscles that he didn't even know existed. They burned both hot and cold.

He tried to raise himself but cried out and collapsed as though he'd been shot. Burning pain exploded in his left arm. Bud retched and gasped for air, trying to steady his balance. He was pinned. Through the blur of pain his memory kicked in, and his heart began to pump wildly. In his mind's eye he saw himself slipping, and in a rush

123

he realized what had happened.

His hand was caught in the winch.

His mind repeated this over and over, not wanting to accept it.

"Noooo," he groaned, closing his eyes. "No, no, no. This can't be happening to me. How could I have been so *stupid? Stupid. Stupid.*"

Bud lowered his head into the crook of his arm. The salty trickle down his face mingled with sweat. Bud wept for the loss of his hand. He wept for the loss of his livelihood. He also wept from fear. For in his heart he knew he'd been wrong to go out alone today, a fool to travel so far out in off weather without a crew. He was pinned here, helpless as a baby. He couldn't get to the radio, couldn't call for help. He was going to die out here.

Bud gulped hard, warding off nausea as he worked up the courage to try again. Not that he wanted to — he had to. He had to fight for his own survival.

Gathering his wits, he figured his arm was dislocated from the fall. Bud held his breath and, grunting with the effort, lifted himself to his knees. Shifting his weight, he paused, gulping for breath as sweat poured down his face. Slowly, he tried to straighten his back, rising in degrees. Blood drained from his head and he almost keeled over from dizziness, but he gripped the winch with his good hand and waited for it to pass.

When he felt ready to face the damage, he wiped his forehead against his sleeve, took a breath, and looked down his left arm. His arm was wet with blood and what was left of his hand was crushed between cable and drum. What had once been a thing of God-given beauty was now a mutilated mass of torn muscle, bone, and blood. He jerked his head up, eyes wide, instinctively looking for help.

The first-aid kit was in the pilothouse. So was the radio.

He felt bile rise in his throat as the full reality slammed into his brain. He was pinned to the winch. He couldn't move, couldn't get himself free. Couldn't call for help. All of the misery, pain, and fear was compounded by the fact he was alone, deathly alone. Bud wasn't a man who shook easily, but he was scared of what might be coming.

"Stay calm, stay clearheaded," he chanted as a mantra. Bud knew his survival depended on it. He'd been in bad patches before. Once Pee Dee had fallen from the rigging and the bone from his leg had stuck clear out from the skin. Man, could that kid scream. Bud had kept his head and done what he had to do to help Pee Dee, but it was harder to help himself. He gritted his teeth and shook his head with a guttural growl. You can do this, he told himself. He had to take stock. Putting on his war face, Bud forced himself to look at the carnage again.

A trickle of blood dripped from his hand to a pool on the deck. It looked like veins were severed. First, he had to stem the bleeding. If it were a major artery, he'd already be dead. A bit of good news, at least. His arm was slightly raised; also good. How much blood had he lost? He squinted and looked closer at the pool of blood. It was surreal to feel so detached, as if the blood had come from someone else. Then he almost retched; a severed finger lay on the deck.

His first thought was to save it. He'd heard stories of body parts being reattached. Pain burst anew as he stretched his good arm toward the finger. Try as he might, it was a few inches too far under the drum. He tried again, then stopped, panting from the effort. It wasn't going to happen. What was the use, anyway? He couldn't get to the ice. Here he was, sitting over a vast hold of ice, and he couldn't get to a single cube.

126

Pee Dee would have a laugh over this one.

"Don't give up," Bud told himself. "Stay alert. I just got to hang on. Someone will figure out where I am. Someone will come. Stay alive . . . that's it. C'mon. I can do this. I can do this!"

He shook his head in disbelief. Was he losing his mind, talking to himself like this? But it made him feel better. And what the hell. Who was listening?

He needed to make a tourniquet. Bud patted his rear pocket, then pulled out the Swiss Army knife Carolina had given to him as a gift years before. No sailor worth his salt would leave home without a pocketknife. He looked at the black and red case lying in his palm. It was a solid knife with a good, heavy feel to it. Thank God it was his left hand that was mangled or he wouldn't live long enough to open this thing, he thought. It was described as a one-handed pocketknife. Bud had never had call to test that claim before and prayed that wasn't just some fancy name. He slumped with relief when he could actually open the knife with one hand.

He was wearing a long-sleeved shirt over his T-shirt. Spots of blood splattered the white cotton. He managed to cut a narrow strip of fabric from the hem. Sweat stung

127

his eyes as he bent his head to grip one end in his teeth, painstakingly tying a tourniquet using his free hand and his mouth. Simple movements he'd taken for granted as a two-handed man took his full concentration with only one.

He racked his brain, trying to remember facts he'd learned about tourniquets. There was a limit to how long he should wear one. . . . Was it an hour? Two? Shit, he thought, his dismay deepening. He wasn't wearing a watch. He wouldn't know when sixty minutes had passed.

"You really did it this time," he muttered. "Going out alone. . . . You didn't have the sense to tell anyone where you were headed. Secret spot, hell. So secret I'm going to die out here with the stinking gulls. Now no one knows where you are! I should have told Carolina. Or Pee Dee."

A thought burst in his head, and he held his breath. Pee Dee knew this spot. They'd been talking about checking it out to see if the shrimp were running. If Pee Dee had his wits about him, he might remember. Surely he would. . . .

Bud jerked his head up, but he couldn't see over the railing. Even if the *Miss Carolina* drifted some, the boat was moving slowly. He took heart, thinking there was a good chance Pee Dee could find him. He'd tied the tourniquet. All he could do now was wait.

The wind gusted, billowing the frayed edge of his shirt. He looked down at it, ripped and spotted with his blood. Once upon a time, this had been his best shirt. Carolina had given it to him back when he'd gone to see her parents in Greenville to announce that they were getting married. It was his first visit. There hadn't been many more.

He lowered his head to rest against his arm, feeling the muscles of his neck stretch. Closing his eyes, Bud let his mind wander back to the day this shirt was new.

February 1975
Greenville, South Carolina
It was a cool night, and the heater in Bud's truck was broken. Carolina cuddled against him, smelling of her own special brand of sweetness, her flame-colored hair blowing in the wind. She'd been chiding herself for forgetting that in the mountains, no matter how warm the day, the air was chilly once the sun lowered. Bud told her she'd been in the lowcountry too long and was getting coldblooded, expecting a retort. Instead, she'd said softly that the lowcountry was

129

her home now. Bud was of the school where a man didn't get giddy, but Carolina made him so damn happy. They were busting with the news that they were going to get married.

The sky was dusky when they arrived at the country club Carolina's parents belonged to. Bud paused at the pretentious black-iron gates. They stood open, more a statement about exclusivity than serving any real function. Bud lifted his arm from around Carolina's shoulders to lean forward and cut off the music. Quiet suddenly descended, save for the truck engine purring like a well-fed cat. Talk ceased between them, too, as anxiety tightened their throats. Carolina sat up and with prim strokes smoothed her pink cashmere sweater.

Bud leaned over to give her a quick kiss. She smiled, seemingly relieved. They both knew they might not get another chance in front of the old man.

With a deep breath, he rammed the stick into first gear. Shadows dappled the winding driveway as they passed a meandering creek, towering hardwoods, and the rolling fairways of the golf course. A couple of die-hard golfers were trying to squeeze in a few holes before the sun set. Bud felt apprehension tighten his gut at seeing the white pillars of the country club, looming like a facsimile of Tara or the White House on top of the hill. Closer, he saw a young valet, probably a college boy from Clemson, leap forward to open the door of a Cadillac for a woman in a fancy dress and high heels. The driver, a middle-aged man in a gray suit, handed his keys to the valet with hardly a backward glance.

Bud ran his finger around his collar. Carolina had purchased the white button-down shirt for him on King Street in Charleston. She'd also bought him khaki pants and a navy wool blazer. "Just because," she'd told him, but he knew full well it was because she wanted her fiancé to make a good impression on her parents. Because he wanted the same thing, he wore them.

"This tie is choking me."

"You look handsome."

He could hear in her voice that she found him attractive in his new getup. "I feel like I'm about to get lynched."

"They'll love you. I promise."

"I don't know why we had to meet them at some country club. Why couldn't we just go to your house for barbecue like normal folks?"

"It's just a local club. We hang out here all

the time. Mama and Daddy like to invite people here for dinner. It's so easy. Between golf and meetings, Daddy practically lives here, and Mama doesn't have to fuss. I think cooking makes her nervous."

Bud looked at her askance. "You're not going to take after your mama, are you?"

"I'm not a good cook, if that's what you're asking."

"Doesn't matter, sweet thing, because I'm a great cook. I'll spoil you with my barbecue."

"Thank God," she said, unbuckling her seat belt. "Our marriage is secure. What does any successful marriage need other than a good barbecue recipe?"

"Don't knock it, babe. No self-respecting southern male doesn't have a good recipe for sauce."

The valet took his keys, uttering, "Cool truck!" Bud put his hand on the small of Carolina's back and guided her inside. He'd give the boy a tip that made him feel as good as that comment did him.

The moment he stepped into the country club, he felt his skin crawl. The boldly colored walls seemed out of sync with the reproduction American furniture and the oriental porcelain that filled dark wood breakfronts. Carolina slipped her arm through his and led him across the black-and-white-tiled foyer toward the main dining room. The club was bustling with activity. Couples in evening dress talked to others dressed in golf shirts who had finished their games and were looking to have a quick drink or two at the bar before heading home. Bud tried to compare it to a night at the Crab Shack back home, then chuckled. Where were the clouds of cigarette smoke and the Jim Beam?

"Carolina!"

"Mama!"

Carolina released his arm and he followed her across the foyer to a tiny woman with blond bouffant hair. She stood trim and erect in a blue silk pantsuit with hefty pearls at her ears and neck. When Carolina stepped back, Mrs. Brailsford's eyes darted to Bud. He noticed they were the same blue as Carolina's, but while Carolina's eyes were as warm as the embers of a fire, her mother's were like chips of ice.

"Mama, this is Bud Morrison. Bud, my mother, Allison Brailsford."

She offered a polite smile. "So, you're the one we've been hearing so much about. Bud is a nickname for . . . ?"

"William, ma'am," he replied, taking her extended hand. "William Morrison III."

Her hand was limp, her smile weak.

"Where's Daddy?" asked Carolina.

"Oh, you know your father. He's got to stop and say hello to everyone he passes." She looked down the hall. "There he is now, over by the Pub."

Bud turned his head to see a tall man about the same age as his father. But unlike the barrel-chested Oz, who loved his plaid flannel shirts, this man looked distinguished in his navy blazer with brass buttons, gray pants, and Italian leather shoes. His hair was the color of burnished copper streaked with gray. His deep voice boomed, and Bud overheard scores shared and quick comments that ended with a burst of hearty laughs and pats on the back. Mr. Brailsford caught his wife's gaze, signaled with his hand that he'd seen them, and broke from his friends.

Carolina trotted forward to be swept into her father's embrace.

"Carolina adores her father," Allison Brailsford said, her gaze on the pair. "She's never done anything to disappoint him."

Bud heard the velvet warning.

Carolina's cheeks matched her pink sweater as she brought her father closer. Bud could see where she got her hair color and height. He saw, too, the same imperial radiance.

"Daddy," she announced as they drew near, "this is my Bud."

He saw her father's brows rise slightly at her emphasis on the word *my*. Bud worried that she was trying too hard.

"Bud, this is the other man in my life, my father, Edgar Brailsford."

"Mr. Brailsford," Bud said, extending his hand.

Edgar Brailsford's eyes were flinty as they inspected Bud, and he let Bud's hand hang in the air for a second too long.

"Hello, young man." He grabbed Bud's hand in his own large paw and delivered a bone-cracking squeeze. In that grip, Bud felt the strength of a man who could deliver a rock-solid punch. No number of years behind a fancy desk in a bank could mask the bully in a man's handshake.

"Your table is ready, Mr. Brailsford."

"Shall we?" Edgar Brailsford said. He placed an arm around his daughter's shoulders and guided her toward the dining room.

"I'll just be a minute," Bud said, excusing himself.

While the Brailsfords walked toward their table, Bud hastily retreated to the Pub down the hall, rubbing the pale finger imprint on

135

his hand. He went straight to the bar, lifted his hand to draw the bartender, and ordered bourbon, neat.

"Are you a member, sir?"

"No. I'm with the Brailsfords."

"I can put it on his account."

"My cash isn't good here?"

"I'm afraid not. I can put it on the Brailsford account," he repeated.

Bud was tempted. "No, I'm good," he said, pocketing his wallet. He walked back to the dining room, cursing the system that wouldn't let a man buy a drink with good, hard cash when he needed one. He didn't like feeling obliged, but that was just what Brailsford had intended, Bud realized.

The large dining room was dominated by an enormous crystal chandelier. Beneath it were dozens of round tables draped in white linen and adorned with flickering votive candles. The low buzz of conversation was spiked with occasional bursts of laughter. Bud spotted the Brailsfords at a prime table in front of a wall of windows draped in pale blue floral chintz. The shadowy outline of the golf course spread out beyond them.

Bud straightened his tie and wound his way through the room, unaware of how many women cast furtive glances at the strikingly handsome, deeply tanned man in a crisp white shirt and dark blazer.

Brailsford stood when he reached the table and pulled out a chair for Bud beside him and opposite Carolina, closest to the impressive stone fireplace in which burning logs crackled. Within minutes of being seated, Bud could feel the heat seeping through his wool jacket.

Edgar Brailsford brought his hands together in a soft clap. "We're all here now," he said jovially, then turned to Bud. "What will you drink?"

"Do you have anything on tap?" Bud asked the waitress.

"Wait, Daddy," Carolina said, placing one hand on her father's sleeve. "Let's order champagne."

Brailsford's gaze shot to his wife. He quickly collected himself. "Are we celebrating tonight?"

Carolina was smiling, but her eyes were blazing, imploring her father not to embarrass her. This wasn't the way Bud had wanted to lay out his hand tonight, but these were Carolina's parents and it was her play.

"Well, I wanted to do this with a champagne toast, but why wait? Bud and I have some wonderful news." She stuck out her hand, revealing a modest diamond. "We're getting married!"

There was an awkward pause while Brailsford sat immobile and his smile hardened on his face. Beside him, Bud could have sworn he heard Allison Brailsford's sharp intake of breath. She released a soft, "Oh, my. . . ."

Bud felt the heat of the fire on his back and looked to Carolina for his cue. She looked momentarily lost.

Bud cleared his throat. "We'd like your blessing, sir."

Brailsford leaned back in his chair. He clearly was not a man who appreciated surprises. He turned to face Bud. "Well, sir, in my day we asked the father for his permission before his blessing."

"I understand that, sir. But the lady already said yes."

"Daddy, don't be old-fashioned," Carolina quickly interjected, striving for levity. "Bud and I love each other and are getting married. That's all there is to it."

"Then my blessing isn't really necessary, is it? Not if you're going to do it whether I approve or not."

"Oh, Edgar, be happy for them. Our baby is getting married!" Allison Brailsford exclaimed. Her icy composure had melted like a spring thaw at the prospect of a wedding. Bud saw that Carolina got her dreamy, idealistic side from her mother.

Edgar Brailsford leaned toward his daughter, showing Bud his back, and placed his hand over hers. Carolina leaned toward him and they huddled close, their gazes locked.

"Do you love him, baby?"

"I do, Daddy. With all my heart."

Resignation flooded Brailsford's features as his shoulders lowered. Gently patting Carolina's hand, he said softly, "You know I just want you to be happy."

"Thank you, Daddy."

Then he turned toward Bud. His face was inscrutable. "Bud, is it?"

"It's short for William," Allison interjected.

"It's a damnable thing to learn the name of your future son-in-law the night you meet him."

"Daddy, that's no one's fault but your own. I've been in McClellanville for six months and you haven't been to visit once." Carolina's tone was gently scolding. Bud could see she had her father wrapped around her finger.

Brailsford put out his hand. "Congratulations."

Bud took the hand and once again felt a firm warning in the grip. "Thank you, sir. I'll take good care of her."

"You'd better."

Champagne was poured, and the rest of the meal was an exercise in submission and respect. Carolina gave a colorful description of how she and Bud had met and fallen in love, and Allison was clearly swept up in the romance of her only daughter's joy.

Edgar Brailsford, however, took every opportunity to let Bud know that this was Brailsford's club, his people, his wife, his daughter. He made sure Bud clearly understood that this was the lifestyle that he'd provided for his family and to which his daughter was accustomed. He set aside the menu and announced that they'd all be having the prime rib because it was the best in town. While ordering the wine, he took pains to educate Bud as to the grape and the vineyard, making certain he slipped in the price of the bottle, and then ordered two.

While the two women huddled on the other side of the table in a giddy conversation about wedding plans, Brailsford grilled Bud on his livelihood, all the while liberally filling his wineglass. Bud took only polite tastes of the wine. He drank water copiously. Sweat soaked his shirt, and no matter how he adjusted his seat, he couldn't escape the heat.

"You know, I believe I knew your father, Oz," Brailsford said.

"Is that so? I'll be sure to tell him."

"How's that rascal doing?"

"He's doing good. The usual complaints."

"You're a shrimper, too, that right?"

"Yes, sir."

"I did some shrimping in my day. You know, my family came from McClellan-ville."

"Yes, sir."

"We weren't shrimpers. My family was in the mercantile business, and we moved to Mount Pleasant before I was born. Only one of us left in town is my aunt Lucille. You know her, of course."

"Everybody in McClellanville knows Miss Lucille."

A swift smile crossed Brailsford's face. "My aunt Lucille is a great lady. She and my late uncle Archie never had children, but they've taken a shine to our Carolina. Who wouldn't, eh?" he said, casting a doting glance at his daughter. Hearing her name, Carolina turned her head and smiled.

"You said you did some shrimping?" Bud asked, trying to maintain the conversation.

"That's right. When I was in college, I worked on the boats for a couple summers. I don't mind telling you I made some pretty good money."

"Yes, sir. We're having some good years now, too."

"Do you own your own boat?"

"I captain one of my father's boats. The *Miss Ann.* She's a fine sixty-footer, named after my mother."

"I was sorry to hear she passed."

"Thank you. My father hasn't taken the *Miss Ann* out since she died."

"So she's an old boat?"

A smile played at Bud's lips. "Yes, she is. But I'm good with my hands and I manage to keep her going."

"How's your crew?"

"The best. My brother and my cousin."

"Did you go to college?"

The hair at the back of his neck felt sticky and wet. Bud resisted the urge to take off his jacket. He didn't want Brailsford to see him sweat.

"I started, but quit after the first year. The money shrimping was too good and I couldn't see putting it off. It's what I wanted to do."

Edgar looked at Bud and seemed to be making a judgment. Then he picked up his tableware and dove into his beef. "So, Bud," he asked after a couple bites, "what do you do for a good time?"

"Sorry?"

"Do you golf? This is a great club. You can't see it now, but outside that window is one of America's top one hundred courses. It was designed by Robert Trent Jones. I could take you out, if you like."

"I don't play golf. If I have free time, I tend to go back out to the water. Carolina and I like to take the jon boat out for some creek fishing. She's pretty good, you know. If I get the chance, though, I do some deep-sea fishing." He cracked a smile. It was his turn to boast. "My pal Trey and I caught a bluefin tuna weighing seven hundred forty pounds. Caught that monster about a hundred twenty miles offshore."

Brailsford's eyes glittered as he leaned back in his chair. "You're quite the fisherman, aren't you, Bud?"

"Yes, sir, I am. When I see a fish I want, I catch it."

Their eyes met and held. Then Brailsford turned his head to the women on the other side of the table. "Well, ladies, that was a fine meal. Now Bud and I are going to the Pub for a smoke."

The two women turned their heads, surprised. Carolina's questioning gaze met Bud's. He shrugged.

Edgar stood and set his napkin on the

table. Bud followed suit and stretched his shoulders, glad to be away from the fire.

"Do you want us to wait for you?" asked Allison, her blue eyes wide. "Or if you like, Carolina and I can head back to the house. We have two cars."

"We'll wait," Carolina answered her mother. She rose and said with a smile, "Don't make it too long, Daddy. I'm tired."

"We're just going for a nightcap. You go on with your mother. Have some cognac by the fire in the lounge."

"Lord, we drank so much wine already I can barely walk," said Allison, rising on wobbly legs.

"Then order tea."

Allison drew herself up. "Come along, Carolina. I need to visit the powder room."

Edgar Brailsford turned and said brusquely, "Come on, Bud."

The Pub was a male bastion of dark paneled wood, rich blue carpet, and shining brass. Several men clustered on leather sofas and in bucket chairs, some with heads bent close in discussion, others leaning far back with drinks in their hands, laughing at jokes. Brailsford led Bud to a far corner of the bar where they could talk. The bartender came to them immediately.

"Yes, Mr. Brailsford? What can I get for you?"

"Scotch. Laphroaig. Straight up. And make it a double."

"And you, sir?" The waiter turned to Bud. Recognition flared in his eyes.

"A beer. Got anything local?"

"The Rainbow Trout Ale is a local favorite."

Bud nodded his approval, then reached up to loosen his tie and unbutton the top button of his shirt. Neither man spoke until the drinks appeared. Bud refused a glass and promptly took a long slug from the bottle. He'd avoided drinking the expensive cabernet during the grueling dinner to keep his wits and was dying for a beer. The ale was cold and crisp on his tongue and slid down his throat like it was quenching a fire. He set the bottle down and, leaning one elbow against the bar, turned to face Brailsford. The ladies were gone. He didn't feel the need for pretense and polish. Bud was on home turf in a man's bar.

Brailsford reached into his pocket to pull out two cigars. He handed one to Bud. It was long and fat and smelled great. They went through the male ritual of tipping and lighting the cigars. Brailsford tilted back his head to exhale a plume of smoke, then squared off and got the first punch in.

"So, you're the man who's going to marry my only daughter?"

Bud puffed out slowly. "I am."

"Well, son, frankly, I'm worried."

Bud looked at his cigar but didn't reply.

"I'm not a rich man," Brailsford continued, and held out his hands to indicate the comfortable surroundings. "But I do all right. I can provide a nice house in a good neighborhood with good schools. I gave Carolina the pretty things a girl likes to have. She never went without. And my daughter graduated from college." He paused, marking the distinction between Bud's and Carolina's education. He pointed his finger at Bud, the cigar extended like a drawn sword.

"I'm worried that you won't be able to provide the lifestyle she's accustomed to. A father worries about such things."

Bud shrugged. "You should ask your daughter what she wants."

"What does a girl know about what she wants at this age?"

"How old were you when you married your wife?"

Brailsford seemed irritated by this question and signaled for the bartender to replenish both drinks. He put his elbows on the bar and steepled his fingers, then turned his head toward Bud, his mouth curved downward.

"I'm asking if you can provide for my daughter."

"If I didn't believe I could, I wouldn't have asked her to be my wife."

"Let me give you a little history. I know how hard the shrimping life is. You work like slaves out there on the boats. It takes raw muscle and grit. I admire that. I do." His mouth twisted in a rueful smile. "I knew early on I wasn't going to be a shrimper. It's a tough life, for the men and the women. Where are you going to live? Do you even own a house?"

Bud's eyes flashed. The small wood bungalow he owned by the creek was stable, but barely. He often joked that the only thing keeping it together was the termites holding hands. It suited him as a bachelor, but he hadn't really given thought to bringing a wife there. His worry must have shown on his face, for Brailsford seized on this.

"Carolina's not as tough as she lets on. Oh, I know she can be brassy and hold her own. But underneath all that bluster is a gentle woman with a big heart who'd work her fingers to the bone for the man she loved and not complain. She'd figure she'd made her bed and had to sleep in it."

He took a long drag from his cigar, the ash about to fall.

"And while we're on the subject . . ." He pinned Bud with his gaze. "I knew your father, and let me tell you, he was one surly son of a bitch. You could hear his voice booming all the way down the creek. A type A personality, if I ever met one. I'm well aware of his reputation with the ladies, too. How many mistresses did he have? How many wives? That's not the life I want for my Carolina. Am I making myself clear?"

"Crystal clear. Now, let me give you a little history. No one knows that Oz Morrison is one mean, swearing, backbreaking, son of a bitch better than me. Who do you think covered for him when he fell asleep at the wheel of the boat? Who do you think stood in front of my mother to take the blows when he came home drunk? After she died, I was glad when he brought a lady home. At least we knew we'd get a home-cooked meal."

Bud leaned forward, his eyes narrowing. "But what you don't know is that beneath that growling, gruff exterior lives a gentleness that'd surprise you. He was a strong provider, always ready to lend a helping hand. But good and bad, that was him. Not me."

Bud clenched the brass railing of the bar, aware that their raised voices were attracting attention. He lowered his voice and said in measured tones, "And with all due respect, sir, this is my father you're speaking about, so I urge you to use caution. I can say what I want about my own father, but nobody else can."

Brailsford's lips thinned. "You won't cheat on my daughter?"

"I give you my solemn word. I won't cheat on your daughter."

"I don't want my daughter heading shrimp or cracking oysters at fifty cents a quart."

"She won't be."

Edgar finished his drink and slammed the glass on the bar. "Frankly, I don't believe you."

"Frankly, sir, I don't care what you believe." Bud set his bottle on the counter and turned to face Brailsford squarely.

"You like to grandstand about how you used to go out on the boats and do some shrimping when you were a kid. You can name a few names, maybe show a scar or two. I'll bet it makes a nice story while sitting around the bar with your fancy cigars and good scotches, going on and on to men who never so much as picked up a cast net in their lives. Men who probably never even thought about where the shrimp they're eating came from.

"You don't know what it feels like to man the winch in foul weather when the rain is pounding your back and the boat is rocking so hard you can barely stand, knowing that if you slip, you could lose your hand, or your leg, or just get sucked in and become mincemeat. You don't know what it's like to dangle on the end of an outrigger, dipping into the icy water, hanging on for dear life. Or what it means to go out, day after day, night after night, fighting the sea inch by inch to get her to give up enough of her bounty so you can come back to port and feed your wife and your kids.

"Sure, you had some fun as a kid. Earned some good money. Got a nice tan. That's nice. I'm glad for you." Bud jerked his chin, indicating the club. "All this might not be my world, but don't pretend that my world is yours. Because it's not. We have an exclusive club of our own. We have our own code." Bud stubbed out his cigar and rose to his feet. "And you're not one of us."

Bud reached into his pocket, pulled out his wallet.

"This is a private club. Your money's no

good here," Brailsford told him.

"Then consider this a tip. Thank you for the dinner and the conversation. It was . . . enlightening. Good night."

Bud left a twenty-dollar bill on the counter and headed out, his heels digging half-moons into the deep carpet. He went directly to the palc aqua lounge and found Carolina sitting at a white French bistro table drinking tea with her mother. She looked up; seeing his stormy expression, her face froze. Bud jerked his head, indicating it was time for them to go.

"I've got to go, Mama," she said, rising.

"I — I'll see you at the house," Allison replied, flustered at the abruptness.

"I don't know."

"Carolina!" Allison's voice was sharp.

Carolina paused.

Allison put her teacup in the saucer and straightened her shoulders, clenching her hands in her lap. When she spoke, her tone was measured. She didn't seem to see Bud standing in the doorway. "Carolina, honey. Bud's a nice fellah. Enjoy his kisses and his protective love. But don't marry him."

Carolina looked stunned. "But I thought . . ."

Allison shook her head with a pained expression, then pinned Carolina with her

151

pale blue gaze. "You can't bring him home for Easter dinner."

"I've got to go." Carolina grabbed her purse and hurried after Bud as he strode away.

She caught up with him in the foyer. He took her hand and they walked at a quick pace out of the club. With his left hand Bud ripped the tie from around his neck.

"What happened?" Carolina asked, looking worried.

"Not now."

Three couples waited in line for their cars. All Bud wanted to do was get in his truck and get the hell out before Carolina's parents came after them and talked them into staying the night. Bud dug into his wallet and pulled out another twenty. He put the bill in the valet's hand with his ticket.

"Just give me my keys and tell me where it is."

The young man pocketed the bill and handed over Bud's keys, pointing to a nearby lot.

They walked in silence across the parking lot. Her shoes made slapping noises against her heels as she trotted beside him. When they reached the truck, he tore off his jacket, opened the door, and angrily threw it inside. Then he leaned against the frame, feeling the night air cool the sweat on his back.

"Bud, what did my daddy say?"

"What do you think he said?"

"I think he said something about how you're not worthy of me."

Bud swung his head around. "Yeah. Something to that effect."

"Bud, he's my father. I'm his only daughter. He says that to everyone."

"I respect him for that."

"Then what's got you so riled? Besides having to wear a tie?"

"Carolina . . ." Bud shook his head, not knowing where to begin. He thrust his arm out, indicating the country club. "I . . . I can't give you all that." He bent his head to collect himself.

A knowing expression passed over her face and she leaned back against the truck. "Ah . . . so that's what this is about."

Bud turned to place his hands on the truck's roof and lean over Carolina. The overhead parking light performed magic on her skin, making it glow pale and unearthly. In sharp contrast, her hair gleamed like fired brick. Her blue eyes were fixed on him, her full lips turned up in a slightly mocking smile, daring him to go on. Carolina had no guile, no false pretenses. She was completely aware of how staggering her beauty could be, but she didn't use it as a weapon. At most, her beauty fed her confidence. He loved her. He wanted her. He was afraid to lose her.

"Do you really know me?" he asked in a low voice. "Know what kind of life I can offer you? Do you know your life isn't going to be country clubs or maids cleaning your house? In fact, if times get real tough, you might be cleaning someone else's house. My mother did. She did what she had to do when she had to do it. That's the way it is in our community. We never know from year to year if the shrimp will be good or bad."

"And you think I'm afraid of that? That I'm too pampered to take it?"

He straightened, dropping his hands to his sides. "I don't know." He said the words slowly, afraid they were the truth.

"I don't know either," she said honestly. "So tell me, then. What don't I know about you?"

"Baby, there's a lot you don't know about me."

"Like what?"

His lips tightened. In the background, he heard car engines revving, tires spinning on gravel as they drove off.

"Bud, tell me anything that comes to mind."

154

He looked up, as though trying to find his answer in the sky. "Do you know I love to read?"

She shook her head.

"I read anything and everything — fiction, nonfiction, magazines, cereal boxes, ads that come in the mail — anything to fill time on the boat while I'm dragging."

Carolina's face eased into a soft smile.

"I'm good at welding," he continued, warming to the subject. "I learned in high school, helping Hambone down at the dock. I did all the dirty work of cleaning up the metals to be welded, grinding, beveling the joints. After a year or two, he let me use a cutting torch. I'd finish my lunch quick and sneak some practice in before Hambone returned." He snorted. "Now I can fix a broken winch and about anything else I need to.

"I'm a decent mechanic. I know how to use a sewing needle, a hammer, and a paintbrush. I might not have finished college," he said, hearing the defensiveness in his voice, "but I spent years apprenticing under accomplished men in their crafts. I learned welding and mechanics because they're good skills for a captain to have. But I love doing the work because of the satisfaction I feel figuring out how to make an engine run and a boat float." He shrugged lightly. "And if I'm helping some other guy out, well, that makes me feel good about myself."

Hearing the words, Bud felt more himself. He stepped closer to Carolina and placed his hands around her waist, tugging her closer. He brought his nose to her neck, feeling the softness of her hair, inhaling her sweet scent. Lifting his head, he spoke in a low voice, inches from her face.

"I don't like getting up every morning in the dark. I don't like not being able to stay up till all hours of the night making love to my woman, then lingering the next morning with slow, deep kisses."

She exhaled a soft moan. He paused and took a step back.

"But I get up and get to the boat, because my absolute favorite things in the world are standing on the deck at first light when the sun fills you with hope, then again at last light when the sun lowers in all her glory. Those are introspective times. Peaceful times that give a man pause to reflect.

"I love my job, Carolina. I love the feel of the boat beneath me like a hundred wild horses plowing through the open water. I love not being stuck in some office without a window, wearing some goddamn coat and tie every day. I love feeling the wind at my face and the whole world laid out before me. I love being my own man. I love that freedom more than I love anything a big paycheck could buy me.

"And I love you, Carolina. I want you to be my wife. I want you to share my bed, have my children, go out on my boat, and grow old with me. *Me,* Carolina. Because everything I'm good at, everything I love, makes me great at my job. I'm a shrimper. That's not just what I do, it's who I *am.*"

He ran his hands through his hair.

"And that's who you're marrying. That's what you're getting yourself into. What you see is what you get. So get out now if you can't handle it or it's not what you had in mind. You'll break my heart, but I'd understand it."

Carolina stood silent before him for a few moments, looking at the small diamond on her left hand. Bud could hardly breathe, his chest was so tight. He felt sure she would remove the ring and hand it back to him.

"Bud, I don't know what kind of spineless, mindless girl you think I am. If I'd wanted to marry a banker like my father, or a lawyer, or a businessman, or anyone else who could buy me a nice house and give me the country-club lifestyle, honey, trust

me — I could have. I came to McClellanville because I chose to settle there. And I
not only want to marry a shrimper, I want
to be a shrimper myself. I want to go out
on the boat with you to see that first light
and last light from the deck instead of being
left behind on shore.

"I knew I was going to marry you from
the first moment I saw you. And if you think
I'm going to let you go now, you've got
another thing coming. Bud Morrison, I'm
going to be your wife, your crew, and your
best friend. I'm going to be your everything.
Because you might be good at a lot of
things, but I'm good at only one. That's loving you."

She reached up to cup his jaw in her hand.
"The rest" — she shrugged — "we'll take
as it comes along."

Bud's sigh was like the steam coming off
a fire after it has been doused.

"Come on," she said, and held out her
hand. "Let's go home. To McClellanville."

Bud drew her to him and kissed her. Not
the impetuous kiss that sealed a conversation, but the unhurried, possessive, endur-
ing embrace of commitment.

September 21, 2008
On board the Miss Carolina

Bud opened his eyes and blinked in the harsh sunlight. He remembered his last vision of Carolina in the wee hours of this morning, sleeping on her pillow, her red hair splayed around her.

He wished now he'd kissed her good-bye.

Bud clenched his hand into a fist. I'm not giving up. Just leave me an opening, he admonished death. I'll beat you. I've beaten you before. He wiped his face with his sleeve and lifted his head. I'm the captain of this boat, he thought. I know these waters better than any man alive. I'll figure a way out of this mess. I'll find my way home to Carolina.

7

September 21, 2008, 10:12 a.m.
Mount Pleasant

Carolina clenched the loops in her jeans, twisting them until the tips of her fingers turned white. The dentist was inserting a needle into her partly numbed gums. There was a pinpoint of pressure, then another. Then it was over.

"That wasn't so bad, was it?" asked her dentist.

Carolina's mouth was held open with a metal apparatus and stuffed full of cotton. She wanted to nod vigorously — yes! But she shook her head.

Dr. Assey sat back on the stool and lifted his goggles. Beside him, his assistant put away the tools with swift efficiency. "Now, you just wait here for a few minutes, Mrs. Morrison," he said. "We've got to give the Novocain a chance to take effect. Are you comfortable? Do you want a magazine?"

She wanted laughing gas, but again, Carolina shook her head.

"I'll be back in a few minutes." He patted her shoulder, then left the room.

Carolina wiggled her foot as her mouth numbed. The lower rear tooth was not going to get better. Dr. Assey had told her that she'd ignored the problem for too long and they'd have to do an extraction. The dentist was a good man and had offered to work out a more modest payment plan, knowing she didn't have insurance. So she'd reluctantly agreed and now was left to wonder how they'd manage to make the payments, no matter how reduced.

Her gaze traveled around the small cubicle filled with dental equipment and posters of various dental procedures that could give her a brilliant smile. Must be nice to be able to afford whiteners, veneers, caps, just about anything to brighten your smile, she thought. From the cubicle beside her came the high-pitched hum of a drill. Carolina shuddered and closed her eyes.

Slowly she began to relax and her breathing came easier. Images from the dream she'd had the night before flitted through her mind. She felt again the tug of nostalgia for those early days of her marriage when she was Bud's deckhand on the *Miss Ann.*

Whenever she thought of that time, she remembered being happy.

October 1975
On board the Miss Ann
Carolina wasn't accustomed to sleeping on a boat. She was roused from a restless sleep by a strange whooshing sound and clicking noises. The room was indigo and close, like the inside of a tent. She blinked, slightly disoriented in the gentle, rhythmic rocking. She heard again outside her cabin the raspy sound of air being forced from a blowhole and water sloshing and slapping against the hull. There must be a pod of dolphins near the boat, she thought. Beside her she heard a fulsome snoring, low and sonorous, and she smiled.

Turning to her side, she drank in the shadowy sight of her husband's beautiful bare back, long-spined and tan. He never wore pajamas and she'd given them up. A good decision, she thought as she carefully tugged the sheet lower, exposing the curve of his waist and the sharp bone of his hip. Next she delicately slid her fingertips over his shoulder and around his chest, relishing the feel of smooth, warm skin beneath, laying down her palm.

Instantly the snoring ceased; Bud was a

light sleeper. He took hold of her arm and tugged her closer so her face lay against his skin. She smelled the maleness of him mingled with the scent of sex and other earthy smells in their tight quarters. She closed her eyes and breathed in the mysterious odors of a boat — wood, mold, fish, oil, salt.

She squeezed her arm tight. "Good morning, husband."

He bent his head to kiss her hand and said in a gravelly voice, "Good morning, wife."

They'd been married four months, and the newness of being Mrs. William Morrison III still delighted her each morning. They were married in June at the quaint Chapel of Ease in McClellanville. Judith Baker and Odelle Williams had been her bridesmaids and Bobby and Lee Edwards were groomsmen. Aunt Lucille was dutiful to every detail, doting on Carolina as if she were her own child. Carolina would never forget the glorious show of pink azaleas, purple wisteria, and waxy white blossoms of Cherokee roses against the chapel's wood shingles, hand-hewn cypress siding, and gingerbread filigree.

Bud rolled over and blanketed her with his weight. He buried his face in her neck. "You're awake early."

"Oh?" she half murmured, half groaned at the feel of his whiskers tickling her neck. "It's nearly four. By your clock, that's not early."

He trailed kisses up her neck to her cheek, obliterating all thought of time from her brain. "You're feeling spry this morning. Usually you complain when I try to wake you up."

"Who wouldn't complain? The sun isn't up yet, so why should I be?"

He kissed her nose. "Because, wife, you're a deckhand on a shrimp boat."

"I am that," she said with a sigh.

He shifted his weight and propped himself on his elbow to peer down into her face. "Are you getting tired of the job?" he asked, concerned. "You don't have to do it. You can quit anytime."

"No, I love working with you," she hurried to reply. "You know that."

"Then what?"

"Nothing. I just couldn't sleep. I was thinking about the house and all that we have to get done. My mother found us a washer and a dryer. They're bringing them down next week."

She could feel his muscles stiffen. "It's not a handout, is it?"

"It's called a gift."

He pulled away and fell on his back with a disgruntled sigh.

"Why is that a problem for you?" she asked.

"Because for your father, it's the same thing. And you know it."

She puffed out a plume of air, sounding much like the dolphin outside her window. Their wedding had done little to smooth over the relationship between Bud and her father. It was a strange rivalry. Whenever they were together, it was like watching two pugilists throw punches. Every statement was a challenge. Every gift a handout. This competition had caused tension between her and Bud, too.

She thought of the ramshackle house by the creek she'd moved into after they married. To say the two-bedroom bungalow needed work was generous. Her father had taken one look at it and declared it was no better than "camping indoors." Carolina took Bud's side and tried to be brave and make the best of it, scrubbing every inch of the place and making curtains. But when a mouse ran over her head while she slept, she'd bawled like a baby. Bud felt horrible and they'd promptly decided to live on the boat while they made fundamental improvements. But not before her father took him aside and let him know how he felt about his daughter living in such a "dump."

It had turned out to be a mixed blessing. Bud and Carolina were having fun fixing up the house together. When they weren't working together on the trawler, they were working together on the house. They had lots of help. Judith was a regular. She was as handy at home construction as she was on a boat. It turned out that teaching elementary school was not for her, so she'd quit and hired on as a striker for one of the local trawlers. Bobby and Pee Dee helped, too, when they could spare the time.

"Maybe we shouldn't have knocked down the living room wall," Carolina mused. It was an ambitious move.

"I thought you liked it open and airy."

"I do. It's just taking forever to build those bookshelves. It seemed easy when we talked about it."

"Judith has her mind set on the design."

"I was wondering, have you noticed how good Bobby and Judith get along?"

"Why shouldn't they? They work together, and both are pretty good with a hammer."

"I mean in a romantic sense."

Bud chuckled. "Ain't gonna happen."

"Why not? Bobby's good-looking. Agreeable. You can't help but like him."

"Until he drives you crazy borrowing money. The guy earns plenty, but he blows it on drinking, pot, and some new girl he picked up in Myrtle Beach."

Carolina couldn't argue. There were so many girls she couldn't get their names straight. Her brother-in-law was like a big, adorable puppy that sometimes did naughty things like chasing cars or going through the trash. Then he looked up with his big brown eyes and smiled his goofy smile, and everyone melted and forgave him for not showing up at the boat in the morning or forgetting that he'd promised to deliver a load of lumber to the house.

"That's why I think Judith would be good for him. She's responsible, frugal, and punctual. Plus she can drink any man under the table, is a natural at sports, and has an affinity for boats. I think Judith and Bobby would be a perfect match."

Bud rolled back on his side and traced his finger along Carolina's face. "Bobby's not like me. He's not the marrying kind."

"Maybe he just hasn't met the right girl."

"And you think it's Judith?"

"She could be."

"They're friends, Carolina."

"Sure, but there are days I can't help but

think something more is sparking between them."

He chuckled. "Yeah, about that. You've got to stop winking at me when they're working. They're going to see you and get embarrassed. Or think you've got a tic."

She laughed and jabbed his ribs. "Did you know Bobby invited Judith to join us aboard the *Miss Ann*? Again."

"You're reading too much into it. She's a good deckhand."

"Good? She's the best damn deckhand you've ever had."

He raised his brows.

"Okay. I admit it. She's better than me."

He chuckled low and tightened his arms around her. "I don't think Judith is inter-ested in being a captain's wife. She wants to be captain."

"Don't be silly."

"Swear to God. She asked me if I knew of a shrimp boat that might come up for sale."

Carolina pulled back, eyes wide with surprise. "For her?"

"I don't know who else she'd be asking for."

"Maybe Bobby."

He shook his head. "Bobby's set. He's go-ing to take over the *Cap'n and Bobby*."

"B-but . . ." she stammered, trying to

digest Bud's words, "*women* aren't captains."

He smirked and said with sarcasm, "So much for your women's lib."

"There's no women's lib on the dock."

"There are some guys who don't even want a woman on their boats. They think it's bad luck."

"That's exactly the kind of comment that really ticks me off. Why can't a woman be a captain if she wants to?"

"No reason. She's just gonna face some stiff competition." His eyes darkened and he ran his hand down her belly. "So you want to be captain, do you?"

Carolina arched slightly into the sensations caused by his hand. "No," she breathed, warming to him. "I never did. But I don't want to be stuck in the galley, either. If a man can do it, then you'd better believe I can."

"Just so you know, there *are* a few female captains out there. Not many. And God knows those saltwater cowboys will make it hard for her. But it's been known to happen."

"Not in McClellanville," she said flatly.

"No, not here," he conceded. "We tend to like the status quo."

"What is she thinking?" Carolina said,

worried about her friend. "She'll be ostracized. By men and women alike."

He brought his body closer and lowered his head to her neck again. "Not by us," he said softly, igniting her cells.

"No," she sighed, and nestled closer, shifting her hips under his. His body was warm and hard and her words were beginning to float in her head. "Not by us."

Bud moved on top of her and slid inside, obliterating all thoughts of Judith and Bobby and the house from her mind.

"Woman, we'll have a late start again this morning," he said, arching above her. "You'll be driving me broke by the season's end."

As he moved inside her, Carolina knew it was enough for her to be Bud's first mate, spending her days and nights on the water with her husband, working side by side, making a living, building a future together. She closed her eyes and heard again the clicking noises of the dolphins and felt the rocking of the boat. She wrapped her legs tight around him and matched his rhythm, exulting in the knowledge that this was her man and her life and she'd never felt as safe or as fulfilled.

They dressed quickly, donning wool sweaters against the early-morning chill, and soon the *Miss Ann* was making her way through the dark creeks toward the ocean. At that early hour, the dark sky and black water seemed too vast. Carolina liked to stay with Bud in the warm and snug pilothouse, where the constant drone of the engines competed with the music of Waylon and Willie. They sipped hot coffee while Bud talked on the shortwave radio to other captains, complaining about the price of shrimp, fuel, and life insurance and figuring where the shrimp were going to show that day. Bud looked handsome in the faint glare of his equipment. He held the wheel and stared at the horizon, unaware she was looking at him.

They reached the ocean as the pale pink of first light stained the purple water. The gulls sat silent in a line high on the rigging, resting as they enjoyed the free ride before breakfast. Carolina and Bud slipped outdoors to watch and listen to the world as it slowly awakened. Bud wrapped his arm around her as they stood on the deck and sipped their coffee. The Milky Way was still a faint haze in the sky beside a ghostly moon.

These were the moments Carolina loved most, being in Bud's arms when the ocean was quiet and full of promise and the outriggers were folded toward the sky like hands held in prayer to the new day. She felt that such moments strengthened their union in a sacred bond more powerful than a spoken vow.

A mile or so out, she saw the dark outlines of several other shrimp boats. Their serene appearance was misleading, for she knew the crews were scrambling, poised to drop nets and begin trawling. Bud gently squeezed her shoulders, signaling it was time for them to get to work. He went to the pilothouse to slow the boat while she readied the nets. It was a time to hustle with lines, ropes, and pulleys. He hurried back to the winch and shouted directions, which she promptly followed. They worked in synchronization, neither needing to fill the silence with empty chatter. Out here their relationship was strictly that of captain and striker. When the red sun burst above the horizon, she heard the growl of the winch as the drum rolled out cable and lowered the nets into the sea.

Bud protected Carolina from the more dangerous jobs, as much as he was able. Anyone who made a living on or near the water knew the hazards of drums turning and ropes tangling. He wouldn't let Carolina work the winch or climb out on the rigging.

If they pulled in a good-size shark, he'd handle the fish.

The sun's light was blanketing the ocean by the time the outriggers' nets were dragging the sea floor. The engine thrummed loudly at dragging speed. Carolina felt the tug and pull as the nets spread out below the surface. She took this time to head down to the galley to cook up a hearty breakfast of shrimp and grits. Bud always had an enthusiastic appetite and praised her fast-developing cooking skills, assuring her Pee Dee's gravy couldn't hold a candle to hers.

After breakfast, they went back to work. Bud checked the try net, a small sampling net that could be quickly hauled up to reveal what the big nets were catching and indicate whether they should stay or move elsewhere. If the sample was scant, Bud's face would pinch and he'd shake his head with disgust and mutter under his breath. Carolina had learned to be silent at such moments and patiently wait as they moved on to another area. She held her breath, looking out at the sea that had turned from dark purple to a steely gray that mirrored the rising sun. When she looked again at Bud, he was grinning and gave her the thumbs-up.

Carolina pulled off her sweater and donned a pair of rubber gloves, adrenaline pumping in her veins. Bud was in constant motion. He was a master at his job, using instinct as much as experience. He'd been shrimping since he could walk, and his movements were so familiar they were ingrained — watching the sea, pulling in the nets, running to the wheelhouse to adjust their speed, always with an eye on the winch.

The winch wailed again as it pulled up the main net. She tensed as the wood plank doors emerged, the cable clanging loudly amid a cacophony of screaming gulls. They formed a white cloud above the net as it slowly emerged, dripping, from the sea. The frenzied birds dove for any spare bits of shrimp or fish that might tumble from the bag, while below bottlenose dolphins arced and dipped alongside the boat, eager for the feast sure to come.

She trained her gaze on the hovering net while Bud maneuvered it over the deck. In a swift movement, he lurched to grab hold of one green webbed bag with a hook and wrestled it into position. Then, with a powerful tug at the drawstring, the net burst open and a bounty of glistening sea creatures slid out, hitting the deck with a shimmering splash. Carolina jumped to grab the small silver shovel and dove in as Bud opened the other net. It was hard work culling through the mound, hard to see so many gasping fish die. Crabs scuttled across the deck to hide under anything in their path and, if lucky, out of the scupper holes back into the ocean. She wished she could stop working long enough to throw the drum, spot, juvenile sharks, squid, urchins, rays, and others back into the sea. Bud often talked about designing a net that would somehow filter out the bycatch, but that was a pipe dream. Time was critical, so she bent to the task, doing her job of tossing the shrimp into baskets.

The gloves protected her hands as she picked through the squirming mess, but the shrimp were prickly and cut through the rubber, leaking juice that stung her tender flesh. Tears filled her eyes, but she didn't have a free hand to wipe them away, so she gritted her teeth and let them flow. Bud came to sit beside her and help cull through the enormous pile. His hands were roughened and moved quickly. She wasn't nearly as fast as him — or Pee Dee or Bobby. It took more than two hours to sort out the shrimp. When they were done, they washed the grime from the shrimp, iced them, and finally stored them below deck.

Then it all began again. Bud returned to

the winch to lower the nets back into the sea. Meanwhile, Carolina shoveled the trash fish overboard to a grateful horde of dolphins and birds. Finally, she scrubbed the decks with a broom. It was hard work, grueling at times, but she loved the freedom of wearing anything she wanted, of being independent, and of getting away with Bud on their boat, alone on the great open sea. On a good day, she had to admit, it was romantic. This was a sentiment shared by most women who worked on the water. But the work was hard, there was no denying it.

While the nets dragged, Carolina could take a welcome break. Sometimes she grabbed a book and read for a while, but today the sea was calm, so she indulged in a favorite pastime. Her arms and legs felt weak from exertion, but she grasped the rungs of the ladder and, with her face to the sun, climbed up to the rigging. When she reached the height of the birds she stopped, clinging to the rigging like a gull. From her perch she could gaze far out over the ocean.

It was nearing eleven in the morning, and the blazing sun had bleached the ocean to a pastel blue. She loved to hear the sounds of the seabirds around her and to watch the pelicans fly in formation like bombardiers on patrol. Below, she spotted three dolphins racing alongside the boat, keeping pace. From time to time, one leaped above the water as if in play. She laughed aloud, delighting at the glistening silver body and the sheer joy of a spectacle that never grew old.

The borders of sky and sea blended into one silvery blue palette that went on to infinity. The vista was so vast it made her troubles seem tiny. She found that oddly freeing, and breathed fresh air deep into her lungs. She loved being out here on the open water. Loved being with Bud. How could she ever give this up? she wondered. No matter how exhausted she was when she began her climb up to her perch, she was always revived by the time she came down.

There were two more good hauls before Bud called it a day. Carolina's arms hung loose at her sides and her back was aching. She couldn't wait to shower. The sun had begun its westward slide by the time they plowed through the endless maze of marsh grass and snaking water, riding the incoming tide home.

Back at the dock, their last job was to unload their catch at the fish house. Some boats stayed out longer if they were catching shrimp, but Bud could see how exhausted Carolina was. They dropped anchor offshore for the night.

The light faded slowly, changing the water of the creek into stained glass. As was their habit, they ate dinner together under the moon and stars, listening to the night music of waves lapping against wood. Some nights they drank beer and talked about the house repairs and news of family and friends, or had deep philosophical conversations, but tonight Carolina was exhausted and went below to their cabin.

She showered with her favorite lavender soap, scrubbing off the slime and dirt of the day, and let the hot water sluice down her aching muscles. The thirsty towel felt heavy in her weak arms. Her hands stung from the pricks of the shrimp horns. She let the towel drop, holding them out before her. Her palms were chapped, scraped, and raw, and they hurt like the devil. Feeling tears sting her eyes, she curled up on the bed, bringing the blanket around her shoulders. From out in the galley, she heard the high whistle of the teakettle and the cupboards opening and closing.

Bud stepped gingerly into the room balancing a steaming cup of tea. She caught the scent of chamomile and honey, and had a sudden yearning for it.

"I thought you might like something warm to drink."

She pulled herself up to sit, murmuring, "Thank you." After arranging the pillows behind her, she reached out for the creamy mug. "This is so nice."

Bud paused, noticing her hands.

"Don't look at them," she said, self-consciously pulling her hands back. "They're ugly."

His brows furrowed with concern. "To me, they're beautiful."

"They're not. They're as red as lobsters."

Bud set the tea down on the shelf and lay down beside her. He gently tugged her hands toward him to study them, then raised them to his lips. He kissed one palm, then the other. Then he slid his arms around her and they settled back against the pillows.

"You smell good," he told her.

"I smell like fish."

"That's what I said. You smell good." He turned to peer into her face. "Are you feeling okay? You're not coming down with something?"

"No, I don't think so. But, oh, Bud, I'm so tired," she said, yawning wide. "My hands hurt, my back hurts, my eyes hurt. Everything hurts."

He tightened his arms around her. His muscles felt like iron straps when he squeezed. "Aw, babe, I hate to see you hurting. This life can be brutal. You didn't grow up on a boat like I did." He snorted. "Hardly. I warned you," he said gently, and she didn't hear any teasing or scolding in the tone.

They'd talked about the dangers of being a deckhand, about the long hours and harsh conditions. For her, it was a whole new way of life. But Carolina had wanted it. She still did.

"I just have to toughen up. I'll be okay."

"You know," he began with a slight hesitation, "there's no shame in quitting. Every year we see some newcomer take it up, then quit before the end of the season. They think anyone with a boat can be a shrimper. They think what we do is easy. I wish it were."

"Well, I *know* it's not easy," she quipped.

"Especially not for a woman."

He looked down, and Carolina stole the moment to study his face, to gauge the sudden seriousness of his tone. His face, so tan and weathered from a summer in the sun, was taciturn. When he looked up, his blue irises shone against the white.

"Hell, most of the guys can't believe

you're even giving it a try. They tease me about it."

"The women tease me," she confessed. "Mrs. Macon told me she didn't think it was decent to be out on the boats, acting like a man."

Bud snorted. "Mrs. Macon, that ol' busy-body."

"I don't care what she says. I don't care what anybody thinks, except you."

"You know what I think. I'm proud of you. But, Carolina, it's up to you. Pee Dee is ready and willing to come back as my striker. Sure, the money we're saving with you working is good. But we can afford for you to quit and have babies if you want. Or you can go back to teaching. You can even be shore skipper and manage the boat's business from dry land. A lot of shrimpers' wives do that. But for you to work on the boat as crew, I have to depend on you. It's got to be your life. A commitment. Other-wise, it's too damn much work, more than it's worth, if you ask me. You have to love it, because it'll take all you got."

"I know *you* love it." Her voice was soft.

"I do. But I love you more. Carolina, I won't stop loving you if you decide to quit."

She sighed heavily and rested her head on his shoulder. His shirt smelled of fish and sweat, a male smell that was all Bud. "Who's talking about quitting? Like I said, I'm just tired."

Bud bent to kiss her. "You should be. It was a tough day. You worked hard. You're the best deckhand I've ever had."

"Sure. . . ."

"I guess I'm not good at telling you this, but it's great having you with me. We make a good team, you know? I know what you're thinking just by the look on your face. You cook a damn sight better than Pee Dee ever could. And I sure as hell can't hug or kiss Bobby when I get the urge." He chuckled. "And I'm tired of hearing about his women."

She laughed softly, thinking of those sudden hugs and kisses that came when the work was at its roughest and she was ready to quit. They gave her strength and the work meaning, and reminded her of why she was doing this. Sometimes something so little could keep a woman going.

"Seriously, Carolina, whether you stay on the boat with me or decide to stay on shore, it won't make a whit of difference how I feel about you. You know that, don't you? What we have is forever."

She looked into his eyes and saw the ocean. She'd married a man more at home on the sea than on land, and she knew if she wanted to be part of his life, she'd have to join him.

"I remember telling you at the start that I wanted to go out on the boat with you every day instead of being left behind on shore. I know it's a tough life, and I wouldn't advise many women to go into it, at least not without knowing what to expect." Her lips twisted into a smug grin. "But I'm not most women. I thought you knew that by now." She dropped her smile and placed her hand on his chest, over his heart.

"I might be new at this, and you've been more than a patient teacher. I don't mean to whine and complain. Bud, I do love this life," she told him, and meant every syllable. "I love working with you, being with you every day and every night. I may be hurting now, but I'd die if you left me behind on the dock."

A myriad of emotions flickered across his face as he stared at her. He raised his hand to stroke her damp hair from her face. His calluses felt rough against her tender skin. Slowly, gently, he kissed her forehead, her cheeks, her lips. Then he lifted away the blanket and his eyes slowly, possessively swept across the curves of her nakedness. Rising above her, Bud bent to kiss her sore muscles, taking his time as her body loosened beneath his lips.

The day ended as it had begun. As so many had before it. She fell asleep to the sound of fish jumping in the racing current that filled the creeks, the sounds, and the estuaries, overflowing the mudflats, rocking the boat gently on the rising tide.

September 21, 2008
Mount Pleasant
Carolina felt a gentle shake.

"Mrs. Morrison? The Novocain should have taken hold by now," Dr. Assey said. "Are you ready?"

Carolina blinked heavily, dragging herself back from her memories. Dr. Assey sat on the stool beside her while his assistant carefully laid out tools on the small metal tray over her chest. The dentist's movements were sure and steady. She could smell the antiseptic on his hands, hear the crispness of his white coat when he moved. As he probed the decayed tooth, Carolina couldn't help but compare those halcyon early days of her marriage to the lassitude she and Bud shared today.

She'd spent six years working side by side with Bud aboard the *Miss Ann*. Oh, she'd felt such passion then. It was as quicksilver as the sea — easy, stormy, serene, turbulent. But her love was constant. Deep and unfathomable.

When had it started to change? In the twilight stage of painlessness, Carolina could consider this question without the usual upheaval of emotions that sparked either fury or heartbreak. She could probe and pick, rather like the dentist was doing with her tooth, to seek out the roots of decay.

She'd have to say that it began with the *Miss Carolina.*

Bud had always wanted to build a fiberglass boat. It was a relatively new concept in McClellanville in the seventies. The guys had read about them in the trade magazines and seen a few in Florida, but no one had anything but a wood hull that fell victim to the worms. Bud's was the first — and Carolina knew him well enough to realize that was part of its charm. He was a proud man. This boat would be *his,* not a hand-me-down.

For two years, he'd spent every spare moment and all of the off-seasons in the abandoned horse arena owned by his friend in Georgetown. The trawler was built hanging upside down inside the facility. She used to joke that she was jealous of that boat, but in hindsight she saw plainly that the building of the boat marked the beginning of his long hours away from her. Her husband spent more time stroking the frame of the hull than he did his wife.

She couldn't deny she was proud of the boat. All the days, months, years of back-breaking work, stinging hands, sunburned skin, pinching pennies came to fruition when Bud arrived with their new trawler in McClellanville. Carolina had stood on the dock with friends and family, cheering at the first sight of the beautiful boat. Her voice silenced in her throat when she saw, boldly emblazoned in berry red on the hull of his dream, the name *Miss Carolina.*

Bud had honored her in the seaman's tradition. It was a validation of her hard work, her support, and his love. She'd blushed and told everyone he ought not to have done it. Inside her heart, however, she was beaming with pride.

Then Carolina became pregnant. Not that she didn't want a baby. She and Bud were both overjoyed at the news. But it marked the end of her shrimping days. She'd tried to continue, but early in the pregnancy she'd slipped on deck, and it scared her. Carolina remembered the day she'd stood on the dock, one hand over her swelling belly and the other lifted in a wave as she watched the *Miss Carolina* carry Bud away down Jeremy Creek with Pee Dee as his crew.

Her heart had broken that day because Carolina knew she was watching her dream of living on the water sail away with him.

She was still Bud's wife. She loved him, tended his house, and raised his child. But ever since the day she was left behind, some vibrant essence of the bond they'd forged on the water had begun slipping away.

Carolina felt a violent tugging and pulling in her mouth. It felt as though roots that went deep into her soul were being ripped out. She gripped the sides of the chair. There was a soft sucking noise and, with a final, prolonged pull, the tooth was out. Immediately, her tongue sought the soft, bloody space where the tooth used to be. Probing, delicately touching the bruised gum, tasting the salt of blood.

All that remained was an empty hole.

8

Lizzy closed the door of T. W. Graham's behind her and tugged the elastic from her ponytail. Her hair fell loose around her shoulders, easing the headache that was forming. She walked toward the docks, stretching her legs and breathing in the balmy September breeze. She smelled rain in the air, full of green and coolness and a hint of moisture.

McClellanville was a village straight out of a Mark Twain novel. She made her way along narrow sidewalks that were cracked and split, especially in spots where the great roots of live oaks burst through like bunions through shoe leather. The sweeping, graceful limbs laden with moss stretched over the streets. Some of the wood houses were grand dames more than one hundred fifty years old, their front porches crowded with rockers and hanging plants. Like White Gables, many showed their age. Other homes were modest cottages supported by bricks or cinder blocks. Here on the coast, rust, rot, and wind were harsh on house and land alike. It was a constant battle of nip and tuck that the owners could not always afford.

This was a community of working families who could trace their ancestors back to the original owners of these historic houses. The families had survived wars and hurricanes, economic downturns and upturns, recessions and the Great Depression. The foundations of the homes were rooted deep in the ground, forever a part of the landscape. Neighbors knew each other's names, were helpful in times of need, and celebrated together in times of joy.

Yet as she walked down the main street, Lizzy saw that the clothing store had closed its doors and two more houses had posted FOR SALE signs on their front lawns.

The wind gusted, tossing her hair. She reached up to smooth it from her face. Above, cumulus clouds were gathering, fat and gray. She strolled past the Village Museum and the Town Hall and through a gravel parking lot to where the land turned to marsh at Jeremy Creek. A professorial-looking man wearing a wrinkled brown corduroy jacket with leather elbow patches, khaki pants, and boat shoes was setting up his easel. He seemed keen to position it for the correct angle of light. When she drew near, he turned his head, and she saw his blue eyes sparkle in welcome behind his heavy-framed glasses.

"Hello, Mr. Dunnan."

"Lizzy! What a nice surprise."

John Dunnan was a local artist and a good friend of Lizzy's mother. He could often be spotted by the docks, painting the boats and the wildlife. Lizzy couldn't figure him out. His paintings were in galleries and museums all over the world, but he preferred to live in the white clapboard house along the creek that had been in his family for generations. She knew if she had his money, she'd be traveling to those places where his pictures hung. But her mama had told her that Mr. Dunnan had lived the high life and had been to all those places and now was happy staying where he was. Growing up, Lizzy and her friends had called him the Guru because he'd spent years in India living in some ashram. And because when he smiled, as he did now, he made you feel that he really cared.

"What are you going to paint today?" she

asked, trying to be neighborly.

"Oh, I don't know. I never arrive with a notion of what I'm going to paint. I let the inspiration come to me."

"What if the inspiration doesn't come?"

"Then I wait." He chuckled as he struggled with the tripod legs. "But what's not to be inspired by?" he added, gesturing broadly toward the docks. "I'm inspired by gazing out to sea, or feeling the breeze of an oncoming storm, or watching the birds soar in the air and the boats lined up at the dock. I'm inspired by people, too — all types of people. I find I get inspired all the time. I just have to open my eyes and really look."

Lizzy wrapped her arms around herself and looked out over the marsh. She wondered how that kind of inspiration made you feel.

"You seem troubled today, Lizzy. Is anything wrong?"

She shrugged. "I lost my job."

"Oh. I'm sorry to hear that."

"Me, too. It's no one's fault. Graham's is closing."

He nodded slowly, and she had the feeling he already knew.

"What's going to happen to us?" she asked. "I mean, shops are closing and houses are for sale. And look out there. See how many boats are docked and for sale? I used to see twenty, thirty boats off the harbor, and now there are only a few. And I'm not that old."

"You sound worried."

"Of course I am."

"And afraid?"

"A little." She felt a deep insecurity well up, almost overwhelming her. "Why does everything have to change? Why can't things stay the same?"

He bent to finish tightening the legs of his easel. "Change is a natural part of life."

"Well, I don't ever remember so much changing so fast."

He straightened his easel on the gravel, then slapped the dust from his hands. "Sometimes it does seem that a lot hits all at once." He turned to face Lizzy, his expression fatherly. "There's always change. It breaks our routine, and that shakes us up a bit. We get nervous and afraid because we aren't sure what's coming next. But change is nothing to be afraid of. It's all in how we face it. If we accept change, it opens us to new possibilities we would have missed if we'd clung to the status quo."

"So change is a good thing?"

"It can be. It can also be hard to face. You have to be willing to sweep away the past and welcome whatever comes in the future. That takes courage. And faith. And love. When it comes to change, there's only one word that matters."

"What's that?"

"Yes."

"Yes?" she repeated, a little disappointed. She'd expected something more profound.

"Think about it. When you say yes, you are surrendering yourself to change. That's a powerful commitment."

He squinted and looked out at the sea, his thoughts momentarily captured, perhaps by some memory. When he turned back, he sighed and looked into her eyes. "So don't say yes unless you mean it with your whole heart and soul."

Her father thought Mr. Dunnan was some kind of out-there hippie. Her mother thought he was a brilliant eccentric. All Lizzy knew was that when he spoke, he made life seem so clear and simple.

She smiled weakly and tucked her hair behind her ear. "Thanks, Mr. Dunnan. I'll see you."

"Nice talking with you, Lizzy. Say hi to your mother."

He went back to setting up his canvas and paints.

Lizzy walked a few steps, then turned and

called over her shoulder, "Do you think a person can change?"

Mr. Dunnan looked up, smiled, and nodded. "Yes. People do — all the time. Oh, and Lizzy? Sometimes change is nothing more than a second chance."

Lizzy waved, then turned and walked to the edge of the small park to sit on the dock. She tucked her arms around herself. Beyond was the Intracoastal, and beyond that the Atlantic for as far as she could see. The shrouded sun seemed to hover between the silvery clouds. Out in the vast steely blue, she saw two shrimp boats with their nets lowered. They bobbed in the ocean like pelicans. It was a sight she'd grown up with, one she'd taken for granted would always be there. Now she wasn't sure.

She leaned back on her arms and looked out and wondered — as she so often did when she saw a shrimp boat offshore — if that was Josh's boat out there and if he was having a good day. She thought back to the last day they'd spent together. Has it been over a month ago already?

August 8, 2008
McClellanville
"Well. Here we are." Josh pushed the gear of his pickup into park. The muffler

rumbled, then quieted. He exhaled and wiped his palms on his jeans. As soon as the air-conditioning quit, the steamy heat of an August morning began warming the cab.

Lizzy glanced at him. She felt as nervous as he obviously did. He'd called the night before, his voice shaking with excitement.

"I have something to show you," he'd said.

She was hesitant. She didn't want to encourage him. But he'd cajoled and begged her to come, and she could tell that whatever it was, it meant a great deal to him. So she'd agreed. When he came by the house to pick her up, she was surprised to see him showered and shaved and wearing an ironed white shirt. He'd taken pains to tamp down his thick, dark hair. The damp locks were brushed flat against his head, and she knew it was only a matter of time before they sprang up again. His dark brown eyes were bright with anticipation, and he was acting as high-strung as he had on their wedding day eight years before.

Lizzy looked out the window, curious. They'd parked in front of old widow Baldwin's house. She'd died a few months earlier.

The truck door squeaked open as Josh climbed out, then trotted around the front to open her car door. Instantly, she felt the crush of hot air. It was like walking into an oven. Josh offered his hand to help her out. She took hold of his fingertips, murmuring her thanks, impressed that he was making such an effort with his manners. They'd dated throughout high school and married right after. At some point in those years, he'd stopped being the gentleman about such things as holding doors open and assisting her out of the truck.

Their marriage hadn't lasted long. It wasn't so much that they'd drifted apart as that Josh's eyes had the bad habit of drifting to other women. He was too good-looking for his own good, and he couldn't resist a sultry come-hither. They'd divorced after only three years. Josh had left McClellanville to try his luck shrimping in Beaufort. She hadn't heard much from him in the following years. She knew little of his daily activities, who he dated, or whether he was making a good living. Nor did she inquire. Josh had broken her heart, and a woman didn't heal from that kind of pain readily. But he was dependable with his child-support payments, and she was grateful for that.

Then, without warning, a year ago he'd shown up back in McClellanville with an old rehabbed shrimp boat he'd called the

Hope. She couldn't deny that he'd grown up a lot in those years he was away. He'd stopped his wild ways and drinking, worked hard, and went to church on Sundays. And he began calling on her, taking her and Will on outings. After every visit, Lizzy had to remind herself why she'd divorced him in the first place and to ignore the pattering of her heart whenever he came near.

Lizzy stepped onto the gravel path and instantly released his hand. The fabric of her short skirt clung to her thighs and she self-consciously shook it free. Looking up, she saw that Josh was standing with his hands on his hips gazing with a hungry air over the Baldwin property. To her mind, the cottage sat on the prettiest acre in town.

"What are we doing here?" she asked.

"You'll see. Come on," Josh replied, taking her hand.

His hand was warm and clasped hers tightly as he led her up the winding gravel path to the front door. Her mind was racing with questions as she took in the old dark-wood cottage. Though solidly built, it needed a lot of work. The front steps slanted dangerously, the paint around the windows was flaking, and a jungle of jasmine, clematis, and trumpet vines seemed intent on climbing the front-porch lattice to devour the roof. He dug into his pocket and pulled out a set of keys affixed to a paper tag.

"Josh, what're you up to?"

He turned to face her, pale with nervous excitement. "Lizzy, I bought it. This house is mine."

Her mouth slipped open in a silent *Oh.*

"I closed yesterday. It's mine!" he repeated, pride shining in his eyes. "You're the first person I told. Come in. I want to show you around."

Lizzy licked her lips, too stunned to speak. She glanced back at the small cottage, seeing it with a whole new appreciation now.

Though dark on the outside, the cottage held more light than she'd imagined it could. Dust motes danced in the shafts of sunlight that poured in through the many windows. It was the house of an old woman without means, permeated with the stale scent of an infirmary. The once-cream-colored walls were dingy and checkered with the outlines of vanished paintings. Most of the furniture had been removed and parceled out to relatives, but a small round table holding a vase of flowers and a wood rocker sat by built-in bookshelves made of the same wood as the floors. Mrs. Baldwin had lived in this house for more than fifty years, thirty of them as a widow on a fixed income. Despite the neglect, there was a homey, welcoming feeling to the house. It held promise, possibility.

"Oh, Josh, it's wonderful."

He exhaled in relief, and she realized he'd been holding his breath. He grinned broadly and began pacing the room, gesturing animatedly as he pointed out the maple floors, dentil molding, and working fireplace. He took her through each room, talking nonstop about his plans to gut the bathrooms, to update the kitchen, to add new plumbing. Lizzy craned her neck from left to right, keeping up with his heady pace. She couldn't help but be caught in his whirlwind of enthusiasm. Josh knew carpentry and, like her father, had a good head for mechanics. She could believe in his dreams.

It was the garden, however, that set her heart yearning. Stepping out on the back porch, Lizzy counted seven majestic oaks on the property. Their branches hung low, laden with silvery Spanish moss. Mrs. Baldwin had been the head of the garden club for almost as long as she'd lived in the cottage, and it was clear this was where she'd spent her money. She'd died in June, and the ensuing summer of neglect had left the garden in a shambles.

Lizzy leaned against the porch railing. Her

experienced eye could see where a sharp spade and a determined will could restore the prized daylily bed and instill order among the host of perennials that circled the murky black pond, the crusted stone fountain, and the tilting, rotting pergola.

As intrigued as she was by the house and garden, Lizzy had spent more time during the tour glancing at Josh's flushed face as he spoke. Hope made his eyes shine like the stars he was trying to reach. And he was reaching for her; she saw that in his eyes, too.

She thought of the bowerbird, an amazing Australian bird that built an elaborate nest of twigs and leaves to attract a female. The industrious suitor took great care to arrange hundreds of objects — shells, flowers, berries, feathers, stones, and bits of discarded glass in bright colors, especially blue — to entice the female's eye. Lizzy knew Josh was presenting this house to her, room by room, dream by dream, as a validation of his ability to provide.

Josh came to stand beside her on the porch and motioned enthusiastically toward the grounds. "What do you think?" His thick, dark brows were drawn together as he anxiously studied her face.

Her heart lurched. It was that same boyish vulnerability that had first made her fall in love with Josh Truesdale when she was a freshman at Wando High School and he was a popular junior and on the football team. She resented that he still had the power to make her heart pound against her ribs like a bird trapped in a cage.

The thought struck Lizzy that she could cut him to the quick with one cruel word. She could pay him back for all the hurt she'd felt years back when the gossip about his fooling around in Florida came flying up the coast.

Lizzy clasped her arms and looked again at the garden. "It's a fine cottage," she said. "I've always thought so. You should do real well for yourself here." She tilted her head, feeling her hair slide against her face. "I didn't hear it ever came up for sale."

"It didn't. I'm friends with her nephew, Billy." He paused. "But you know that."

She nodded.

"Anyway, we were out on the boat back when old Mrs. Baldwin took sick again. Billy told me how it weren't looking so good for her and how they were fixing to put the house on the market. She had a lot of medical bills to pay, and even if she made it through that last bout, he said she'd be unable to take care of herself. They'd have to place her in a home of some kind."

"I'd heard she was sick. I'm sorry I didn't come by to check on her."

Josh shook his head. "From what Billy told me, it hit her fast and hard. It was a blessing in a way. She didn't suffer."

"She had a nice funeral. I never saw such flowers." She looked out over the bountiful garden, evidence of the woman's lifelong passion. She imagined Mrs. Baldwin had had many hours of happiness among those lilies. A wistful smile eased across her face. "It surely is a pretty place."

He smiled, heartened. "I was hoping you'd like it."

"I didn't know you were looking to buy a house."

He shrugged and leaned back against the railing, facing her. The red brick steps that led to the garden separated them. The sun was rising higher, and already the heads of the lilies were drooping in the sweltering heat. But in the shade of the porch and the bough of a mighty oak that hung danger-ously close to the roof, the air was cool.

"It was time. I've been frugal. Saving up." He gave a self-deprecating laugh. "It's a wonder how much I could put away once I stopped drinking."

She darted a glance at him. "What made

you stop?"

He raised his brows in surprise. "Don't you know?"

Lizzy straightened and walked to the far corner of the porch. The waxy white, tubular blooms of the jasmine against the lustrous dark green leaves reminded her of her wedding bouquet. She breathed in the cloying sweetness and was transported back to their wedding day. The entire church had been perfumed with the scent of jasmine and gardenias. She'd been giddy with love for Josh and couldn't wait to put his gold ring on her finger. She'd truly believed that it was the first day of many years of happiness for them.

Turning, she found Josh had straightened and stood waiting anxiously for her response. She read both hope and fear in his eyes.

"Why'd you show me all this?" she asked.

"I . . . I thought you'd like it."

She didn't turn away her gaze. "What does it matter if I do or don't?"

His face fell and he stared back at her, dumbfounded. She saw his throat constrict. Then he said in an injured voice, "You know it matters."

She saw the truth of it in his eyes and

closed her own. "Josh . . ." she said on a sigh.

He crossed the porch to her side and reached for her, but she held her hands up to stop him from taking her in his arms. His hands hung in the air awkwardly before he let them fall and took a step back.

"Lizzy, I'm trying hard to show you I've changed."

"Josh, don't. Please. It's too late for us."

"Don't say that."

"You hurt me!"

"I'm sorry I hurt you. I was a stupid, idiotic, shit-faced kid. I threw away what we had. But I'm not the same person I was then. I've changed."

She searched his eyes. "You say you've changed. I'd like to believe you."

"You can."

"But will it last?"

He grabbed her hands, entwining their fingers as tightly as the jasmine vine around the trellis. "Yes. I promise you."

She felt herself respond to his touch, coming alive like the drooping head of a flower at the taste of rain. It caused a rush of grief and her throat strained against a sob.

"Oh, Josh, I'm sorry," she said, slipping her hands away and bringing them to her face. "I can't trust you. I don't want to trust you."

She heard his heavy exhale of disbelief.

Lizzy dropped her hands, letting him see the tears on her cheeks. "You did more than hurt me," she told him accusingly. "You stole my innocence about love. It was girl-ish and naïve, I suppose. I want to believe love is forever, but I can't anymore. You cut me deep, and that scar, it might have healed, but it changed me! *I'm* changed! I don't believe that love is all that matters anymore. And you know what? It hurts to feel so jaded. I feel used up, and I hate it that I won't feel that again." She swiped the tears from her face and took a long, steady-ing breath. "Besides, I'm a mother now, and I've got to think about Will's future."

His face betrayed a flash of anger. "And you think I don't worry about that?"

"I don't know. We didn't see you for five years. After you left, I don't know what I'd have done if it weren't for my parents. They put me up, kept me going while I patched my life back together."

"I didn't think you wanted to see me. And I sent my payments."

That was true. His child support came on time every month. "I'm grateful for that."

He swung his head to look out at the

garden, but she felt sure he wasn't seeing the carefully planned contours of the garden beds or the puffs of dandelions floating on the soft breeze. His gaze was turned inward, his lips taut. Then he looked at his polished brown shoes and wearily shook his head.

"I don't know what else I can do," he said in a low voice.

They stood with their arms locked around themselves, staring out at the garden. After several minutes, Josh spoke again.

"Those years you didn't see me? I was working. Like a galley slave on one trawler after another. I lived like a pauper, saving every penny till I could buy a boat. It isn't much, I know that. But she's a trusty vessel and I knew I could make something of her. I named her the *Hope,* and I guess you know why. When I moved back here, I came with the purpose of showing you I'd changed. I started working all over again and saved enough so I could put a down payment on this house. It's not much, but I know I can make it into a place you'd be proud to live in."

"What did you think I'd do? See the house and just ask when we were moving in? Did you think I'd fall under your spell again like I did when I was fourteen? I'm not a little girl anymore. I can't take any chances."

Josh held her gaze, and she saw the struggle in his eyes. He reached out to wipe away a tear from her cheek. "Well, that's all I'm asking for. A second chance."

He slowly turned and went to lock the back door, jiggling the handle to make sure it was locked, then headed down the stairs to the yard. She felt the sun on her back as she followed him wordlessly along the gravel path to the front of the house and the pickup truck waiting in the street.

"I'll be right back," he said after opening her door. "I've got to lock up."

The cab of the truck was sweltering when she climbed in. She glanced at the clock — only an hour had passed since they'd arrived at the house, but it felt like much longer. She squeezed her eyes closed for a moment, then startled when she heard the driver's-side door open and inhaled raggedly.

Josh climbed in and promptly fired the engine. The air-conditioning blasted out hot air. He quickly turned the power down. "It'll take a minute to cool down," he said apologetically.

"That's fine, thank you."

He nodded, then jammed the gear into first and pulled away. Lizzy turned and, with an ache inside, caught a final glimpse of the sweet cottage nestled under a thick canopy of oaks. Neither spoke as they drove down the narrow street, but Lizzy was aware of how many inches lay between them, of cold air blowing across their sweating skin, of each cough, movement, breath Josh took.

When Josh pulled into the driveway of White Gables, he didn't cut the engine. It rumbled loudly and shook the cab as it idled.

Lizzy licked her lips. "It's a really pretty house," she said softly.

He didn't look at her. His hands still gripped the wheel. "I'm glad you like it."

"I'm sure you'll make it a jewel with all your plans."

"We'll see," he said, without any of the excitement he'd shown earlier. It pained her to hear it.

"Josh, I'm sorry. I didn't mean to hurt you."

He swung his head her way and gave her a sad smile. "I know that, Lizzy. That's not your way. Can I come by for Will tomorrow? I promised I'd take him to his game."

"Sure. He's looking forward to it. He'll be glad you're moving closer," she said, trying to add cheer to her voice. "He'll be able to ride his bike to your new house. It's a real nice house," she repeated.

They both knew there wasn't anything more they could say. Lizzy pushed open the door and stepped out into the dog-day heat. She stood in the sun and watched him raise his hand in a silent farewell. The gear thunked loudly as it shifted to reverse and he backed away.

As she watched him drive off, she wondered whether he was returning to the sweet cottage on Oak Street. She saw again in her mind the small house and heard his voice as he walked her through each room. What color would she paint the kitchen? Did she like the black-and-white tile in the bathroom? She saw again the blue flowers on the table and knew that Josh had arranged them in a vase and carefully set them out, like a bowerbird, to please her.

September 21, 2008
McClellanville
On the dock, Lizzy felt a cool breeze lift her hair. She could taste the rain coming. The two trawlers in the distance were surrounded now by clouds of birds, and she imagined the crew culling shrimp. It had been a tough season, one of the worst. Josh had been working round the clock to make his child-support and house payments.

She thought of what Mr. Dunnan had told

her about change. How she'd have to be willing to sweep away the past and welcome the future. Did she have that kind of courage? That kind of faith? Did she love Josh enough? She wondered, too, if Mr. Dunnan was right about second chances.

9

September 21, 2008, 11:45 a.m.
White Gables

The front doorbell chimed. Carolina closed her eyes and sighed. Who could that be? she thought, glancing up at the clock. Her hands rested on a ceramic bowl full of frosting. She had these cupcakes to finish and bring to Will's class before snack time. She took a breath and considered not answering, but the bell chimed again. I'm no better than Pavlov's dog, she thought peevishly as she licked the creamy frosting from her fingers. Then, grabbing a kitchen towel, she hurried down the front hall. After a quick wipe of her hands, she opened the front door.

"Odelle!" she exclaimed, surprised to see the slight woman in seersucker shorts and a white cotton shirt. She was still trim, but in middle age the size of her waist was no longer a source of pride for her.

They'd been friends since the seventies

when they'd started teaching together, and Carolina would swear Odelle hadn't gained a pound in all those years. Her hair was as dark as the day Carolina had met her, but the evenness of the color made it obvious it was no longer natural. She had cut her hair short years before in what she liked to call a pixie style. Carolina thought it accentuated the sharpness of Odelle's nose and chin. Some people compared Odelle's delicate features to a bird's. Others, less charitable, conjured up the image of a wasp.

Odelle had been one of her first friends in McClellanville, and they'd been through a lot together. Odelle's kindness could be surprising, as could her quick temper. But she was always careful with Carolina not to push too far, knowing Carolina would reach a boiling point and push back. Over the years their friendship had grown comfortable. Yet almost from the beginning, Carolina had known that it would never be the close bond she shared with Judith.

"Aren't you going to invite me in?"

"Come on in," Carolina said, stepping aside. She was slender herself, but she felt like a giant towering over her petite friend. Odelle hurried in, fanning her pale face with a handful of papers she was carrying.

"Honey, I'd kill for a glass of water,"

Odelle said, her dark eyes quickly scanning the front room. "I'm about to faint, I'm so parched."

"Come on back." Carolina brushed flour from her jeans as she led Odelle to the kitchen at the back of the house.

Odelle lifted her nose. "Smells good in here. What are you baking?"

"Butter cupcakes for Will," she replied, going to the cabinet for a clean glass. "Lizzy made them from scratch. The school is strict about not too much sugar and nothing artificial."

"I used to whip out a box of Betty Crocker and bake up a batch of cupcakes in no time."

"Me, too," Carolina replied with a laugh as she filled the glass with cold water from the fridge and handed it to Odelle. "Forgive the mess. I had to go to the dentist this morning and raced back to get these cupcakes frosted for Lizzy." She grabbed the milk jug and an open carton of eggs from the table and put them in the fridge. "It's been that kind of morning."

Odelle picked up a few dishes and spoons and carried them to the sink along with her glass. She found the sponge in the sink and rinsed it, talking loudly over the noise of running water. "I'm glad to hear you got that tooth taken care of. What did he do?"

"He pulled it. I've got this big hole in my mouth, but at least the pain's gone."

Odelle made a face. "Ow. Poor baby. Poor, stubborn baby. I told you to go see the dentist way back when you might've saved it."

"Yeah, well . . ." Carolina shrugged. She returned to the big yellow ceramic bowl. "You know how it is without insurance. . . ." She let the sentence hang. It was a common enough situation in town. Odelle had divorced Lee Edwards before he got rich, so she was pinching pennies like most everyone else. "We'll just have to find a way to pay over time. Same as always."

Odelle began wiping the flour from the counter. "It's going to be harder than ever now."

Carolina looked up from the bowl. "Why's that?"

Odelle's eyes, made up with black eyeliner even at this early hour, widened with surprise. "You heard what Lee's done at the fish house, haven't you?"

Carolina's hand stilled. "No. What did he do now?"

"He canceled all credit, is all. It's a cash-only basis now."

The news took Carolina's breath away.

She stood for a minute with her mouth open. She couldn't believe it was true.

And yet, she could. She'd worked for Coastal Seafood for years. She'd virtually run the place before she quit. Having done the books, she knew better than anyone the tenuous interdependence between the fishermen and the fish house. The shrimpers needed to keep their boats running so they could go out and bring in the product, and the warehouse needed a product to sell. But sometimes the tabs grew beyond what a man might need for fuel or ice or a piece of equipment. She'd seen Lee's credit extend to covering a hospital bill for an injured captain or surgery for his wife.

"It'll run most of us out of business," Carolina said in a matter-of-fact voice. "No one will be able to pay him back." Her thoughts went immediately to Bud, then to Josh.

Odelle rubbed the sponge on the counter. "I'm no longer privy to inside information, but I heard he's thinking of selling out." She glanced up, her dark eyes taking Carolina's measure.

"No. He'd never sell the fish house."

"Lee made his money in real estate, and I can only imagine the fat offers he's fielding for that prime dock space."

Carolina shook her head, feeling a buzzing between her ears. "He knows if the fish house goes, it all goes."

"Don't get upset, honey," Odelle said. "I'm just telling you what I heard. It's probably only temporary. You know, he's tightening things up for a while, trying to hang on like everyone else."

Carolina gave her a look that said that tidbit didn't soften the blow. She pulled out a chair and slumped into it, leaning her elbows on the table. "If he does shut down, it'll be as devastating as Hurricane Hugo was."

Odelle pulled out a chair across from her and joined her at the table. "Funny you should mention that today."

Carolina looked at her questioningly.

"Don't you know today's date?"

Carolina looked up at the wall calendar. September 21. She blanched. "My God, I've been so busy it didn't register. How many years has it been?"

"Nineteen. Next year is the twentieth anniversary of Hurricane Hugo. Hard to believe, isn't it?"

It *was* hard to believe so many years had passed since that devastating hurricane. Anyone who'd lived through Hugo would never forget the monster storm that had hit the town with screaming 140-mile-an-hour winds and a storm surge that had destroyed homes and tossed boats like toys. The swath of destruction extended hundreds of miles inland and had essentially blacked out most of eastern South Carolina.

"I used to measure time by before Hugo or after Hugo," Carolina said. "To think I finally let the trauma slip by and actually forgot it."

"You didn't forget it. You just got past it." Odelle's voice went soft. "You'll never forget it. Or the sound of the wind."

Carolina responded to the change in tone and drew in closer. Talking about the hurricane was like picking at a scab — you couldn't stop yourself. In the whole of Charleston County, whenever the hurricane was mentioned, heads drew close and stories were shared. Everyone wanted to tell where they were when Hugo hit.

"You were one of the ones in Lincoln High School, weren't you?"

Odelle's face went still. She nodded, her gaze glassy as she traveled back to September 21, 1989. "I don't like to think about it much. It's like a lifetime ago. I remember I wanted us to go to my family's house in Moncks Corner, but Lee didn't want to leave town. So we boarded up the house and settled in, but when we heard houses on the water were in danger, we went to the shelter like we were told. Us and about six hundred others. When we saw how crowded it was we wanted to go back, but it was too late to leave."

She rubbed her arm and a shaky smile crossed her face. "You know how I am in cramped places. I have a touch of claustrophobia. I couldn't breathe. Let's just say I wasn't at my best. Lee was getting angry at me, telling me to be calm and not scare Tressy. He told me how the school was sixteen feet above sea level, so we were safe."

"No one knew that wouldn't be high enough," Carolina said. "How could they?"

"Easy to say now. We'd been there for hours when we heard someone shouting, 'Water! Water!' Of a sudden I felt cold water swirling around my feet, and it just felt so wrong, you know? Everyone was looking at their feet, trying to make sense of it. Then the water broke through the doors of the building. I grabbed hold of Tressy and we all scrambled to climb on tables and chairs, any place we could to get out of the rising water. It was a stampede. I reached for Lee but he ran ahead. I saw him climbing up on a file cabinet, so I sloshed through that water and screamed for him to take Tressy.

He had this look in his eyes, round and glassy, like he didn't hear me. The water was up to my knees so I screamed again, and this time he pulled her up. I was pushed away, but some nice man grabbed my arms and pulled me up on the stage."

Carolina was entranced by Odelle's words. It was like she was telling a ghost story.

"When the water reached our necks, parents began lifting their children into the air-conditioning ducts and onto the roof rafters. I screamed for Lee to take care of Tressy, but I doubt he heard me in that mayhem. Truth was, I wasn't sure he would."

"That's a harsh thing to say about a man."

"That's a pitiful fact to face," Odelle whispered, as though shocked she was talking about her own husband, not somebody else's. "He's her father, for God's sake. I wasn't sure he'd put her first. Can you believe that?"

"Sweetie," Carolina said, "sometimes all our ideas of what a man should be shift and change in an instant."

"We thought we were going to die, and we couldn't depend on him."

Carolina reached out to place her hand over Odelle's. She'd heard some version of that story many times over the years, but she'd never before heard about Lee's cowardice.

Odelle paused to collect herself. Then she took a deep breath and shrugged. "God heard our prayers that night. We all survived."

Carolina offered a smile of understanding. "They say you find Jesus in the face of death."

"They say you can learn a lot about yourself in a situation like we were in, too, and I can tell you that's true," Odelle said, her eyes blazing as her dander rose. "Not only about yourself, but about others." Her lips thinned and her voice lowered in a tremble. "After that night, I never saw Lee in the same light. The thought of staying with him truly made me *sick*. I knew our marriage was over."

Carolina paled at that admission. As nosy as Odelle could be about everyone else's business, she was never one to reveal unpleasant truths about her own life. "But, Odelle, really, there were other reasons you got divorced. . . ."

Odelle straightened and settled a wry smile back on her face. "Why, sure, honey. We lost our house and everything I owned. I guess you could say that brought on a lot of stress. And, of course, there was that other woman he wanted to marry." She laughed, a harsh and brittle sound, and said irreverently, "What the heck, I was tired of picking up his underwear." She laughed again, but it sounded forced. Immediately she deflected the attention back to Carolina. "Here I am carrying on about me. You lost your home, too."

"You can always replace a house," Carolina said, not so willing to relinquish this rare moment of honesty between them. "But from your account, you lost a husband. That's far worse."

Odelle's brows furrowed, and she said with sincerity, "But *you* stayed married. I'd bet my last dollar Bud would never have left you alone in that black water to fend for yourself. He'd have carried you and Lizzy both on his shoulders if he had to."

Carolina swallowed, hearing the truth in that statement. That horrible night, when the wind and water had threatened their lives, she'd never doubted that Bud would have gladly died to save her and Lizzy.

"I don't remember where you went. Did you stay at White Gables?"

Carolina nodded. "Bud and I heard the same reports as you. We were living in our bungalow by the creek." She smiled to herself. She hadn't thought of that ramshackle place in years, but this morning it had come to mind twice. Carolina cupped her chin in her palm, seeing it all again like it was yesterday, not nineteen years ago.

"I remember Bud and I were standing by that little TV in the front room listening to the weatherman tell us we had to get out, *now!* That put the fear of God in me, I'll tell you."

Odelle nodded, her eyes glittering with memory. "It's funny how you remember specific moments."

"Bud figured this old house had already survived a few wars and hurricanes, it could survive one more. We huddled upstairs in the middle bedroom. Why, I think it was your old bedroom." They both smiled, remembering that time when they were housemates. "That wind kept screaming till I thought I was going to lose my mind. Then around eleven we heard this horrible ripping noise, like a tree was falling and its roots were being torn out, only it wasn't a tree. It was part of the roof. We felt like our fortress had been breached. The wind started ripping through the house, knocking down bureaus, hurtling paintings off the wall, shattering chandeliers — everything."

"You must have been terrified."

Carolina nodded. "But it got worse after

the eye passed and we got hit by the tidal surge. We felt the whole house shudder, then the sound of terrible crashing downstairs. Bud and I crept down the hall to check it out. We'd started down the stairs when Bud stopped me. The first floor was under three feet of water. It was dark, but we could see Aunt Lucille's antique chairs, tables, lamps, books — everything was bobbing around. Creepy. Bud jumped into that icy water and I screamed for him. He came sloshing back a few minutes later from the kitchen carrying a stepladder and his toolbox. I grabbed the toolbox and we ran back up the stairs. The water was rising at our heels.

"Like you, we were trapped. Bud climbed up on that ladder and began pounding the ceiling like a man possessed. It couldn't have been more than minutes before the water reached the second floor. By the time Bud broke through the plaster, we were already knee-deep in water. It just kept rising. But one by one, Bud got all of us into the attic before it reached our heads. Aunt Lucille was feeling poorly and Bud had to carry her all the way up to the attic. Poor thing, she was frantic about her cat. Bud doesn't even like cats, but he grabbed hold of Aunt Lucille's tabby and carried it up while it spat and clawed his arm bloody."

Odelle's mouth slipped open in a short laugh.

Carolina paused, caught by an image she'd held close throughout the years. The following morning when she'd opened her eyes, gritty with sand, all was still. After hours of the incessant howling of the wind, she was struck by the purity of silence. She felt the damp heaviness of sodden blankets and Lizzy's arm across her chest as she nestled close in their nest up in the attic. The sun was already bright. Looking up through the hole in the roof, she saw a blue sky. It seemed otherworldly after the long storm. Her body ached from being curled up for so many hours. She stretched her legs, and Bud stirred beside her. He reached up to mop his face, then turned toward her. His blue eyes, red-rimmed and tired, seemed to drink in the sight of her before he smiled.

"We made it," he'd said.

"I knew we would," she replied.

He snorted and said, "I'm glad one of us did."

She smiled and wanted to tell him that she'd known because she had faith in him, that he would see them through the tempest, but he was already rising and taking stock of the damage. Now Carolina wondered if she ever had gotten around to telling him.

"That was the longest night of our lives," she told Odelle. "But you're right. I knew he'd take care of us."

Odelle's mouth closed in an introspective smile. Carolina could see in the way her eyes glazed in bitterness that she was comparing the two men. And something more. Carolina swallowed and wondered in that one instant if Odelle knew about what had happened between herself and Lee. Then Odelle's expression changed and Carolina wondered if she'd only imagined it.

"Odelle, you can't judge a person by one incident. Everything isn't always as it seems. We're not all heroes all the time."

Odelle didn't reply, but her cherry-tipped nails strummed the table.

Carolina sensed Odelle's sadness, maybe even jealousy, and strove to equal things out between them. "In the end, like a lot of other people we know, we lost everything."

"Everyone suffered in that storm." Odelle's lips twisted in irony. "Everyone except that son-of-a-bitch ex-husband of mine."

Carolina laughed loudly. "Oh, my God, Odelle, I've never heard you talk like that."

"Well, it feels good. That storm made Lee Edwards a rich man. When else would he have been able to buy that fish house for next to nothing?"

"Be fair. He was simply at the right place at the right time. A lot of good deals were made back then by folks who seized the opportunity. You can't make him out to be a villain. Frankly, I wish we'd have invested in the fish house when we had the chance."

Odelle, however, could only see Lee's faults. "The point remains, while he was making backroom deals, the rest of us were pulling up our sleeves and digging ourselves out of the mud. That terrible tragedy brought out the best — and the worst — in us. And we can't ever forget how people came from all over to bring us food and water and to help. It was a testament to the kindness of strangers. You know, we should have some kind of commemoration to mark the twenty-year anniversary."

"Oh, Lord, Odelle. No one wants to go back and remember all that. We've got enough problems in the present to deal with."

"I just thought it'd be nice for us all to come together."

"We do that during the shrimp festival. But if you want to try to pull something together, you know I won't rain on your parade."

"Well, maybe you're right. I've got enough to do organizing the Blessing of the Fleet festival. That's why I'm here, by the way. Can I sign you up to help?"

"Of course."

"Good." She added Carolina's name to her list. Then she pulled a sheet of paper from her pile and set it on the kitchen table. "This here's a list of names and phone numbers of people you can call. We want to get a real good turnout. And this," she added, handing her another sheet, "is a list of possible sponsors. We need to see who wants to contact who." She glanced at her wristwatch. "Listen, I've got to scoot. I'll call you later to talk more about it when we aren't so busy." Her face softened as she leaned forward to give Carolina a hug. "Thanks, Caro. I knew I could count on you."

The hug lasted an extra second, enough for Carolina to know that Odelle appreciated the moment of confidence they'd shared.

"You bet," Carolina said as they separated. "And it was good to go over all those memories of Hugo. It's cleansing."

Odelle pursed her lips. "It is, sort of." She rose and gathered her purse and papers.

"Oh, wait," Carolina exclaimed, and she

took one of the finished cupcakes from the counter and gave it to Odelle. In some small way, she wanted to thank her for the confidences shared.

"Won't you be short one for the school? I don't want to be accused of stealing sweets from a child."

"I've got extra. Go ahead, enjoy. I'm not making homemade cupcakes again anytime soon."

"Thanks. It looks delicious. I'll need the boost as I make my rounds." Odelle wrapped the cupcake in a paper napkin and started out of the kitchen. She paused at the door, her ruby-tipped hand on the molding. "You know," she began, looking back. She hesitated, as though trying to decide if she should go on.

Carolina looked up as her stomach tensed. "What?"

"We've been friends for a long time. I was a bridesmaid at your wedding. Hell, girl, I met Bud practically the same moment you did! So . . . I feel that gives me the right to say this." Her dark eyes had lost their sharpness and were filled with earnest concern. "I don't know what's going on between you and Bud, but things seem a little, well, strained."

Carolina was stunned. She hadn't seen

this one coming and felt sure her face showed it. She didn't reply.

"Take it from me," Odelle said kindly. "Don't lose what you have." She leaned forward and said in an urgent whisper, "Fix it."

Carolina couldn't begin to explain to Odelle the complexities of her problems with Bud. Even though, like Hugo, one whirlwind series of events had brought devastating damage to their marriage, the storm between them had started years before.

"We aren't getting divorced," she said in a flat tone.

"I'm not saying you are. I'm just saying being divorced isn't all it's cracked up to be. I'm not sorry I got divorced," she hastened to add. "It was the right thing for me. But you and Bud, I don't know, you have something rare. I saw it — we all did — right from the start. See, that's the difference between you and me. You married a true man in Bud." She shrugged. "And I got stuck with Lee." She blew a kiss. "Gotta go."

Carolina watched her leave, unable to speak more than a perfunctory good-bye. She shut the door, then turned and leaned against it. The waves of emotion that had been swamping her all day, ever since she woke from that dream, swept over her again. She closed her eyes tight and stood still for several minutes. When she opened them again, she let her gaze travel around the familiar front room of White Gables.

The house wasn't large. She often thought it was a grand house in miniature. Across the room sat the Victorian blue velvet sofa stuffed with horsehair that was so uncomfortable no one ever sat on it, but that Carolina could never bring herself to get rid of. Beside the small fireplace bordered with the original delft blue tiles was a modern and comfortable upholstered chair in a navy check. In her mind's eye, she saw Bud sitting in his favorite spot, one leg crossed over the other, a television remote in one hand, a beer in the other. An oriental rug, generations old, warmed the room with its muted colors. Across the hall, a Sheraton dining table scarred with scratches, its pedestal legs chewed by countless puppies over the years, sat under a crystal chandelier.

Today, on this anniversary of the hurricane, she remembered how she and Bud had carried each of these pieces of furniture out of the sodden rooms into the sunlight. The front porch was in shambles, the roof was gone, and uprooted trees left gaping holes in the waterlogged soil. She'd spent weeks washing acres of pluff mud off any piece of furniture that could be salvaged. The rug hung on the clothesline next to curtains and blankets, the reds, blues, and greens dotting the muddy vista. The original chandelier had been smashed beyond repair.

She sighed as she saw in today's light the neat and tidy rooms of this once broken and muddied house. Odelle was right. They'd worked it out. They'd saved what they had. She and Bud had worked hard side by side, day after day, month after month, year after year, restoring their home. They'd never lost sight of its original beauty.

Her eyes filled as she brought her hands to her face. How could she have forgotten? Not merely the date on a calendar, but the important, fundamental truth of that storm. In the course of all the fear, uncertainty, and doubt of that storm, she'd maintained her faith in her husband. Amidst all the destruction of a hurricane, that one truth was left shining.

How could she have forgotten that vital truth? Where was her faith in him, in their marriage, in herself?

Her thoughts turned once again to Bud, as they had so often this strange morning. For years, he'd grumbled that this old house was nothing but an albatross. Nonetheless, he'd worked in the mud, long before they took ownership of the house. Bud had restored the broken foundation with his own hands, brick by brick. He'd sweated over the chainsaw, cutting away the tree limbs that had fallen across the porch and lawn. Year after year since they'd inherited the house in 1990, Bud found some chore that needed doing — maybe a loose plank on the stair, a leaking pipe, a moldy piece of siding — and repaired it without anyone ever asking.

Carolina released a ragged sigh of hope. Surely their marriage was worth, at the very least, an equal effort at restoration?

10

September 21, 2008, 12:00 p.m.
On board the Miss Carolina

Bud avoided glancing at his injured arm. He wasn't the queasy type. He could treat the open wounds of his crew at sea and not flinch. Funny how it was different with his own body. But he had to take charge of his own survival.

"If you don't look, who will?" he demanded of himself.

He turned his head, and small black spots swam again in his eyes. He closed them and took a long breath, steadying himself. Then, gritting his teeth, he lifted his gaze to his injured hand. The ragged tourniquet was soaked in blood, but only a slow ooze dripped to the deck.

He slumped in relief. Good, good, Bud told himself. He might just make it. He tried to clear his head and focus. He knew the body contained eight to twelve pints of blood. And he was a big guy. With a slow rate of blood loss, he calculated he could last several hours yet. He squinted and peered at the sky. Sailors were supposed to be able to tell time by looking at the sun, to search out when the shadows were shortest. Right now, the sun seemed to be at its highest. That meant it was about noon, give or take a half hour. Pretty soon, someone at Coastal Seafood would notice that his order hadn't been filled. They'd start asking questions. Maybe Pee Dee would show up at the docks. It wouldn't be long before somebody figured out he was out here alone and overdue. That'd start them worrying.

It could happen, he thought, gaining heart.

Maybe Doc Beckham will even be able to fix my hand when I get back, he thought. Or he'll send me to the hospital. There's got to be some specialist at that big medical center in Charleston. The pain in his arm had dulled to a throbbing. It was probably going numb from loss of blood. He remembered again the warnings he'd read about not keeping the tourniquet on too long, lest the limb die. What the hell? — there wasn't a chance of saving his hand, really. He would have laughed if it weren't so tragic. Whatever, as long as he made it back alive.

Of course, he didn't have medical insurance — any kind of insurance, for that matter. They couldn't afford it. Bud sighed heavily, thinking of Carolina's bad tooth. If he survived, this would put them under for sure.

He'd just have to pay them whatever, whenever he could, the way he always did. If Carolina couldn't get her old job back teaching, she could clean houses for the tourists at Pawleys Island. It was good, honest work. One thing for damn sure — she'd never go back to work for Lee Edwards.

They'd had tough times before. They'd make it if Doc could sew up the loose ends of his hand. He thought of Woody. He'd lost a foot and was able to run his trawler. He could, too. He *had* to work or he'd lose this boat, and Carolina would lose her house.

He closed his eyes tight in a grimace. Who was he fooling? Things looked bleak.

"Aw, geez, Carolina," he said wearily. "What are we going to do now?"

He'd promised her better. If not in words, then in the shared dreams they'd forged when they were young. Back when she'd believed in him. Back when he'd believed in her.

Moving day was usually tough on his back, but this time, Bud only had a few suitcases to carry into White Gables. Carolina walked from room to room like one in a trance, her eyes glittering. She took in the fresh paint, the pretty new curtains, the family's beloved antiques cleaned of mud and reupholstered.

When Bud looked around the same rooms, he was more practical. The hundred-plus-year-old house had suffered a lot of damage in the hurricane. Bud inspected window frames, wiring, and foundations, watching for any sign of the dread mildew. He knew that taking care of this house would be a never-ending series of chores and money spent. He also knew how much this classic house in the heart of the old village of McClellanville meant not only to Carolina but also to the Brailsford family.

Carolina began stacking books from a box on the shelves. Her face was radiant and she moved like a young girl again after months of anxiety. When she'd slipped the last book into place, she walked to the center of the room, sniffing the air like a hound on the scent.

"I still smell a little mildew," she said.

"Honey, this house was underwater," he

replied. "That smell's going to linger for a while."

"Well, let's keep the windows open, then."

Allison Brailsford walked into the room carrying a tray of coffee and cookies. "Opening the windows, Bud? It's getting chilly in here."

Bud looked over his shoulder at his mother-in-law. Even while baking and sweeping floors, the woman looked like she was going to the club. She even ironed her jeans. But she was a trouper, he had to hand it to her. She'd come with Edgar to help them move in and was a whirlwind. For the past few days, she'd made beds, unpacked linens, cooked meals, done the dishes, and even gone out in the yard to plant flowers. She was okay in his book.

"I got my orders," he told her with a grin.

"Just for a little while, Mama," Carolina told her. "The mildew smells mixed with the paint smells are overwhelming. I don't want Lizzy to get sick."

Allison stopped in the front hall and lifted her nose. "It's not so bad. I like the smell of fresh paint." She set the tray down, and her gaze swept the freshly painted front rooms. The tables were polished and the new chandelier, though not as grand as the original, sparkled in the late-afternoon sun.

"Oh, sweetheart, the house looks wonderful, doesn't it? Who'd have thought after that horrible storm this house could have been put back to rights? It's better than ever."

"Thanks to you and Daddy," Carolina said, coming closer to press her cheek against her mother's.

Bud yanked on the stubborn window. The paint was sticking.

"We love this old house, too, you know," Allison said, taking a seat on the blue Victorian sofa. "I only wish Aunt Lucille were here to see this." Her bright blue eyes threatened to fill at the thought of her favorite aunt. Aunt Lucille had survived Hurricane Hugo but died a few months after. The doctors said it was her heart, and they'd all agreed, but not for the same reason. Everyone believed Aunt Lucille had died of a broken heart, seeing her beloved White Gables and the town of McClellanville so devastated.

"She's here in spirit," Carolina said softly. "I can feel her."

Lizzy skipped past them humming a song with the running lyrics "Moving day, moving day."

Allison watched her granddaughter move from room to room, her face a picture of maternal adoration. "Look at the child. She's just so happy to be here!"

"And out of the awful condo in Myrtle Beach. We all are. I hated that place."

"It's been a long six months, Carolina, but you're home now," her mother said.

The window rattled up the frame.

"Place is looking good!" Edgar Brailsford said as he came down the stairs. He'd cleaned up after painting the trim on the back porch. In his khaki pants and white polo, he looked like a typical banker on holiday. He stepped into the front room and clasped his hands before him, grinning like a man before a feast. "It sure is great to be back in this old house. God, we love it here. So many great memories. Now that you're living here, we'll come down more often. Family is all that matters, right?"

Bud grinned but didn't say anything. He couldn't get past Edgar's claim that he'd be coming to visit more often.

Edgar eased himself into one of the newly upholstered armchairs and sat back, crossing his legs and looking around the room like he owned the place. "Can you believe it? We got here in less than four hours. 'Course, with your mother in the car, I had to go slower."

Allison began pouring coffee. "Your

brother and his wife have been like hens, worrying over you ever since that hurricane. They'll be so glad to see the pictures." She handed a cup to Carolina beside her. "Oh, that reminds me. Greg wanted me to ask you if July was okay for them to come down for a visit. The kids are out of school then."

Carolina looked at Bud for confirmation. He shrugged and lowered himself into the other armchair.

"I guess that's all right," she replied. "I mean, we are only just getting settled. I'll call him."

"July is months away," her mother said breezily. "You'll be settled in by then. We wish we were closer to you, so we just have to come down more often."

Bud met Carolina's gaze. Carolina raised her brows as if to say, *What can I do?*

Everyone had been served coffee, and Bud was the only one who reached for one of Allison's chocolate-chip cookies. They were still warm. They were having "tea," as Allison put it, but there seemed to be some important family topic on the agenda that Bud wasn't aware of, and it made him apprehensive. They'd all come a long way since that first tense meeting at the Brailsfords' country club. But Bud still didn't trust his father-in-law. Something was bubbling in that old badger's mind, he thought.

"Well," Edgar began. "Carolina and I talked, and she wanted me to speak with you about a matter that came up recently that concerns all of us."

Bud swung his head to look at his wife. Carolina had her hands clenched in her lap. "She didn't tell mc about this. We don't keep a lot of secrets from each other. So my curiosity is piqued."

"It's no secret. More a surprise," Carolina rushed to clarify. "Daddy, let's not have a preamble. Just tell Bud what you propose."

Edgar took a small sip of coffee, then set his cup on the table. "I don't need to tell you the precarious nature of the economy these days, do I, Bud?"

Bud didn't reply.

"In my day, when an opportunity came my way, I seized it."

Bud's eyes narrowed. "Where are you going with this, Edgar?"

"Where I'm *going,* as you put it, is to this point. Lee Edwards is buying the Coastal Seafood Company."

"Yeah, I know." Bud's tone was incredulous. "He's my best friend. How do *you* know this?" Bud looked at Carolina. She half-smiled and shrugged. "Oh."

"I know a lot about it," Edgar answered.

241

"I have friends, connections who keep me apprised. Everyone recognizes the importance of the Coastal Seafood Company to the town and the region. And, as you already know, Mr. Edwards —"

"Lee," Bud interjected.

Brailsford shrugged. "Lee is putting together an offer to buy it. The timing is excellent, as the place is in ruins and the owner is looking to get out. Any businessman would admit that Edwards's timing — stepping in to buy the destroyed warehouse from a traumatized seller at a rock-bottom price — is financially brilliant. Now, Lee's willing to consider a partner in this venture. It's a large operation, and he could use another investor to help the company meet its projected goals. The man has big plans."

"I know his plans," Bud said flatly.

Carolina looked at Bud, hopeful.

"Anyway," Edgar continued. "We had a good discussion. That young man trusts my judgment and is willing to take my advice. And I agreed to provide the collateral for you. You and Carolina, of course." He looked around the living room at his family with an expression of magnanimity.

Bud stared back at his father-in-law, incredulous. "That's a good one, Edgar. I have to admit, I didn't see that one coming.

But I'm pretty sure you know Carolina and I can't afford to make an investment like that. Especially not now."

"Yes, well, I do happen to be aware of that. However, if I help out with the procurement of the —"

Bud's face was implacable. "No."

"I beg your pardon?" Edgar was not accustomed to being interrupted.

"You heard me. The answer is no." Bud turned to Carolina, cutting her off with a look before she could speak.

"You're being unreasonable here," Brailsford said.

"And you're being insulting."

"Insulting? How?"

"By offering to loan me money to buy a business I can't begin to afford."

"Bud, be reasonable," Carolina said. "We're not going to get this chance again. It's right in front of us. My father only wants to help us. Consider it my inheritance."

"Your father paid to renovate your aunt Lucille's house for us to live in. That was your inheritance."

Edgar sat back in his chair, mulish. "It's my own goddamn money. Why don't you let me decide what I will or won't give my daughter?"

"Carolina's my wife."

"Bud —"

"No. This house is already a stretch for us. Now you want me to invest in Lee's company? How do we know it won't go bust?"

"What does it matter?" Brailsford said coolly. "It's not your money Carolina is investing. It's hers."

"Daddy!"

"That's it," Bud said, slamming his hands on his knees. He rose to his feet and walked away from the group to stand at the front window.

"Bud . . ." Carolina said, perched forward in her chair.

"Don't make a decision you're going to regret," Brailsford said in a menacing tone.

"That's enough, Edgar." Allison's voice, though soft, was as firm as iron. A moment of stunned silence followed this declaration. Then she continued in her honeyed voice, "I'm sorry, Bud. We don't mean to interfere. This is entirely your decision, of course. Yours and Carolina's. We just want the two of you to be happy. It's been such a hard time for you both."

Allison rose gracefully and smoothed her jeans with even strokes. "Well, enough said, I should think. Edgar, won't you help me in the kitchen? I think that roast is about ready to come out."

She smiled prettily and turned toward her husband; Bud couldn't see the *Get up and get out* look he was sure Edgar was receiving.

Edgar's face flushed and he rubbed his jaw in consternation. "It's your decision," he said in defeat, and followed his wife to the kitchen.

Bud rested his hands on the white wood and looked out the window at the lawn. Six months ago it had been a mess of dead marsh grass, pieces of pier and boats, and junk washed in by the hurricane's tidal surge. They'd lost just about everything. Their house was demolished and everything in it, and though they were lucky with their boat, it still had suffered some damage. It was a season that had tested him as a father, a husband, a fisherman, and a man. They'd been renting the only place they could afford. But they weren't the only ones. Nobody in McClellanville hadn't been hammered by the storm. As much as he hated to admit it, he was grateful to Carolina's parents for coming through in the pinch.

Carolina joined him at the window and looked out. They stood side by side for a few moments while the tension dissipated

245

in the fresh air.

"I don't smell mildew," Bud said.

"You don't think your socks smell after a few days on the boat, either," Carolina chided.

He laughed, relieved by her humor. A peace settled between them. "No, really, it's not bad."

"It's better than it was a few months ago, that's for sure. But it'll take a few weeks with the windows open to really air it out." She sighed. "Thank God it's spring."

"I didn't mean to be rude to your parents."

"My father wants to give the money to help us. It might be a good idea. It would give us security for the future."

"*I'm* your security."

"I know."

"They already put out a small fortune to fix up this house," he argued. "Did you see the way they look at this place? It's like they own it. They're planning their vacations here!"

Carolina smirked. "I did notice that. They're just excited, Bud. We all are. We'll be lucky if they come down for a week in the summer and every other Christmas. I hope they do. We have plenty of room, and I miss them."

"I don't care about that. But this other. Caro, I can't take a handout from your father."

"It's not a handout."

"Okay, call it a loan. Either way, your father will lord it over me and Lee will lord it over me, making me feel small. The bad blood would spill over and come between us. You know I'm right."

Carolina was silent.

"Look," he said, his voice conciliatory, "I love you. I want to take care of you. Provide for you and Lizzy. But I can't take your father's money."

"Are you sure my father's the only reason you won't take it?"

Bud tilted his head, not understanding what she meant.

"Is it because the company is being bought by Lee?"

There had always been a deep-rooted rivalry between Bud Morrison and Lee Edwards. Though they were best friends coming up, they'd battled over everything. Oz still joked about how they were always arguing as boys over who ran the fastest, who could catch the biggest fish, who could pop the most shrimp heads. Truth was, Oz had encouraged the rivalry. He was never hesitant to push Bud, to test the mettle of his elder son.

As they grew older, the competition had become more subtle but even more pointed. Lee liked to needle Bud on how he'd gone to college and Bud hadn't. Unlike the Morrisons, the Edwardses always had money, and Lee had a knack for making more.

Bud put his hands on his hips and considered that. "Honestly, maybe a little. Look, Carolina, this might be a good investment. But we don't have the money. We're in hock up to our necks with repairs to this house and the *Miss Carolina.* And this house, as much as you love it, is going to cost us. Then there's Lizzy's school tuition. Yeah, yeah," he said, holding up his hand and stopping Carolina from interrupting him. "I know your parents are helping with her tuition. That's another handout I have to deal with." He moved his hands to her shoulders and looked into her eyes. "Carolina, I don't want to go into business with Lee. I don't want to go into debt to your father. We can take care of ourselves, you and me. Like we always have. Look what we just got through! The hurricane of the century clobbered us, and we're standing here on our feet. My boat's back in the water. I'm making a good living. When we got married, I told you what I've got is what

I am. That's still true today. I hope that's enough for you."

Carolina moved closer and rested her head on his shoulder. He wrapped his arms around her.

"Isn't nature resilient?" she said, looking out. "Six months ago, this street looked like a bomb hit it. Now look at it. The grass is green and there's even some moss back in that live oak tree. I thought we'd lost those gardenias, but they're coming back. And soon, so will the hydrangeas." She closed her eyes and sniffed. "I can smell the gardenias. My favorite."

Bud brought his cheek to her neck. "This's *my* favorite smell."

She leaned back into his arms to look him in the face. "We'll be happy here, won't we?"

"Why wouldn't we be?"

She put her head back on his shoulder with a sigh. "No reason."

Bud knew she was worried about the future and money, and he wished he could promise her the moon and more.

"Don't worry, Carolina. We're going to be okay."

September 21, 2008
On board the Miss Carolina
The family had survived, Bud thought as

249

the boat beneath him rose and fell with the waves. They'd survived a lot of ups and downs over the years. They'd survive this accident, too. He'd promised Carolina he'd take care of her, and that was a promise he intended to keep.

Carolina's parents had come through for them after Hugo. That's what families did. His own family had always taken care of their own, too. He remembered back to when he was very young and sat in the big kitchen of his grandmother's house. Grandma Ellen had had seven children and regularly cooked for fifteen to twenty people. To step into her kitchen was to enter a world of women cooking cornbread, fried chicken, turkey, pork chops, and some kind of fresh fish brought in from the boat. And there was always a pot of hot coffee on the stove. Folks called it the house of milk and honey. At Grandma Ellen's table, there was talk of everything from the price of shrimp and the condition of boats to the antics of their beloved children and grandchildren. The Lord's name was never taken in vain at her table, nor was cussing permitted. Children were welcome but dared not be rude, lest a wooden spoon suddenly appear to slap their hands.

There were always working men ambling

in from the docks or the shed in back where improvised repairs on engines and machinery were made by his grandfather, a kind of MacGyver of the docks. These were the men who worked for the Morrison family. Some did well; others didn't earn enough to support themselves, much less a family. Those few would sleep in a bunkhouse above the shed during the season. If they didn't make it in shrimping, they'd leave. When Bud was growing up, it had seemed everyone in the extended family worked for his grandfather, and later his father, at some time — men like Pee Dee just looking for a second chance. Every able-bodied Morrison fished — shrimp, oysters, clams, crabs. His grandparents had passed on the tradition of looking out for family and friends to his parents, and they'd passed it on to him.

The seasons flowed one into the next like the creek outside their home. White roe shrimp in the spring, brown shrimp in the summer, then the white shrimp that hatched in the spring came back again in the fall. Life was good. In his mind, Bud could hear the women's voices from the shrimp house as they sang spirituals and headed shrimp.

He felt himself drifting off with the music. His grandparents, his mother, Bobby, they were all gone. Yet they seemed to be just beyond the clouds. He sensed they were waiting for him. There was so much love. He felt a white light of their love around him.

11

Rutledge Academy was a small, sprawling school set back from a country road amid a cluster of old oaks. There were only a few cars in the lot; many of the faculty had gone to lunch in town. Carolina spotted Lizzy's green VW bug and pulled up beside her, lifting her hand in a quick wave. As she turned off the ignition she saw Lizzy's car door open, then the familiar red-gold hair emerge. It caught the wind as Lizzy stepped out of her old car. Her hand darted up to tuck it behind her ears as she came around to meet Carolina.

"Hey! You made it," she said when Carolina swung open the car door.

"Breaking speed limits all the way." Carolina reached to the passenger side to grab the large, flat Tupperware container that held two dozen cupcakes. She hoisted it

253

over the steering wheel, then handed it with care to her waiting daughter.

"Thanks, Mama. Will really appreciates this. His class is staying after school to practice for the play and these will tide them over."

"Happy to do it. When's the play?"

"October seventh," Lizzy said in a tone that implied she'd told her mother this many times before.

"Hey, be nice to your mama. I've got a lot on my mind. I'll be there. Don't worry."

"Will Daddy be here?"

Carolina paused, not wanting to get into this well-worn argument again. "Well, honey," she said, hedging. "You know how it is with his work. If he gets back in time, he will."

Lizzy's eyes flashed. "Mama, this is Will's first time in a lead role! He'll be so disappointed if Daddy doesn't show. Can't he skip working for one night? It's only one night."

Carolina cringed, reliving a moment that had occurred years before, when Lizzy was Will's age. And again when she was ten, and fifteen.

"Don't get mad at me," she said. "This is nothing new. You know how your father is."

"Yeah, I know," Lizzy said, but her tone

implied anything but understanding. Her face clouded, and she said, "You know, it's one thing for him to not show up to *my* programs when I was a kid. But this is for Will. His grandson. You'd think it would mean more to him. He'll never change. You can tell him for me that I'm pissed off."

Carolina didn't want to get between the two again. "Tell him yourself. I've told him plenty of times."

Lizzy shook her head with frustration. "I don't know why I even bother to ask."

"I'll be there," Carolina said as an offering.

"I know you will." Temporarily mollified, Lizzy leaned over and kissed her mother's cheek. "You always are." She hoisted the container of cupcakes in her arms. "I better go. Thanks again, Mama."

"You sure you don't need help with those?"

"I'm a waitress, remember? We're one-armed wonders. See you later."

Carolina held the doorframe of her sedan and watched her daughter sail through the door, balancing the cupcakes like the pro she was. The heavy metal door closed behind her with a loud click. It seemed only yesterday that Carolina was the young mother orchestrating Lizzy's schedule with her own work schedule. Then she laughed lightly at the vagaries of fate. As a grandmother-in-residence, she still did.

She climbed into the car but paused, resting her hands on the steering wheel. She'd long since stopped making excuses for Bud. He'd be out late, trying to make his day. She used to ask him to change his schedule, back when Lizzy was young. But over the years, she'd just stopped asking.

That was about the same time he'd stopped listening.

October 14, 1993
Rutledge Academy

It was a big night for Lizzy. Carolina was proud that her daughter had a major role in the seventh-grade play. For weeks beforehand, she'd helped Lizzy practice her lines. At night, Carolina had spent hours on the sewing machine stitching up an early-American costume.

Carolina was sitting on one of the dozens of gray metal folding chairs that had been set up in the gym for the play. Parents scrambled for what they believed were the best seats for pictures — the front, the middle seats on the aisles. Most of the seats were filled and the buzz of conversation began to rise with excitement as the curtain time approached. Carolina chewed her lip and turned to search the back of the room for any sign of Bud. She had a sickening feeling in the pit of her stomach that he wasn't going to make it for the performance. She waved to a few friends who caught her eye, feeling a twinge of envy at seeing so many couples sitting together, excited to see their child onstage. She turned back to face the front and checked her watch.

"Bud's not coming?"

Carolina turned toward the voice. Sitting at her right was Sally, the mother of a sweet boy both Lizzy and Tressy had a crush on. Carolina shrugged.

"I hope he makes it. Lizzy has a lead part," Sally said. "The play starts in five minutes."

Carolina put a smile on her face. She knew exactly how many minutes were left before curtain. She was relieved when Sally went back to her conversation with her husband.

Carolina's gaze swept the room as she tapped her foot. From the corner of her eye she caught a commotion from the stage. Looking over, she saw three girls peeking out from behind the curtain — Tressy, Zoe, and Lizzy — all in costume. Lizzy's hair was pulled up on top of her head in a kind of bun to make her look older, and her blue eyes were accentuated with matching makeup. They shone like searchlights as she scanned the seats. Her face blossomed into an excited smile at spotting her mother. Carolina saw her eyes move to the empty chair. Lizzy looked again at Carolina with a question in her eyes. Carolina could only shrug and mouth, *Sorry.* Her own heart broke as she saw her daughter's smile fall and the curtain close.

Damn you, Bud, she thought. While making his breakfast that morning, she'd told him how important it was to Lizzy that he be there tonight. "Please, don't forget," she'd begged. Before he left, he kissed her cheek and told her he'd try. "Try hard!" she'd called to his back.

He obviously wasn't going to show. She knew Bud worked hard for them and that this was an important end-of-season push. But he had his priorities screwed up if he couldn't find the time — just once — to come to his daughter's play. She was so mad at him at that moment she could hardly think clearly. She released the chair she'd reserved for him, taking her purse from the seat.

A moment later, she heard a familiar voice. "Is this seat taken or can any late father have it?"

She swung around to see Lee Edwards standing in the aisle, his hand on the back of the empty chair. "Lee! Hey, nice to see you. Go ahead and take it." She bent to move her purse under her chair.

"You sure Bud's not coming?"

"I wouldn't bet on it. One guess . . ."

"Still out?"

She nodded.

Lee slipped out of his brown suede jacket and folded it over his arm before taking his seat. It wasn't a showy jacket, but the suede was creamy smooth and expensive.

Lee was more than an old friend, he was now her boss. Carolina had gone to work for Coastal Seafood after Hugo. After a few years Carolina was running the office. She had a good head for numbers, but even more, she was familiar with the captains, their crews, and the world of shrimping. She knew to the pound how much fish each captain landed and to the dollar what he was paid for it. She recorded to the penny who owed how much to the company for fuel, ice, rope, cable, and other necessities. She became the gatekeeper or, as the men at the docks had taken to calling her behind her back, the ballbuster.

"It's cold out there tonight," Lee said. "He

must be freezing his ass off."

"I hope he is. Lizzy's so disappointed he's not here. And so am I. You alone, too?"

He adjusted his seat. "Yep."

"Where's your wife?"

He shook his head. "Melissa doesn't see herself as the mother type. More the aunt for Tressy. Or the big sister. This kind of thing isn't her style."

"Uh-huh," Carolina replied, holding her tongue but disliking the woman even more. Lee had married a wealthy socialite from Charlotte whom he'd met while showing her some coastal real estate. It was inconvenient that he was still married to Odelle when he and Melissa met. According to Odelle, Lee had dated this woman on the sly, still sleeping with Odelle while at the same time making plans to divorce her. It wasn't a friendly divorce, and it made for awkwardness for months afterward while Bud and Carolina tried to reestablish their relationships with Odelle and Lee as separate people.

"Odelle's here."

"I know. She shot me a few arrows as I came in."

"Yeah, well, as ye sow . . ."

"Don't *you* get started on me," he said, settling back and crossing one ankle over the other knee. Carolina noticed that his boots were made of fine brown leather. "I'm here, aren't I?"

Carolina nodded and felt another prick of anger at Bud. The room was full of fathers, many of them shrimpers, who'd found the time or just plain made the effort.

Lee leaned closer and said companionably, "I just got out of the office. You'll never guess what happened."

She looked over, curious. "What?"

"You know how Digger Davis came in earlier in the week to ask about credit?"

"Sure. I did all the paperwork."

Digger Davis was having more trouble with his boat than a street dog had fleas. His winch needed repair, and on his last trip out his engine had blown and he had to be towed in. Digger worked hard, but everyone knew he drank hard, too.

"I told you, I don't think he's a good credit risk."

"Well, I like ol' Digger and I thought he needed a break."

"Uh-huh," she repeated, sensing where this story was headed. "So, what happened?"

"I got an urgent call from the bank. Apparently, ol' Digger was trying to charge a pickup truck to my credit."

Carolina's eyes widened with surprise. "What?"

Lee's lips twisted as he held back a laugh. "Yep. Hard to believe, huh? But wait." He tapped her sleeve. "It gets better. When I talked to Digger on the phone to ask him to explain what the hell was going on, he said he didn't think I'd mind. His truck broke down and he needed to get to work so he could repay the loan, and he thought it all made sense. Besides, he said it was an old, beat-up truck and he was getting it for real cheap."

Carolina looked at Lee and held his gaze, dumbfounded. Then they both burst out laughing at the same time.

"Unbelievable," she said, wiping tears from her eyes.

"Yeah. I gotta admit, that's one for the books."

"Speaking of the books, you didn't lend him the money?" She had to ask. Lee could be generous to a fault with loans, and she wasn't sure.

Lee looked at his boot and shook his head. "Couldn't. Not this time. If word got out, I'd be more a bank than a fish house. I had to draw the line somewhere."

Carolina worked close to Lee most every day. She'd discovered that he had offered a line of credit to most every captain at the dock. Doing the books, she knew, too, that virtually all of them owed Lee money. He made sure they got the ice, fuel, and gear they needed to keep afloat, and let them pay back what they could when they could. He didn't want everyone to know about it, but in a small town, that kind of information couldn't be secret.

Carolina had come to admire Lee Edwards. What kind of man gave so much of his time and wealth to his hometown? she'd often wondered. She thought him generous and loyal, even noble.

"Unfortunately," Lee added, "there's a pile of paperwork on your desk waiting for you."

"I'll take care of it."

"What would I do without you? You're the best."

"That's what I hear."

"No, really." Lee's voice lowered. "You really are the best. And don't think I don't know it. You'll find a more tangible expression of my thanks in your paycheck."

Carolina was surprised. "You didn't have to. But I'm glad you did. Thanks."

The principal of the school, Mrs. Granger, took the stage, and immediately the buzz of conversation died down.

Lee bent over and muttered under his breath, "Don't get too excited. It's not much of a raise."

She returned a smile, then faced the stage. As the lights dimmed and the principal began her long-winded welcome to the parents, Carolina's thoughts turned inward. In her heart, she knew she deserved that raise and it had been a long time in coming. She'd started working for Lee soon after he'd purchased the company. In the beginning it didn't bother her to be just another employee. But as her responsibilities increased, Coastal Seafood became more successful.

Carolina practically ran the fish house, but she didn't get any benefit of ownership. If only they'd taken Lee up on his offer to invest when he was buying it, she thought for the hundredth time. Sure, it had been a bad time. Hurricane Hugo had hit them hard. They were in debt for the boat's repairs and they'd just taken possession of White Gables. But she knew it had been more than just a matter of money. It was Bud's pride, too. Because of Bud's pride, they had not accepted help from her father to invest in Coastal Seafood — and she'd ended up working for the company anyway. Bud didn't seem to recognize that owning part of the company might have given Carolina some pride for her labor.

Lizzy appeared onstage, and Carolina's troubled thoughts disappeared at her daughter's first word of dialogue. The play told the story of the Revolutionary hero Francis Marion — the Swamp Fox — who had fought the British in the neighboring forest that bore his name. At the play's end, parents made a mad dash toward the stage as flashbulbs lit up the gymnasium.

Lee turned to Carolina, smiling. "Hey, Lizzy did you proud."

"She did, didn't she? And ditto for Tressy."

"We're lucky, you know?" he said, referring to their daughters. "Well, I better go."

He bent to give Carolina a farewell hug, his arms around her shoulders in a friendly manner. But Carolina thought he held on a fraction of a second too long.

In that one extra nanosecond, she was acutely aware of the feel of his skin against her cheek. His musky cologne set her blood racing. When they pulled back awkwardly, neither of them could look at each other. Carolina felt flustered and turned to retrieve her purse from the floor in a kind of retreat.

"See you tomorrow," she heard him say. It was clear to her that Lee felt it, too.

Carolina rose slowly to see Lee walking

away. Other parents were crowding the stage to pick up their children. She heard high-pitched voices and laughter, sensed the crush of movement around her. Yet Carolina felt rooted to the spot, unsure of what had just transpired. Dangerously intrigued.

When Carolina and Lizzy returned home to White Gables, Bud was sitting in his favorite chair with a plate of food on his lap, watching television. His muscles were clearly visible under the T-shirt when he turned toward them. His eyes were red with exhaustion, and there was a rich stubble on his face.

"Where's my star?" he called out, lifting his legs off the ottoman and setting the plate down so he could open his arms.

Lizzy stood at the door and pouted. "Where were you? I looked for you."

"Aw, honey, I was working. But I was thinking of you every minute. In fact, when I saw this shell, I said to Pee Dee, 'Stop everything! I have to save this beauty for my Lizzy.' "

Begrudgingly, she walked closer. "What is it?"

Carolina leaned against the doorframe and watched Bud work his magic on Lizzy. She adored him, and it was mutual. When Bud pulled a beautiful sea star from a plastic bag on the floor, Lizzy's sulk vanished.

"Oh, Daddy. That's a keeper." Then she gave him a decidedly feminine look of feigned anger. "But I'm still mad at you."

"I'll be there next time, okay?"

"Promise?"

Bud didn't reply. Instead, he gave her a kiss on her cheek. "You better get to bed now, honey. It's late."

Carolina pushed away from the wall. "Daddy's right. Go on up and wash all that makeup off. I'll bring you up a plate of something to eat."

When Carolina returned to the living room a half hour later, Bud was nodding off. His legs were stretched out on the ottoman and his arms hung loose. The empty beer bottle had dropped to the floor just beyond his grasp. Looking around the room, she saw his half-eaten sandwich going stale on his plate on the floor, his flannel shirt strewn across the sofa, and his muddy boots lying in a puddle by the door. Was this what their marriage had come to?

She bent to pick up the plate and retrieve the bottle from the floor. Then she gave his shoulder a hard nudge. Bud's eyes immediately blinked and opened.

"Bud, you should go up to bed."

He mopped his face with his hands.

"Yeah. Okay."

"Lizzy really missed you tonight. She was great."

Bud dropped his hands and released a heavy sigh. "Wish I could've been there."

"You could have."

His sigh this time was born of irritation, not fatigue. "Caro, it's late. Let's not get into this now."

"That's the problem. You're never here to discuss it."

"Hey," he said sharply. "This is what I do! What do you want from me?"

"I want a little of your time. Lizzy wants a little of your time. Bud, we *never* see you."

"I told you what it was going to be like," he said with heat. "It wasn't going to be country clubs and cocktails."

Carolina groaned. It was always the same. Whenever there was a discussion of money or the demands of his job, he threw her more privileged background at her as though the fifteen years of their marriage hadn't carved a dent in her pedigree. The joke of it was, her parents weren't rich. They were comfortable and could help their children, but far from having any real wealth — even though they sometimes acted like Rockefellers. Yet Carolina knew that beneath Bud's harangue was a tiny barb of truth that still stung. What he didn't say but implied was that she wasn't from a shrimping family, so she didn't and couldn't understand. Otherwise, she wouldn't complain about his long hours at sea.

"You know what? Tonight there were a lot of guys at that school who took time off the boat to be there for their kids. So don't give me that old line about being a shrimper."

"It is what it is."

"Maybe that's the problem."

"What's that?"

"Just that things aren't the same now as they were when we got married. We have a child now. That makes things different."

She saw his big shoulders bow up in defense, and she felt suddenly weary of this old, pointless argument. They'd both thrown the same hurtful lines back and forth so often that they no longer heard the words. It was just annoying, like his mess strewn across the room.

"I'm beat. I'm going up."

"I know you're exhausted," she said with softness. "I don't think it's safe for you to be out there so long, and I worry about you."

His shoulders lowered, and he acknowledged her words with a tired nod.

"I'm just wondering . . ." She laid the

plate on the coffee table and sat down in the easy chair beside it. She rubbed her palms, then clasped her hands tightly in her lap. "I know you and Pee Dee have been making plans about taking the *Carolina* to Florida after the season ends."

"That's the plan."

"I know it's been hard for you since Bobby died, but . . ."

Bud's face hardened. "This ain't got nothing to do with Bobby."

She didn't believe him. He'd been struggling with his brother's drowning, working long hours and brooding in silence. She didn't want to drag him into that painful topic and changed course. "Maybe if you think about it from my side for a change. From May to December you're gone, on the water from sunup to sundown. That's your job, and I know that." She took a breath. "But you have a duty here, too. To your daughter and to me. Maybe you could find a different job for the off-season? Something that will keep you in town?"

"Don't want to do anything else."

"But you're good at welding, machinery. Bud, you're smart. You could do anything you put your mind to."

Her stomach clenched at seeing him already shaking his head. It was this constant roadblock to change that infuriated her.

"But Lee said —" His eyes flashed, and she realized her mistake in bringing up Lee's name.

"What did *Lee* say?" he asked in a low voice.

She licked her lips. "He just said that it wasn't a good year. The shrimp aren't out there."

"He's a real genius. Lee says it's not a good year. Let me alert the media. Maybe if that tight-ass would pay us a decent price for our shrimp, we wouldn't have to break our backs all day and night out there."

"Bud, I know better than anyone what you guys are getting for shrimp at the dock. That's my job. I know who's having a good year and who isn't, down to the dollar."

Bud's face showed that he didn't like that she worked at the seafood house, didn't like the names he heard the guys calling his wife. He especially didn't like that she had to work for Lee.

Carolina looked in Bud's eyes. "I'm just saying, business isn't so good now. Maybe it's not a bad idea to look for something off-boat."

Bud raised his eyes and his anger glittered through the red. "I'm no white-collar, part-time hobby shrimper," he ground out. "And I'm sure as hell not going to trust Lee Edwards's opinion on how I should run my business."

"Forget Lee. This is about me and you. And Lizzy. Our family!" She was trembling with suppressed rage. "We need you, too."

"It's all arranged, Caro."

"You can change your plans. You haven't left yet."

He stood and made a slicing motion in the air, cutting off all further conversation.

"I don't want to change them. Now, I'm tired. I've got to get up in a few hours. Good night."

Carolina sat in the front room for a long while, her hands folded in her lap as she stared at the carpet. Generations of feet had trod over that expanse of wool, all of them dead now. Children, parents, grandparents. Couples who had shared long marriages. Husbands and wives who sat here by the television, or the radio, or maybe just the fire, having the same discussion. She was sure they must have. Every family faced the same pains and joys. There'd be talk about their money problems, or laughs over the antics of their children, or plans for their future. She'd always believed that the glue of any relationship was communication.

Sometimes, just sitting side by side without speaking a word was contact enough.

Carolina sat for a long time, not wanting to go up to bed and lie next to the man who was becoming a stranger.

September 21, 2008
McClellanville

A short beep from a car that had pulled up beside her in the parking lot startled Carolina. She looked over to see Georgia Tisdale waving hello. Carolina smiled and waved back, then checked the time on the dashboard. Bud should be arriving at the dock soon. She'd better get moving if she was going to help him unload.

As she drove along the narrow country road that led to the docks, Carolina passed under a thick canopy of leaves tinted with hints of red, yellow, and orange. It was going to be a beautiful fall. Driving through the dappled light, Carolina reflected on how differently things might have turned out if Bud had stayed home in those winter months rather than heading south to Florida on the *Miss Carolina*.

12

Pee Dee arrived at the dock as skittish as a feral cat. The tide was low and the tips of countless oysters gleamed in the mud, sharp and menacing. He squinted and looked overhead. The slate-colored sky was now streaked with black clouds, blocking the sun.

He'd awoken to sun shining through the blinds into his eyes and bolted upright in a surge of panic. He'd overslept, and he knew it immediately. Pee Dee didn't own an alarm clock. He had one of those internal clocks that usually served him well. It had to. With Bud, you were either at your post ten minutes before you were supposed to report or you were left at the dock. But he'd scored drugs the night before and passed out. It didn't happen often, maybe once every five years.

Bud Morrison was gonna hang his hide high up on the rigging for making the *Carolina* late. Pee Dee reached beneath his seat, taking a quick glance around for cops, then pulled out a fifth of discount whiskey and took a couple long swallows, his large Adam's apple pulsating with each gulp. He wiped his mouth, then screwed the top back on and stashed the bottle. There was nothing left to do but face the music.

He peered into the rearview mirror. He looked a good ten years older than his fifty years. Pee Dee smacked his lips, revealing stained and battered teeth. With a withering sigh, he pulled back his thin blond hair into a ponytail, slapped on his cap, pulled the keys from the ignition, and headed toward the dock.

Limping slightly on legs that were scarred from hooks, rope burns, and cuts that just wouldn't heal, Pee Dee zigzagged across the weedy, gravel-strewn path. As he neared the dock, he felt the wind gust, carrying the scents of salt and fish and the shrill, savage cries of the gulls mocking him for showing up at this late hour.

He paused beside the weathered gray warehouse to pull a solitary Marlboro from his shirt pocket, the last from a crumpled pack. The low voices of several men rose and fell in conversation out front. Pee Dee peeked around the corner. Five old men were clustered under the rusted awning of the welding shop. He knew them all. Pee Dee also knew they'd take turns assaulting him with their verbal barbs until he was deflated. They sat in cheap plastic garden chairs, beer cans nestled in their gnarled hands, cloaked in thin rain jackets and caps with various insignias.

Pee Dee pulled his head back, safely out of view. He took a long drag from his cigarette, exhaling hard from his nose like a peeved bull. These were the old captains, venerable shrimpers too aged, too injured, or too broke to go out to sea. So they sat at the dock, morning after morning, to rage over the regulations and laws that were ruining the industry and to talk about how it used to be "back in the day." As usual, it was Oz's voice that boomed loudest. Pee Dee leaned closer.

"Hell's bells, I give up," he said, his voice sounding like small pebbles were grinding in his throat. "You used to be able to hunt for shrimp. Use your wits. You can't afford to ride around no more. You gotta drop your nets and hope you don't pull up a load of garbage or worthless fish."

"My boy, Donnie, won't go to his best

spots no more. Can't."

Pee Dee recognized Captain Woody's voice. For thirty years he'd managed to work on a prosthetic foot after a wire cable snapped and lashed off the one God had given him. This was a minor inconvenience for the old sea dog. In a couple of years he'd learned to maneuver around, and if you didn't know about the accident, you would never have guessed he had just the one. Woody could do most things better than men half his age with two able feet. He danced, sailed, and helped run the boatyard with an iron fist. But the nickname Woody had stuck.

"He just skims where he can, hoping to catch whatever he can," Woody continued. "It's all he wants anymore, just to get by. Don't think his heart is in it no more."

"Don't matter," a nasal voice replied. It was a beloved old captain known as the Hagg. "The shrimp, they ain't out there."

A few other curmudgeons muttered their agreement.

"Oh, they're there," Oz pontificated. "But who can afford to go out and get to 'em? It's a damn crime what they're charging for diesel. They're choking us out of business."

"Don't go there," said the Hagg, heaving a sigh. "We talk about the same bullshit every day. We sound like a women's red hat club, or whatever the hell they call it. My blood pressure's already sky-high today."

Pee Dee heard a loud slurp from a can, then Woody said, "Well, there's no denying, back in the day we caught a lot."

"A lot of crap," Oz said with a chuckle. "I remember the time we drew up a twelve-foot shark. Near lost my foot to that son of a bitch. No offense, Woody."

They chuckled, each having a sea story with some sort of danger attached, usually embellished over the years.

"Shark, hell, that ain't nothin'," said Clay Cable. Unlike Woody, whose scruffy hair and clothes had the disheveled look of a man who couldn't be bothered to look in a mirror, Clay was usually dressed in a tan coverall freshly laundered and ironed by his diligent wife. He still had a twinkle in his eye that could bring life to any story, even an old one. He chuckled. "Did I ever tell you about the time we drew up an old bomb?"

The men grumbled that they'd heard that story plenty of times before.

"Well, I'll never forget it, that's for damn sure," Cable continued, undaunted. "We all went white, like we was already dead in the water."

"It was a different world back then," Woody said. "It mattered if you knew the water. My daddy could read the stars. Used a sextant. Now it's all GPS."

"And rules and regulations," added Oz.

Another round of curses and grumbles. The conversation heated up, one voice talking over another.

"I'm sick of being told how to shrimp. How much I can catch and what I can catch."

"Crabs are gone."

"Scallops, too."

"A man can't hardly make a living without breaking the law."

"It's not worth going out no more."

"It's a damn shame."

Pee Dee leaned against the dry, splintered wood and closed his eyes tight. The familiar smells of the working dock — dead fish, murky water, salt, mold — rose up to choke him. He couldn't listen anymore to their incessant ramblings. It was always the same. But hate 'em or love 'em, these were his people. Icons of the creek. And what stuck in his craw was that this morning he felt like an intruder.

Pee Dee had been coming to this dock ever since Oz took him on as a striker when he'd run away from home at fifteen. He'd been a skinny, snot-nosed kid with bruises and broken bones from a man he wouldn't call father and a shrunken woman who couldn't protect him.

From the moment he'd stepped aboard the *Miss Ann,* Pee Dee felt he'd come home. Long hours in the sun, hot meals on the boat of fish, potatoes, garlic, tomatoes, and grits, and nights of sleep unbroken by the cursing and howling of a drunken brawl had filled him out. His wounds had eventually healed. Even after Mrs. Ann died, with the Morrison men he experienced the only real peace he'd ever known. When he was young, Pee Dee had hoped he'd be something like a son to Oz.

But the old man blamed him for Bobby's death, and now he darkened every time Pee Dee's shadow crossed his path. Like a black cat or a broken mirror, Oz looked at Pee Dee as the devil's luck.

Bobby had died more than fifteen years before, but Pee Dee remembered it as fresh as yesterday. Bobby's mother used to tell the boys not to drink on a boat. She said you never knew what was coming. She was a saint, God rest her soul, but she also knew what she was talking about. She'd worked on Oz's boat when they were first married and had sewed his nets till the day she died.

They should've listened to her. Things would have turned out different for everyone.

December 1992
Bulls Bay

It was early winter. Pee Dee and Bobby were looking to make some off-season money, same as usual. Pee Dee had the old bateau he'd bought from Charlie Pickett. Oystering, like shrimping, made for some long and brutal days. They'd been lucky and had made some decent money the week before. So this morning they headed out with high expectations.

It was damn cold, with biting winds that froze his nostril hairs. They wore long johns under their hip waders, and heavy parkas over their slickers. Pee Dee had three or four beers just to wake up, and Bobby was keeping up. By mid-day Bobby was feeling the beer. He started singing to while away the time. Not the heavy metal they liked to listen to, but some ribald songs of the sea he must've learned from his dad, or maybe even his grandfather. Bobby had a good voice, though not many knew it. He came across as a charmer, but that hid his gentler side. Few folks but him knew that Bobby was shy about things that mattered to him.

Pee Dee liked to tease Bobby about his romantic soul. For sure, Oz had no inclination to the softer things in life. And Bud? Forget it. He was smart and liked to read books without pictures, but if Bud had a soft side, he was keeping it to himself. Pee Dee used to catch Bobby squirreled away in his bunk, writing in a notebook he kept hidden under his mattress. Once Pee Dee stole a peek at it, just to see what Bobby was up to. He didn't know what he expected to find — porn, scribbles, whatever. He sure as hell didn't expect to find poetry. And it was good, too. Even a know-nothin' like him could tell that. Pee Dee figured some people felt things more deeply. Bobby was one of those, and he loved him for it.

There was no such clutter in his own mind, Pee Dee thought as he took another swig from his can. He looked over to the other side of the bateau and watched as Bobby hauled a cluster of oysters into the bateau with the tongs, a cigarette dangling from his mouth. Bobby knocked one oyster off the cluster, then tugged off his thick rubber glove and pulled out a pocketknife. He slipped the blade inside the edge of the oyster, prying it open, then handed a half shell to Pee Dee, careful not to spill the briny liquor.

Pee Dee cupped the shell and tipped it back, tasting the succulent meat, salty and sweet, as it slid down his throat. He turned and gave Bobby the thumbs-up. Bobby laughed and went back to work.

Man, this was the life, Pee Dee thought. Aside from his work with Bud, this was what Pee Dee lived for. Pee Dee looked up at the clouds gathering close to shore. He didn't like the looks of them. "We're done here," he shouted. "Skiff's full. We got maybe fifty unculled bushels."

"Not yet," Bobby called back. "Just a bit longer. There's a big demand for Christmas. I could stand to make some money."

Pee Dee rubbed his back. They'd already spent hours slogging through the soft mud bottoms and swinging tongs to get those oysters out of the cold water, and the tide had turned. It was backbreaking and dangerous work. But he went along, as he always did. And the beer was hitting the spot.

A short while later the wind started picking up and the strong, treacherous tide brought water rushing over the flats. Pee Dee scrunched his face in worry as he looked over his bateau. It was heavy with shells and mud and sat dangerously low in the water. He figured he only had eight inches of freeboard. Any ten-foot wave could sink the bateau.

"We gotta get outta here. Let's make a run for it!" he called to Bobby.

Bobby was bringing in a load of oysters. He looked up when the wave hit, swamping the low-riding bateau. Pee Dee shouted for Bobby as the boat quickly sank beneath them. He caught a glimpse of Bobby flailing in the water, grasping at the sky. His hip waders were filling fast, pulling him under. Pee Dee's own waders were dragging him down, too, like they were filled with frigid cement. In a panic, he lurched to grab hold of the gas tank floating by and clung for his life. Pee Dee was tossed around like a bobber on a fishing line. He lost sight of Bobby and tried to call for him, but saltwater scalded into his throat. His chest felt like it wanted to burst.

It all happened fast, but it seemed like slow motion. Maybe a minute had passed from his sight of Bobby until he was gone, but it felt like hours. Hypothermia was setting in fast and the current was pushing him. He was about to give up when he realized he could put his feet down on the mud. He didn't remember walking in to shore.

The rest of the day was a blur. Pee Dee

awoke in a nearby hospital, but for the life of him, he couldn't remember how he got there. Shortly after he'd regained consciousness, the doctor came to see him. His death was interrupted, the doctor told him. What they called a near drowning. Pee Dee had taken on a lot of water, and some had collected around his lungs. But he was lucky, the doctor told him. He'd survived.

September 21, 2008
McClellanville
Pee Dee leaned his head against the warehouse and felt the sting of salt in his eyes. That sting was one of the most vivid memories of Bobby's death. The saltwater had burned his eyes, his throat, his chest. The memory still stung like salt on a fresh wound. Time had never dulled the pain. If anything, the pain had intensified. On that day, he'd lost not only Bobby but Bobby's father. And a good part of Bud, too.

This was what people couldn't understand. How could two grown men who'd spent their lives on the ocean get caught in such a rookie situation? If it was Pee Dee who'd died and Bobby who came home to tell the story, nobody would have been talking about it fifteen years later. But it was Bobby who'd died, and Pee Dee would never be forgiven.

Pee Dee couldn't blame Oz for hating him. He hated himself. Pee Dee still couldn't look back on the accident without trying to figure what he might've done to save Bobby. How he could've handed Bobby the gas tank. Not once didn't he wish it was him who'd died that day, not Bobby.

Pee Dee dropped his cigarette to the ground and crushed it with his boot. Then he cleared his throat and spat. It was time to face the music. He wiped his sweaty palms on his pants, feeling the grime, then shuffled with slumped shoulders out onto the dock. He smiled weakly at the old captains, lifting his hand in a meek wave and a show of respect, wincing when all talk came to an abrupt stop. Pee Dee's gaze went straight to Oz.

The old man sat slumped in his chair. His once-massive shoulders were soft and rounded and his barrel belly protruded from his black slicker, revealing one of the plaid shirts he always wore. Under his long-billed cap, dark eyes narrowed with hostility at the sight of Pee Dee. He swung his head toward where the *Miss Carolina* usually docked, beside a trawler with a FOR SALE sign tacked on the hull. Oz turned back, puzzlement etched on his face.

Yanking the pipe from his mouth, he growled, "What are *you* doing here? Why aren't you on board the *Carolina*?"

Pee Dee reached up to scratch nervously under his cap. "Yeah, well, I . . ."

Woody leaned forward in his chair to offer Pee Dee a cigarette. At close range, his pale gray eyes were sad. Pee Dee was taken aback at the kindness and stepped forward to take the cigarette, nodding his thanks. His hands shook as he patted his pockets for a match. Woody tossed him a pack. Pee Dee caught it clumsily and lit up, aware that the eyes of all the captains were on him.

"It's kinda late for you to be coming by, ain't it?" Woody said.

Pee Dee took a long drag, feeling the burn before he exhaled, looking down. "Yeah. I guess." He shot a glance at Oz. The old man's meaty knuckles had whitened into hard fists.

The Hagg's face hung as wrinkled and soft as a basset hound's. "Someone else go out with Bud today?"

Pee Dee hung his head and shrugged.

"You don't think he went out alone, do you?" asked Woody.

"Not in this weather," answered the Hagg. "He knows better."

"Wasn't bad earlier," said Woody.

287

"Who's out there with my boy?" asked Oz with heat.

Pee Dee shrugged again, shaking his head, unwilling to look Oz in the eye.

"I'm asking you a question," Oz growled, gripping the arms of his chair and leaning far forward. "And you'd damn well better give me an answer or I'll flick your head off like a goddamn shrimp."

Pee Dee's gaze drifted down to Oz's scuffed boots under frayed khaki hems.

"I dunno. Honest, Cap. Bud, he don't like to go out with anybody but me. We always go out together. I came here direct to check on him, to see if he come back. I ain't never missed the boat before, I swear to God. Leastwise, not for a long time."

"You really missed the boat this time," Woody said with exaggeration, sending the men into tense laughter.

Pee Dee looked down the dock at the empty space where the *Miss Carolina* should have been, to confirm that what Woody had said was true. He turned back, feeling hunted. "M-maybe he did go out on his own."

The fury in Oz's eyes cooled to worry. Pee Dee saw that same look in the eyes of all the old captains. They knew Bud was a worthy seaman. They understood that once

288

in a while, a captain would take his boat out alone.

They also knew what it meant to be out on the ocean alone when the sky turned black and the water muddied.

13

September 21, 2008, 1:10 p.m.

On board the Miss Carolina

Bud looked up to see the darkening clouds moving in. The sun was a dim globe hovering in the leaden sky. Even though the day had been overcast, the skin on his face, neck, and arms was burning. Thirst tightened his throat so he could hardly swallow. His shoulder ached from holding the awkward position over the drum for hours. His head was swimming in a fog. He knew these were signs of blood loss. He had to face the possibility that he might not make it.

He lowered his head, feeling anger well up like a new pain in his chest. It wasn't fair. He was only fifty-seven. This wasn't how he wanted to go — helpless and broke. The goddamn regulations, he thought. The quotas. The licenses. The costs. The fuel. The companies dumping foreign shrimp into the market. His body shook with dehydration and his gut churned as he directed his anger to the heavens.

"Why me?" he cried out, balling his fist and pounding the deck. "What did I ever do to piss you off? I may not have been a saint, but I wasn't that bad a sinner, was I? I worked hard all my life. Never asked for help from no man, but gave it when it was asked of me. I was true to my wife. Good to my daughter. I didn't smuggle drugs — and we both know the money woulda been nice to have. I stayed clean. I stood tall. What more can a man do? What do you want from me?"

The skies answered in a low, grumbling thunder. He squinted and saw a fleet of clouds the color of gunmetal moving closer. The wind was picking up, too, whistling through the rigging. White tips crested the choppy waves. It was a fast-moving front and would be here soon.

Bud rested his head against the steel winch. He had no choice but to weather the oncoming wind and rain. Not that he was afraid. He'd seen his share of storms. He gazed up at the gloomy sky as the *Miss Carolina* began pitching in the swells. It was the squalls of his relationships, the bruises of words, the deceptions and consequences, that had proved hardest to endure.

March 2, 2001
Off the coast of Florida

Back in the day, Port Canaveral had been a
thriving shrimp port in Florida with hundreds of working vessels docked. From up
in the pilothouse, Bud counted fewer than
fifty. He maneuvered the *Miss Carolina* into
a space between two seventy-five-foot trawlers. He turned off the engine and could feel
the sudden silence. Pee Dee and Josh tied
off the lines. They knew their jobs and
didn't need Bud to holler instructions. He
sighed with relief and scratched his head,
feeling the salt in his hair.

The sun was setting and his men were
tired after twenty-four hours on the water.
They had by his estimate some six hundred
pounds of shrimp to unload from the hold.
All in all, it was a good day in a good two
weeks. He was looking forward to a long,
hot shower and a cold beer at a motel.

The air-conditioning in the lobby of the
dumpy motel was broken, but the clerk, an
old man so pale and fat Bud guessed he
rarely moved far from his chair, assured Bud
that all the room units worked just fine. A
fan was whirling noisily in the lobby and
the front doors were wide open to the balmy
night. Pee Dee and Josh smoked cigarettes
at the entrance and waited, watching the

female tourists walk by. Bud knew Pee Dee didn't have the guts to talk to any of them, and Josh didn't have to try. The girls always smiled at him.

Sometimes his crew acted like high-school boys, Bud thought, pocketing his credit card. But they worked as hard as men, and this had been a long season. They needed a night off. Bud lifted his worn duffel bag and walked out of the lobby. He tossed a key to Josh, who snared it.

"Rooms are around the corner. You're in one-seventy-one. I'm in one-seventy-three. It's on my card, so you best not be breaking anything or walking off with towels."

They shuffled toward their rooms like zombies. Josh clicked open the lock and pushed the door open with his foot. Pee Dee tossed his bag inside their room, then immediately turned to head back out.

"Going on a beer run," Pee Dee said.

"Get some tequila, too," called Josh.

"Don't get hammered tonight," Bud told him. "I need you tomorrow."

"What time?"

"Five a.m. sharp."

Bud closed the door to his room and dropped his bag. He took a slow look around. The room was no different than the hundreds of motel rooms he'd stayed in near various docks over the years. It was dingy, but convenient and cheap.

He couldn't wait to get clean. He peeled his grimy clothes from his body and climbed into the shower. Turning on the hot water, he placed his hands on the tile, closed his eyes, and let his head drop as the hot water pounded his back in a poorman's massage. It'd been a long two weeks on the boat. He was so tired he felt he could fall asleep standing up.

The mirrors were steamed when he stepped out of the shower. He treated himself to a slow shave, taking care to trim the moustache that trailed in a thin line to his chin. He could thank his father for his full head of hair — most of his pals were thinning at the top or bald. Turning his head from side to side, he stared at the bits of gray feathering at his temples and mingling in the dark brown of his sideburns.

"It is what it is," Bud said to his reflection, but he knew that for a fifty-year-old guy, he still looked good. Hard muscle filled out his broad shoulders.

Lowering the brush, he caught sight of a long red hair dangling from the bristles. Bud carefully plucked the one hair and held it between his rough, calloused fingers. A surge of longing brought a wistful smile to his face as he let the hair float down to his palm. He missed his wife.

The thought surprised him. And pleased him. He hadn't missed her, or even thought much about her, for days. Sure, they'd been busy on the boat, but Bud knew his apathy went deeper than that. The closeness had gone out of their relationship. So had the fun. They didn't talk much, except when they had to about a job or the routine. A hot topic around their house was what she'd make for dinner.

And the physical . . . Bud snorted. There wasn't much of that, either. He'd gone from feeling lonely for her touch, to frustrated, to just plain angry. Carolina didn't seem upset about it at all. He thought she liked things the way they were. Except she was angry, too. All the time, it seemed.

But there were moments . . . a smile when he needed one, her bringing him a beer when he was working, waiting up for him with a warm dinner on nights he returned late. Despite everything, he always knew she was on his side.

Bud looked at his watch. It was almost eight o'clock. He hadn't called to check in for almost a week. On impulse, he wrapped a towel around his waist and went to the phone by the bed. He picked up the receiver and dialed home. Carolina answered after three rings.

"Hello."

"It's me."

There was a pause on her end of the line so cold he felt the chill in Florida. "So, you finally called."

"I've been on the boat."

"You could have called from the dock."

"I know. I'm usually so beat . . . you know how it is."

"Uh-huh."

Bud felt his longing for Carolina shrivel in his heart. There was another pause, longer this time. Neither wanted to be the first to speak again.

"Well, if you wanted me to know you're alive," Carolina said briskly, "I know. You can go drinking with the boys now."

"Okay, Carolina, what's wrong?"

"Nothing."

Bud sighed wearily. When Carolina was in this mood, nothing good was coming. "Okay, then."

"When are you coming home?"

"I dunno. I'm figuring to stay on maybe another week."

"Another week?" Her voice rose. "You've already extended a week. It'll be over . . . two months you've been gone!"

"Don't nag. You know how bad the season was. The hopper is running good here. I'm trying to catch up."

"You're *always* catching up."

Here we go, he thought.

"It's bad enough during the season." He could hear her anger bubbling under her forced calm. "But you're pushing the limits, Bud. You're never here! Not for me. Not for Lizzy." She took a shallow breath. "What about your daughter? She's got a new baby. Where's Josh? She needs her husband now more than ever."

"All the more reason we need to keep working. He gets little enough money as it is, and now he has a child to raise. Hey, you both married into the life."

"You always say the same thing, over and over like a broken record. The fact is, we don't have any kind of life. You're gone all the time."

"I thought you liked it that way."

She *tsk*ed in frustration. "I'm telling you I'm lonely, Bud. And . . ."

"And *what?*" His tone was asking her, *Is this a threat?* He was starting to get angry now.

"You're not listening!"

"I've heard it all before. I call home to check in, and you give me hell for working

297

my ass off here. Then you wonder why I don't call."

"Bud, I don't want to fight." Her voice trembled, and he felt bad knowing he was making her cry. "I'm so tired of fighting. All I'm saying is, your being gone so much isn't good for us. It's no way to have a marriage."

He looked at the slender strand of hair in his palm. "Caro, I've got to stay while the shrimp are running. I'm down to the fish house for two thousand already for fuel and ice, and now the motor is giving me trouble."

"We've always had money troubles and we've always managed."

"It's just a week. Two at the most. We're going to go a ways offshore."

"Come home, *please*."

He hated to hear her voice break. "I can't."

"You won't."

His sigh rattled his chest. "See it the way you want to, Carolina."

"Well, when *are* you coming home?"

Bud was sorry now that he'd called. His head ached and he was dying for a beer. "I'll get home when I get home," he ground out.

"Fine," she spat out. "I may not be here when you get back." She hung up.

Bud clenched the hair in his fist as he

stared at the phone in his other hand. He hung up slowly, then opened his palm, watching as the red hair slid from his hand to float to the floor.

He needed a drink. He dressed quickly in the cleanest jeans he could find and a fresh shirt, then walked down the cement walkway and pounded the boys' door. "I'm not getting any younger. If we're going, let's get going."

Pee Dee emerged from the room looking like he had going in. But Josh had showered and shaved and was wearing a clean T-shirt with a skull and crossbones. His dark eyes had that eager shine that Bud recalled from his own youth.

The Conch House was part grill and part tiki bar and boasted some of the best hush puppies in the South. It was a local place that welcomed families and tourists, but after nine the joint was getting wild. Pee Dee found a booth near the pool tables and, with a sweep of his tattooed arm, raked the half-dozen empty beer bottles to the edge of the table. The young waitress hurried by to pocket the tip before scooping up the bottles and placing them on her tray.

"Evenin', gentlemen," she said, red-painted lips smiling at Bud and Josh as they slid onto the seat. Her skintight black T-shirt and large breasts gave maximum exposure to the red lettering *Get Freaky at the Tiki.*

"Why, hello, darlin'." Josh beamed, sitting far back in the booth. "How are you on this fine evening?"

"Looks like my evening just got better," she replied with a toothy grin.

"What's your name?" Josh asked.

"Marlene."

"Marlene, huh?" Josh replied. "You mean like Darlene, only with a *mmmm.*"

"Oh, the shit's flying early tonight," Pee Dee said. "Round of beers here."

"And a basket of those hush puppies," Bud added.

"Shrimp looks good tonight," the waitress said, eyes on Josh as she handed out menus.

"I don't wanna see another goddamn shrimp today," Josh said.

Bud chuckled. "Just bring three burgers around, well done. Slaw on the side. And don't forget those hush puppies." He handed her the plastic-covered menus.

"Don't worry, they come with the plate. But I'll bring extra," she said, heading off to the bar for the beers.

"We should have ordered some shots," Josh said. "I'll ask that little honey for some when she gets back."

"Quit acting like you're eighteen," Bud said.

"You jealous? You had your chance."

"You had your chance, too," he reminded Josh. "When you're single with no responsibilities, you can act like those monkeys out there." He jerked his head to indicate the drunken guys dancing with giggling women. "But when you're married, you owe it to your family to sit on the sidelines. And you're a married man now."

Josh swung his head to look over at the bar, his fingers tapping the table.

A few minutes later, the waitress returned with the beers. "Hope you fellahs don't mind, but I took the liberty of buying you handsome men a shot of whiskey. Bought it with my own money." She smiled and set the shots down beside the beers.

"You and me," Josh said, "we're on the same wavelength, honey." He picked up his shot and tossed it back.

"I thought so," she replied flirtatiously.

Bud frowned and took a long swallow from his bottle. Josh acted like any other handsome young buck out for a night, except that he was married to Lizzy. That put Bud in a tough position. Why couldn't Josh be more like Pee Dee? he thought, looking at his cousin across the table. Pee

Dee was happy as long as there were good tunes on the juke and cigarettes in the pack.

As if he'd heard Bud's thoughts, Pee Dee shook his nearly empty pack and rose from the booth. "Gotta get some smokes. Be right back."

Pee Dee wandered off in search of a cigarette machine, passing tables with families finishing their meals, couples talking and laughing, and a group of young men and women on the prowl dancing close to the jukebox.

Bud leaned forward and kept his voice low, but his irritation was clear in his tone. "Cool it with the womanizing," he said to Josh.

"What?"

"The waitress. The flirting. It's embarrassing."

"Give me a break. Can't I have a good time?"

"You can have a good time. Just have some respect."

"Respect for who?"

"For your wife. For *my* daughter."

Josh drank from his bottle, staring at Bud. "Look. I'm just trying to relax. Sorry if it's not up to your standards. By the way, don't talk to me like I'm some kid. I may work on your boat, but you don't own me."

"Never said I did."

"Yeah? Then don't tell me who I can and can't flirt with."

"That's where you're wrong. You're not out with your buddies chasing some skank. I'm your father-in-law. I'm your captain. I'm telling you to quit it."

"This is bullshit. We're off the clock."

"Funny thing about being a father — you're *never* off the clock. And if you don't like the way I'm talking to you, you can quit. Pay for your own room. Your own beers."

"Yes, *sir.*" Josh downed his beer and scooted out of the booth. He headed toward the mechanized dartboard, fished in his pockets for some quarters, and jammed them hard into the game.

"You ride the kid hard, Bud," Pee Dee said as he slid into the booth across from Bud. "Be cool. He's family. Not like me."

Bud looked up at Pee Dee in his stained T-shirt, gazing out over the room beneath lids heavy with fatigue. He looked like an older, worn-out version of the scrawny, half-starved fifteen-year-old who'd fled to their home years before. Oz had let the boy live in their house. He'd fed and dressed his nephew. But the old man had never treated Pee Dee as anything more than a deckhand.

"You're family," Bud told him.

303

Pee Dee's Adam's apple bobbed and he ducked his head.

Bud looked across the room and, catching their waitress's eye, indicated he wanted another round of beers. Bob Seger's "Katmandu" blared over the speakers. The noise level in the restaurant rose as the alcohol flowed. An attractive woman at the bar, not more than forty, met his eye and smiled seductively. Bud felt a flare of interest, then looked away.

Their waitress came by with two long-necked beers in her hand and a basket of hush puppies. The day's work had sharpened his appetite, and he popped a few in his mouth. Bud closed his eyes and savored the warm cornmeal as they practically melted in his mouth. They cooked them right, he thought. Carolina made the best hush puppies. She always said the secret was a little bacon grease.

He thought of Carolina and wondered if she'd eaten dinner alone in that old house. After doing the dishes, she'd probably pay some bills, read, then go upstairs to their room to watch television. He pictured her in their bed, leaning limp against the pillows, the gray and white flashing light on her face. Bud pushed back the basket, his hunger gone.

"What's eating you?" Pee Dee asked, chewing.

"I had a fight with Carolina."

"Again?"

Bud took a long swallow from his beer. "She's mad we're not coming home."

"That don't sound like her." He shrugged. "But we been gone a long time."

Bud looked out over the room. The kids dancing, playing darts, getting drunk — they all seemed so young. Or maybe he was just bored with the scene.

"I don't know, Pee Dee. Sometimes I think I'm getting too old for this kind of work. My back hurts from bending over squirming fish, my bum knee gives out all the time, and the sun and wind have turned my skin to leather. For what?"

"You're a good captain," Pee Dee said, his eyes blazing. He didn't like to hear his captain so down. "The best. When no one else finds the shrimp, you always do."

Bud appreciated Pee Dee's loyalty. He knew Pee Dee was proud to work on the *Miss Carolina* as his deckhand. Not just because, as Bud's cousin, he was aligned with the respected Morrison name.

"We haven't had a decent season in three years."

"That the shrimp's fault. Not yours. They

not there. Or they got that black gill rot. Man, that's just ugly."

"It's just one more problem. I can't get ahead. Seems I'm working just to pay off last season's debt. And now when I'm coming into some money, my wife's on my case for not being home. What the hell am I working so hard for?"

"You're born a shrimper, you die a shrimper. It's simple. You know that."

"Do I?"

Pee Dee whistled. "She done a number on you, that's for true. I'm stayin' single forever. That's it."

"Speaking of single . . . you see Josh?"

Pee Dee motioned with his head. "Last I saw, he was on the dart machine with some young thing."

Bud leaned over, trying to catch a glimpse of Josh and whatever mischief he was bound to get himself into. It was a big place. Someone had cued up a favorite Hack Bartley song on the juke, and guys in the crowd started singing the chorus:

Don't wait up on the shrimp boat baby
'Cause I'm comin' home with the crabs.

The waitress arrived with the burgers and placed them in front of Pee Dee and Bud.

"You're missing one burger here," Bud said.

"I gave that other one his burger by the darts. He asked for it there." Bud could see she was miffed at Josh's request. "Guess he prefers blond bimbos." She turned her charms on Bud, making eye contact. When she bent closer, it was a pose of invitation. "Can I get anything else for you? Anything at all?"

Bud frowned and shook his head dismissively. "I'm fine. Thanks."

The waitress walked off in a huff while Pee Dee chuckled into his burger.

Bud's gaze followed her as she walked past the dart game, searching for his son-in-law. "I don't see him."

Pee Dee wiped his mouth. "Let him blow off a little steam. He's not hurting anyone."

Bud silently cursed and bit hard into his burger.

"Why don't you like Josh? I like him."

"Never said I don't like him. I do. Like the son I never had." He wiped the ketchup from his mouth. "I just don't trust him."

Pee Dee laughed. "You don't trust no one. You barely trust Carolina."

"I do trust Carolina," he replied seriously. "With my life."

Pee Dee nodded, catching the change in

tone. "Yeah, you got a good woman there. Hard to believe she picked a goat like you."

Bud laughed, relieving the tension. "Don't think I don't know it."

He ate his burger in silence. He might know how much he loved his wife, but he didn't show it. He'd heard Carolina say to a friend how he wasn't the romantic type. That was true enough. He'd be the first to admit he wasn't one for coming home with flowers, or for candlelight dinners with wine. More often they'd watch a movie over beer and pizza. But they'd had their sentimental moments. She loved it when he took her out on their boat, and they'd anchor in shallow water and eat dinner on deck. They might not have had candles, but they dined under stars.

And no hearts or flowers could beat the awe and wonder they'd shared when Lizzy was born to them. Milestones, that's what they'd shared. Over the years they'd buried her aunt and Bud's brother, held each other through miscarriages, endured Oz's and Lee's divorces and remarriages, celebrated the marriage of their daughter and the birth of their grandson. They'd made it through the good years when the shrimp were running, and the bad years when they were scarce. Milestones like these kept them together.

But Carolina was right when she said these long absences weren't good for their marriage.

In his mind he played again his phone conversation with Carolina, heard once more the tremble in his wife's voice. *Come home, please.* He scowled and felt shamed. She was a good wife, loyal and true. She could've picked any man, and she'd picked him. She deserved better than what he'd offered, he decided. A woman shouldn't have to beg her man to come home.

"To hell with it," he said, setting his burger on the plate. His mind worked quickly. "The winch has rusted brakes that need replacing, and I've got patching to do on the nets. We'll do a couple more runs; then we're heading home."

"Sounds good to me, Captain."

Bud pulled a paper napkin from the metal holder, grabbed a pen from his shirt pocket, and began writing a list of things he had to get done before he left Florida.

The waitress returned to collect the burger baskets and dropped the check. "You fellahs can pay me whenever you're ready." She gave Bud her tried-and-true smile and wink, hoping to boost the tip.

After a quick look at the bill, Bud reached into his wallet and dropped cash on the table. "Leave the rest for the girl," he told Pee Dee. "Don't be picking up the change for some smokes."

"Where you headed so early?"

"I'm going back to the motel. I want to call Carolina, and I don't want the jukebox blaring in the background."

"Well, if you're off, I'm gonna play me a game of pool. Got any quarters?"

Bud dug into his pocket. "What am I, your father?" He handed four quarters to Pee Dee. "I feel like Chase Manhattan."

Bud went to his room and directly to the room phone. He sat on the mattress and punched in his home number. His foot tapped the floor as the phone rang once, twice, three times. He glanced at the clock when it rang four, five times, before he heard the click of the answering machine and his own voice asking him to leave a message.

He replaced the receiver slowly in the cradle, then fell back on the mattress. Music thumped through the thin walls from the adjoining room. He fell into a restless sleep asking himself, *Where was Carolina?*

Later that night, Bud roused to the sound of cats fighting. He rubbed his eyes, waking slowly. The room was dark and the air conditioner was whirring loudly. When a loud crash pounded the wall, Bud jerked up, whipping back his covers. Those weren't cats. He heard men shouting and a woman screaming. It took a second before Bud realized the disturbance was coming from Josh and Pee Dee's room. Another loud thump against the wall toppled the cheap print of a shrimp boat onto his bed.

Bud grabbed his jeans, rammed his long legs in, and zipped as he ran to the door. Opening it, he heard glass shattering next door. What the hell kind of fight were those two jerks in?

Several motel guests were coming out of their rooms onto the narrow cement walkway. Men without shirts and women clutching robes stared blankly, afraid but curious to check out the commotion. The door to the boys' room hung twisted from the frame, splintered and wide open. Rushing over, Bud saw a huge skinhead, with shoulders that stretched his flannel shirt like a sausage, whaling on Josh in the corner. This wasn't a fight, it was a slaughter. Whatever opposition Josh had offered a minute ago was over. On the bed, a blonde Bud remembered seeing at the bar was hopping from foot to foot, the sheets pulled half over her naked chest, screaming. "Stop it, Joe! You'll kill him!"

Bud launched through the door and reached the brute in two steps. His arms came down on the man's head with the force of an alligator's jaws. The blow froze the man not so much in pain as in shock. When he turned his head, Bud pulled him off Josh like he weighed no more than a sack of shrimp.

The man ripped away from Bud's grip and stared at him, snorting like a bull. His eyes were red with rage. Bud knew the type, more animal than human. The man charged with a guttural growl. Bud staggered back, then lifted his fists at the ready. Bud knew his own massive hands could land a punch like a mule's kick. When the man roared back at him, Bud aimed carefully, landing a solid hit in the gut, hearing a satisfying *woof* of pain, then followed fast with a hard uppercut that sent him flailing back into a heap on the floor.

The skinhead was groaning. Outside, someone was calling for the police. Bud swore under his breath. He was too old for this. He grabbed the guy by his torn shirt, yanked him up, and guided him toward the door. With a final shove, Bud sent the man stumbling into the gawking public.

Bud turned to the girlfriend or wife — he still didn't know which. She was more or less dressed. He jerked his thumb toward the door. She grabbed her spiky heels and, screaming words at him no lady should ever utter, scrambled out the door. Bud kicked it closed behind her, but it hung from the frame at an awkward angle on its broken hinge. He kicked it again, just because he was mad.

The air conditioner was whirring loudly. Taking a breath, Bud turned his angry eyes toward Josh. The kid looked pale, frightened.

"He was gonna kill me," Josh said.

Josh was standing in his boxers, his face swollen and bloodied, and Bud guessed he'd broken a rib or two. He would have black eyes he'd have to explain to Lizzy. Then Bud's gaze swept over the tangled mass of sheets on the bed, the broken furniture, the smashed mirror, the hole punched into the drywall — all of it an open confession of his son-in-law's infidelity — and his sympathy shriveled in his chest. Bud began pacing, rubbing his bloodied knuckles.

Josh pulled on a T-shirt, moaning softly with the movement. "I'm sorry. I know I messed up."

"Shut up."

"She was the only one. I swear."

The lie detonated his fury. Bud spun on his heel. "I said, shut up! Don't play me for a fool. I don't want to know how many there were before this one. But you're not going to hurt my baby anymore."

They heard sirens in the distance. Josh's eyes darted to the window.

Bud faced Josh again, all business. The kid was still his crew. He was still family. "That guy. He busted in here, right?"

Josh nodded.

"Then you were just defending yourself. Got it?"

"Yeah."

"What about the pot? I can smell it. Is there any left in here?" When Josh nodded, he shouted angrily, "Flush it."

Josh emptied his duffel bag and, finding a small plastic bag, took it to the bathroom. A few seconds later, Bud heard the toilet flush. Josh came back out, nervous, arms wrapped tight around his chest.

"Thanks, Bud."

"Don't thank me. I'm not doing it for you. I'm doing it for Lizzy. Now, get your damn pants on."

Bud looked down at his own bare chest and feet. He had to get some clothes on before the cops got here. He turned to the door, then stopped. "Where the hell is Pee Dee?"

"I, uh . . ." Josh finished pulling his jeans on. "I asked him to take a walk."

Bud snorted in disgust. He put his hands on his hips and gathered his thoughts. "The cops will be here in a minute, so listen up. I'll help you through this mess. Get you to a hospital. Then Pee Dee and I will take the *Carolina* back. You can take the bus home or whatever the hell else you want to do."

Josh stood silent as the words crashed into meaning. "You're kicking me off the boat?"

"That's it."

"Well . . . what about my pay?" He looked miserable.

"Tell you what I'm going to do. I'll give you a hundred dollars cash for bus fare. Then I'm going to pay off the damages to this room. The rest I'm giving to Lizzy to pay her bills. You got a problem with that?"

Josh swiped his hand through his hair. "You won't . . . tell Lizzy? About this, I mean."

Bud tightened his lips, holding back the torrent of words he wanted to shout at the kid. Bud was deeply hurt by this betrayal. He could only imagine the boatload of hurt his Lizzy would feel. "No," he replied. "Because by the time I get back with the boat, *you* will have told her."

"She'll leave me." Josh's voice was a hoarse, scared whisper. "I'll lose my son."

As far as Bud was concerned, that was something Josh should've thought about before he cheated on her. "I don't know what she'll do. But that's between you and her. I'm done with you. Pee Dee will deliver your stuff. You're off the *Carolina.*"

Tires screeched in the parking lot as the sirens went silent. It would only be a few moments until the cops were at the door. Bud turned to face Josh and saw the heartbreak and disillusionment on the boy's face.

"I messed up bad. I'm sorry, Bud. I'll make it up to you. To her. I swear."

Bud was struck by his sincerity. Images flashed in his mind of Josh and Lizzy on their wedding day; the proud parents bringing baby Will home to meet his grandparents; Josh aboard the *Miss Carolina,* his fingers flying as he culled the shrimp faster than any deckhand Bud had ever seen. He was a natural on the sea, destined to be a captain — if he didn't get himself killed first. He was a boy Bud had loved like a son. He was a kid who'd got married too young. The boy's testosterone was screwing up the man's judgment.

Carolina's words came back at him again.

We shouldn't be apart so much. Bud felt the sunken weight of guilt. Carolina was right, as she usually was. He shouldn't have kept the boy from home so long. He was partly to blame if Josh's marriage broke up.

Outside the room he heard the heavy footfalls of the police. Bud sat down on the mattress and rubbed his weary eyes with calloused palms. So much lay in ruins — the room, his hopes for a son to take over, his daughter's marriage. Dropping his hands, he thought bleakly of the three more times he'd roused and tried to call his wife, and how each time he'd got the answering machine.

He was left to wonder if his own marriage didn't lie in ruins as well.

September 21, 2008
On board the Miss Carolina

Bud tightened his grip on the winch as the boat began to pitch in the swell of the waves. A burst of pain shot through his arm with each jerk. Maybe he was going to die at sea, he thought. Like Bobby. Josh was a lot like Bobby — fun-loving and irrepressible. Too good-looking for his own good. Maybe that was why he'd always liked the boy. And why he missed him, too.

He swallowed hard at the thought of his

317

brother. In fifteen years, the pain of losing
him had never lessened. Bud thought about
him often, especially when he was sitting
alone in the pilothouse, staring at the vast
sea. He never could figure out what kind of
guy Bobby was. He was handsome, and the
girls called him romantic. But Bud just
knew he was his dearest friend in the world.

Bud loved to read Hemingway, and he
remembered telling Bobby when he was a
kid the story of the old man who'd caught a
huge fish — bigger than his boat. Bobby
loved the story, even though he'd said the
old man should've motored home and made
himself a burger or something. But Bobby
kept going back to that story over the years
whenever times were tough. He'd remind
Bud of the old man who hung on to that
fish until his hands bled.

Fishing had kept Bobby and him together,
and it had also taken him away. After Bobby
died, Bud never felt the same about it. Some
of the passion had died along with his
brother. When times got bad on the boat or
with Carolina, he no longer had the hope
he did before. Maybe that was why his
father had stopped shrimping after Bobby
died. He just didn't have the heart for it
anymore.

Bud had worked hard all his life and

provided for his family. He never complained. But the past years had been difficult. It was like being caught in a riptide. The harder he worked, the farther behind he got. Now he was drowning in debt. He didn't want to leave Carolina this way. He needed more time. He'd promised her better.

Bud scowled and looked down at his mangled arm. This wasn't how he wanted his story to end. He didn't want to die like Bobby in some fool accident before his time. Or like that old man with the big fish. He didn't want to end his life with nothing but blood on his hands and the skeleton of a fish.

14

September 21, 2008, 1:15 p.m.
McClellanville
Carolina arrived at the docks and parked in the lot of Coastal Seafood. The office was a small wood building nestled behind the enormous warehouse that bordered the creek. Several trawlers lined the dock, but the *Miss Carolina* wasn't in yet.

She walked slowly around the weathered buildings wondering — hoping — Bud had a good day. Gusts of wind carried wafts of the rich, fertile scent of the marsh. At the water's edge she peered past the pilings and the hulls of boats down Jeremy Creek. There was no sign of the *Miss Carolina*. Carolina crossed her arms and looked up at the darkening sky, frowning.

"Lookin' for Bud?"

Carolina swung her head toward the familiar voice. She spied Judith high up on deck of the *Miss Ann*. She was stockier now than she'd been as the young PE teacher, and instead of a dress she wore jeans and an old oil-stained sweatshirt bearing the phrase *Friends Don't Let Friends Eat Imported Shrimp.*

Her old friend Judith Baker preferred to be called J.B. by the working crew. She was the first — and only — female shrimp boat captain in McClellanville. Probably along the South Carolina coast. She'd purchased the *Miss Ann* from Bud after he'd built the *Miss Carolina.* Judith had bucked a lot of nasty comments and prejudice from both men and women who believed no decent woman would try to act like a man. She'd laughed and replied that she wasn't trying to be a man. It was rough going at first. Judith couldn't find a man who'd serve as crew for a woman. So she'd worked alone for several seasons, proving her mettle as an able captain. Though she wasn't born into shrimping like Bud, Judith was a decent carpenter, mechanic, painter, and tailor. She persevered and brought in the goods, haul after haul. Captain J.B. later hired on a crew and earned a begrudging respect, both on the docks and in the community. Over beers at the Shack, the guys owned that J.B. might be one of the best captains on the dock, man or woman.

"Hey, Judith!" Carolina called, returning the wave and walking toward her. "I didn't expect to see you here. Thought you'd be out."

Judith came to the railing of her trawler. Her face was ruddy and tan. Spiky wisps of her short salt-and-pepper hair poked out from under her cap. "Couldn't afford to take her out today. Your man's not back yet, but I hope he gets his ass back in soon. A low pressure system is developing."

Carolina looked up at the blue-gray clouds smearing the sky. "He was due in around noon."

"Then he'll be here soon. Maybe he's having a good day. Sure as hell hope somebody does. Come on up and wait here. I just made coffee."

"That's an offer I won't say no to."

Judith leaned over and lent Carolina a strong, slightly calloused hand. With a firm yank, Carolina climbed aboard. Her gaze swept the boat on which she'd once been a deckhand. The *Miss Ann* was an older wooden boat that had always been lovingly maintained by Oz, Bud, and now Judith. The tools of the trade — ropes, cable, nets, winches, pulleys — were all neatly stored and in place. No one could ever fault J.B. for being lax.

"She looks good," she told Judith.

Judith's eyes shone with pride. "Yeah, she's a sweet boat. I'm lucky to have her."

Carolina's face softened, feeling the spirit of the boat. "I had some of my happiest days on board this old girl," she said in a wistful tone. Her gaze drifted up to the ladder she used to climb to survey the vast ocean. She hadn't felt that soaring exhilaration in a long time.

"Whoa. You sound as moody as that sky up there."

"Do I? It's been a weird day."

"Must be the weather. Barometric pressure can do strange things. How about that coffee?"

Carolina followed Judith below deck to the galley. She'd been in many galleys over the years, and most of them were pigpens with cans of motor oil, girlie magazines, and dented pots cluttering the counter. Judith's galley was as impeccably neat as a navy brig. When she handed Carolina a mug of coffee, the brew was fresh and the cup clean.

"Sit down," she said with a brusque gesture.

Carolina slid into the small booth and cradled the warm mug between her fingers.

"What are you staring at in that coffee? Reading your fortune?" asked Judith.

"I wish," she replied with a short laugh.

Judith sat across from her and leaned against the back of the bench. "What's the matter, Caro?"

Carolina hesitated. She didn't like bringing up her personal business, but Judith was her closest friend. "I saw Odelle today."

Judith gave a short laugh. "That explains a lot."

There was no love lost between Judith and Odelle. Judith made no secret of the fact that she found Odelle to be a bottom-feeder, and Odelle was openly disdainful of Judith's being a boat captain.

"It was a nice visit, actually," Carolina replied. "But strange. I'd completely forgotten the date. Did you know it's been exactly nineteen years since Hurricane Hugo?"

Judith merely shrugged. "I guess."

Carolina wondered why the date had made such an impact on her, but obviously not on others. Maybe others just didn't want to be reminded. She'd been skittish about storms ever since.

"We started talking about our experiences that night and she got into how Lee had acted during the hurricane. We've all talked about this a zillion times, but today she told me things I'd never heard her say before."

Judith leaned forward. "Like what?"

"Well," she began slowly, careful not to betray Odelle's confidence, "it was more her attitude about Lee. She was much more open about her anger with him. Which is good, right? But she went on to say how great Bud was, how he took care of his family and how he was more of a man than Lee." Carolina stared at the clouds in her coffee, seeing Odelle's face as she talked. "You know, sometimes I catch a flicker in her eye when she mentions Lee, and I think, What does that mean? I wonder if she knows about what happened between Lee and me."

Judith waved her hand dismissively. "She was probably just comparing the two men and Lee came up lacking. Let's face it, Bud's a hunk. Always was. Odelle had her eye on him from the first day."

"It wasn't like that! She wasn't jealous."

"But maybe a little envious?"

Carolina cracked a small smile. "Maybe a very little."

"Don't ever tell her what happened," Judith said bluntly. "She can't keep a secret. Even if she wanted to. The truth just busts out of her, and she might regret it, but it'll be too late. This is a small community. It'll spread through town faster than a plague. It's just guilt you're feeling — let it go."

Carolina put her elbows on the table and sipped her coffee, wondering how to do that.

"Is that what's got you so wound up?"

"No," Carolina replied with a sigh. She lowered her mug to the table. "All day long I've had this nagging feeling something's, I don't know, wrong. I woke up with it. I had this dream last night of Bud and me." She looked up to see Judith's brows rise. "Oh, never mind. I know people hate to hear about other people's dreams."

"No, go ahead." When Carolina demurred, Judith said more forcefully, "Really."

"It's just that this one felt so real. And the feelings . . ." She took a breath, reliving the girlish rush of love for Bud she'd had in the dream. "They were so strong."

"What was it about?"

"Me and Bud, back when we were young." Her eyes roamed the small galley, and in a flash she saw herself cooking shrimp in tomato sauce over the electric burner and Bud coming up from behind to slip his arms around her. "Back when we were together, here on this boat. Sometimes, I think it was a mistake for me to ever leave the water."

"You had Lizzy."

"I know, but maybe when she got older, I could've come back to be Bud's deckhand again. We were happy then. It was never the same after I stayed ashore. We lost that closeness. We used to tell each other everything. Now . . ." She looked down and let her fingers drum the sides of the mug. "I don't know if we can get it back."

"You can try, honey."

"I have been trying, but it's like he's shut me out. Ever since . . . you know. I don't think Bud's ever forgiven me."

Judith was the only person she'd confided in. Her old friend never judged her. She'd advised Carolina to stay the course.

"Have you talked to him about it?"

"We've been to counseling. We're trying to work it out, but I sense him holding back." Carolina fidgeted with her wedding ring. "I hate to ask, but I have to. Has Bud ever fooled around?"

"What? Damn, no! Not that I know of, anyway."

"You'd tell me if you knew, wouldn't you?"

"Yeah, I would," Judith replied. "You're talking crazy now, girl."

"Am I? I used to head south with Bud, don't forget. I've seen with my own eyes what went on in those bars. Lord knows we've both heard the stories. No woman ever thinks it will happen to her. But it can. And it does."

"Carolina, Bud loves you. Always has. I've

never seen him with another woman."

Carolina put her hand over her eyes and shook her head. "I don't know whether hearing that makes me happy or makes me feel worse."

"Would you forgive him if he did fool around?"

Carolina stared at Judith, slack-jawed. She honestly didn't know what to say. Judith was staring back at her with a look that said, *Don't worry, honey. I don't expect you to answer.*

Judith slapped her hands on the table and pulled herself out from the bench. "I'll go up and check on the *Miss Carolina.* You finish your coffee. Be right back."

Carolina leaned back and let her eyes graze across the galley. Among the pictures posted on the bulletin board with plastic pushpins, she recognized the photo of Judith wearing the corny old captain's hat that Carolina and Bud had given her the day she took possession of the *Miss Ann.* She squinted more closely at a photograph of herself and Bud standing beside an enormous rust-encrusted anchor from an eighteenth-century sailing ship. They'd snagged it in their nets, and she remembered Bud had had a hell of a fight bringing it up. Carolina recalled the day they'd donated that monstrosity to Coastal Seafood, back when the Morrison and Edwards families were friends. Oz had cooked barbecue and the whole extended family and friends had shown up with cornbread, boiled shrimp, greens, and more to celebrate the dedication. They used to laugh a lot back then.

She closed her eyes and felt the memories drag her, one by one, like links of a rusted chain, to a time she didn't like to return to. Remembering how one mistake could act as an anchor, crusted with bitterness and recrimination as thick as barnacles, keeping her unrelentingly mired in the mud.

March 2, 2001
McClellanville
Bud's cold dismissal had cut Carolina to the bone. *I'll get there when I get there.* His insensitivity was bewildering. All week long she'd been staring at the phone, willing it to ring. He hadn't called, and she'd begun imagining every kind of accident that could happen to a shrimper.

And now, when he finally had called, they'd quarreled. She squeezed her eyes shut and put her forehead in her palm while her mind screamed, *Why? Why? Why?* Another fight was the last thing she'd wanted. Why hadn't she told him how much she missed him? Why hadn't he told her the same thing? She had a sickening feeling the answer was obvious.

Carolina was a woman with a grown child, but she'd flopped across her bed and sobbed like a little girl. When at last she wiped her eyes and looked around her bedroom, though it had only been a matter of minutes, it seemed as if everything had changed.

She shook herself as if from a trance. The house suddenly felt like a tomb. She needed to get out, maybe have a drink with friends. Anything to feel a little better. She washed her face with cool water and applied a little blush and lipstick. Then she brushed her shoulder-length hair and pulled it up into a twist. She leaned closer to the mirror and touched the tender skin along her cheek-bones. Too many hours spent in the sun had left their mark in fine lines at her eyes. Still, she was slender and firm in her jeans and looked far younger than her forty-nine years.

It was a short drive to her favorite restaurant. As she walked from her car to the old wooden building with a huge red crab painted on the sign, she could hear thumping music and laughter pouring from the open windows.

It was a busy Friday night at the Crab

Shack. Some of the couples at the tables were tourists with accents from all over the country. Most were locals. Carolina recognized a few faces. She smiled and stopped to chitchat as she made her way to the bar. She felt a little conspicuous. She'd been to bars many times, but always with Bud or a group of friends.

"Carolina!"

Carolina turned to see Lee Edwards standing at the bar waving her over. The last person she'd expected to see at the Shack tonight was her boss. She made her way to his side. Lee was casually dressed in jeans and a navy V-neck cashmere sweater. When he bent to kiss her cheek in a friendly greeting, she caught the familiar scent of his cologne.

"What are you doing here?" he asked.

"Nothing much. I was alone and just needed to get out. Maybe have a drink."

His brows rose. "Well, come sit down. Let me buy you one."

Carolina was torn between wanting someone to talk with and her desire to be alone. "Thanks."

Lee propped himself on the stool next to hers at the bar and lifted his finger to summon the bartender. A young man with a bored expression and two piercings in his ear stepped up to take their order. Lee asked for a vodka and tonic, and when he looked at Carolina, she ordered a margarita.

"I've never seen you here alone before. Is everything all right?"

"Why wouldn't it be?" she replied, trying to sound airy but hearing the pain in her own voice.

The bartender set the drinks before them with a bowl of nuts. Lee clinked his glass against hers. The liquid was simultaneously salty and sweet, and for one moment she was able to take her mind off the anger and hurt that felt palpable in her chest. It hurt to breathe in. It hurt to breathe out. She wondered what it'd be like to not breathe at all.

Lee's brows gathered as he searched her face. "Where's your lesser half?"

"In Florida somewhere."

"Still?"

Carolina heard the surprise in his voice and felt vindicated for her earlier anger.

"When is he due back?"

Swirling her drink, she thought of Bud's response on the phone. "He gets back when he gets back. And I quote."

"Ah," he said, nodding. "I heard the shrimp were running. He should be bringing in a good haul."

"So I understand." She turned her head to look at him. His expression was eager. "Do you mind if we don't talk shop tonight?"

He lifted his shoulders, indicating that he didn't care. "What should we talk about?"

Her emotions were on a roller coaster and she felt herself plummeting downward, so she pushed for levity. "Well, it's Friday night and you smell good, and I'm guessing you're supposed to be meeting someone tonight. You're a free man again, after all."

"True enough."

From the sound of his voice, she gathered being free wasn't all it was cracked up to be. Despite his financial success, Lee had never found happiness in his personal life.

"You don't want to waste your time sitting here with me." Her gaze traveled down the bar from person to person, resting on an attractive thirtysomething blonde with a nice, open face. "There's a pretty girl hanging out with her friends. Oh, look. I think she's noticed you. Maybe you ought to go say hello."

Lee glanced down the bar and immediately found the blonde, who was, indeed, looking at him. He raised his glass in acknowledgment, then returned his attention to Carolina.

"I could," he said smoothly. "Or maybe I could just sit here for a while. I'm enjoying the company."

Her heart skipped. That simple remark struck home. It was nice to know *someone* enjoyed her company.

Lee and Carolina talked for more than an hour — a little politics, a little about films and music. They talked about everything except Bud. She looked at him as he spoke, bent forward with his hands gesturing, and realized he was really interested in what she thought. Lee always was a good conversationalist. At work they'd often chat across the office about the headline news, good movies or books, or some obscure medical advance that brought ethical concerns. Talking with Lee was one of the things she enjoyed most about her job.

Tonight, however, sitting side by side at the bar felt different from sharing an office. While she spoke, Lee looked at her earnestly and his eyes roamed her face in a way that made her feel pretty. He listened like he actually cared about her opinions and found her fascinating. Didn't men know this kind of attention was an aphrodisiac? From time to time his hand would seemingly absent-mindedly rest on hers, or on her arm. Once he reached up to tuck a lock of hair that had slipped from the clasp back behind her ear. With each touch, her blood raced in a way she hadn't felt in such a long time.

After her third margarita, Carolina's head was swimming and she thought in horror, Oh no, I'm getting drunk. "I better go." She rose slowly and felt the room teeter.

"Let me drive you home."

"I'm okay," she said, digging into her purse for her keys.

Lee put his hand out to restrain her. "No. You're not. It's not safe. I'll drive you home. We can pick up your car tomorrow."

Carolina knew he was right. The roller coaster in her head was careening and looping wildly.

He paid the bill, then lightly took her arm and led her out the door. When the cool, fresh air hit her, Carolina wobbled slightly. Lee's grip tightened as he guided her toward his car.

"Easy does it," he said. "Watch out for that puddle."

A red vintage Cadillac shone eerily under the cobra light fixture. She'd not seen this one before but wasn't surprised it belonged to Lee. Everyone knew Lee loved old cars. When he was young, he'd always been in the backyard tinkering under some vintage car up on cinder blocks.

"This is a beauty," she said, feeling the alcohol thicken her tongue.

"A sixty-five Coupe deVille," he replied, and she heard the pride of ownership in his voice. "It's just a hunk of tin," he added, gently slamming the door after making sure her legs were safely inside.

She sank into the vast interior of the old Cadillac, amazed at how roomy and plush it was.

Lee closed his door and watched her hands slide across the white leather. "As soft as a baby's bottom," he said with a smile. Then, pointing to a pair of fuzzy dice hanging from the rearview mirror, he added, "They were a joke from my ex, and I kept them."

"You never talk about her much."

"Melissa? There isn't much to tell."

"You were married five years."

"The longest years of my life."

He was being flippant, trying to deflect this line of questioning. Usually Carolina would have backed off, but tonight she felt reckless and pushed on. "Why did you marry her?" When he shrugged, she said, "You know what some people say, don't you?"

"That I married her for her money." His tone was flat.

"Did you?"

He turned his gaze from the road to search her face. "No. And yes. I was very attracted to her, to her lifestyle. But more than that, we both enjoyed the same things. And we both loved real estate. It was a turn-on for us. Especially during those boom days when every property we flipped made us a small fortune."

"And it didn't bother you that you were married to Odelle at the time?"

"Of course it did," he replied sharply, and she thought she'd gone too far. Then he added, "But I didn't think it would lead to anything at the beginning, and I didn't want to hurt Odelle. She was the mother of my child . . . but there were troubles there long before I met Melissa."

"Every marriage has troubles, but you work through them," she replied, then turned her head to stare out at the dark night, feeling morose. Her answer sounded so pat in her ears tonight. So false.

"Yeah, well, maybe that's the difference between me and Bud. He was always the steady one in our group. The one we all relied on." His voice grew introspective, and she turned to look at him, a silhouette dimly lit by the green light of the dashboard.

"Bobby was the kidder," he went on. "A

goofball. He and I liked to fool around a lot, but Bud . . . ol' Bud always seemed above it. Amused. We used to call him the old man, even back then."

"Bud can be fun," she said, feeling defensive.

"Oh, sure. I don't mean that. He was just a loner. Kinda moody, too, like James Dean. Only he wasn't so much cool as old-fashioned." He laughed and looked at her. "I mean that in a good way. But he played fair. One thing about Bud — we always knew we could count on him."

Hearing him talk about Bud made her feel sad. What Lee was saying about Bud was true, but it felt like he was talking about someone she had known once, long ago. Someone she'd cared deeply about but who was gone.

Lee seemed to be having similar thoughts because his voice changed again, losing its reflective tone. "So," he said as though in answer to a question, "it makes sense that he'd be the kind of guy to stick with his marriage and work things out, while I . . ." He shrugged. "I'm not. Or maybe I wasn't as lucky as Bud and never met the right girl."

Carolina considered that comment in silence as they pulled into her driveway. He cut the engine. The big car rumbled then went still.

"It's been years since I've pulled into this driveway," Lee said. They both knew his and Bud's friendship had waned. He leaned forward to peer through the windshield at the house. "Remember the touch football games we had on Sundays? You and Bud always won. Damn, he could throw a football."

They both stared at the trees. The moon was bright and the air was cool. The front porch light was on, illuminating the interior of the car with a hazy yellow cast. Neither made a move to leave. Maybe it was because she'd worked side by side with Lee at the seafood company. Or perhaps it was because he was a friend. More than likely, it was the margaritas. But when he asked her again what the problem was, she told him about Bud's phone call and how it had made her feel rejected and dismissed.

"Well, he *is* in hock up to his eyeballs," Lee offered as explanation for Bud's decision to stay in Florida.

"I know what we owe. What's that got to do with anything?"

"I'm just saying you can understand why he'd want to stay on, that's all."

"I don't understand. I think he likes it out

there with the guys in Florida, bacheloring it up. I've been there, don't forget. They're drinking and having a good time on the docks and God knows what else." Carolina saw in her mind's eye the wooden tables along the murky water, the jukeboxes and games of darts, the waitresses in tight T-shirts giving the good-looking men the come-hither. "He doesn't miss me. I don't think he loves me anymore."

"What? He's crazy about you."

"Sure, he loves me," she said dully. "I'm his wife. Maybe it's like you said. He's old-fashioned. He's hanging on because he doesn't want to hurt me. But what's so awful is that, in the end, it hurts all the more." She cast Lee a slanted glance. "You hurt Odelle badly, you know that, don't you?" She looked down at her hands and shook her head. "I don't think he's in love with me anymore. If you want to know the truth, I don't think I'm in love with him, either."

He didn't reply, but he was staring at her with fiery eyes. They both fell silent.

The spring night was damp with chill and the air in the car was getting colder by the minute, yet neither of them seemed eager to leave. The darkness made talking easier and cloaked the brutal honesty of the words. Carolina tucked her bare hands under her arms for warmth.

Lee reached into his glove compartment and retrieved a silver flask. He opened the top and took a drink, then offered it to Carolina. She took the flask and, tilting her head back, tasted the smoky burn of a good single-malt scotch. Coughing, she handed it back to him and watched him take another swig.

"Are you happy? With him?" he asked.

"I used to be. Very," she replied.

"But now?"

"But now . . . we're not even particularly good friends. After all these years, isn't that sad?"

"Yeah. I've been there. Twice."

Anger flared in her — at him. At herself for being in this position. "It's nothing to be proud of. All it proves is you men are alike. You don't know anything about commitment."

"Now you sound like my ex-wife."

"Which one?"

"Both."

They laughed aloud. It was a relief. She'd always heard that laughter released tension and pain. Tonight, Carolina felt she could cry for hours.

"Are you happier now? Divorced, I

mean?" she asked. "Does it make your life better?"

He considered this. "It's easier because we're not fighting anymore." He snorted ruefully. "I've had a bellyful of fighting."

Carolina felt that comment to her bones. She reached for the flask. The scotch tasted smoother this time. Less burn and more smoke. She wiped off the top with her palm and handed it back to him. Their fingers grazed, and she felt the sensation travel down to her stomach.

"But it does get lonely at times," Lee added. He shifted his weight to lean back against the door and face Carolina. She heard the leather creak in the darkness. He took another drink from his flask, then lowering it, asked pointedly, "Are we talking divorce here?"

She turned to look at him, startled to hear the word spoken aloud. *Divorce.* It sounded so final. She'd never entertained the thought before. The idea of leaving Bud, leaving the fighting and the money problems and the walking on eggshells, had always fluttered about in the dark corners of her mind, more as a fantasy of escape than anything real. She'd never pulled the word forward in the light to consider it.

Carolina's silence was enough of an answer.

Lee whistled softly. "He'll never let you go."

"He can't stop me," she blurted.

"Carolina, are you serious?"

She took a deep breath. Was she serious? Or was it the margaritas? Slowly, she nodded.

Lee seemed blindsided. "Shit. I thought you and Bud . . . we all thought you were the one couple that had it made."

"I'm not saying it's *definitely* going to happen," she replied elliptically. "I only know I can't go on like this. I'm so . . . unhappy." Her voice broke, and she hated the short, choppy cries that she couldn't contain.

Lee set the flask aside and slid across the length of white leather to wrap his arm around her in a consoling hug. She fell against him, feeling the softness of the cashmere, cocooned in his musky fragrance. In the dark, his arms felt comforting. She knew this could lead to something, but she was beyond caring.

"What happened to you guys?"

"I don't know," she replied, bringing her fingers up to wipe her tears from her face. But she didn't leave his shoulder and instead relaxed into it. Then, in a moment of clarity, she knew. She missed *this.* The laying of her head on a man's shoulder while he stroked her back and listened, really listened to her. Feeling appreciated. Cherished.

"How long has this been going on?"

Carolina knew why he'd asked. In the past several years, as Bud became less of a presence in her life, Lee's presence had loomed large. She'd become aware of an undercurrent of attraction between them since that night at the play. For years, the tension had come and gone — nothing overt or dramatic. It was more a series of simple accidents — a touch of hands, a bump of shoulders, a meeting of gazes over the rim of a coffee cup — that sent jolts of electricity through her. Carolina had always dismissed it as the harmless attraction one sometimes felt for a friend. Just innocent flirting. But now she knew that Lee was asking how long she'd been considering divorce because those feelings had not been one-sided.

"I can't pinpoint any day when I began thinking of leaving him," she answered honestly. "But I remember resenting it when Bud left me behind on the dock that first time he took out the *Miss Carolina.* He cut me out of a major part of his life." Carolina felt the wound as though it had happened yesterday. "Then Bobby died. He changed after that."

"Bobby's death hit us all hard."

She shrugged. "The indifference grew over time. Our marriage is like a mountain after years of being pounded by waves. Rather than a landslide, it wore down rock by rock."

"What happened to set you off tonight? Was it because he extended the trip?"

"That was only the tipping point," she said with resignation. "But it hurt. It felt like he'd made the call more out of duty to the old ball and chain than because he missed me." She sighed, feeling the heat of tears in her eyes and the hurt billowing up again in her chest. "I lost my temper. But, God, he was so cold. He didn't care if I was lonely."

"He's a jerk."

"Oh, it's not all his fault. He probably just wanted to hang up. I'm angry a lot lately," she admitted. Her lips trembled, and she brought her fingers up to still them. "It hurts, you know? To not feel attractive anymore."

Lee tightened his arms around her. "You're a very attractive woman, Carolina. One of the finest I've ever known."

She felt the blood rush to her cheeks, hearing the emotion in his voice. It felt so good to be thought attractive again. Desir-

345

able. The air between them thickened. His hand stroking her back dug deeper along her spine. She was heading into dangerous territory. The alcohol swirled in her brain, breaking down her inhibitions.

"You know," he said softly by her ear. "I've often wondered how things would've turned out if you'd stayed with me at the dance. I've wondered a lot."

Carolina held her breath. She'd always known Lee had a thing for her, but this was the first time it was presented in words. The next moment seemed to hang between them. Her mind screamed that she should get out of the car now. Her body muffled that warning with a recklessness that was new and exciting and dangerously frightening. She turned her head. His face was a breath away.

"Carolina . . ."

Their mouths came together so hard she felt bruised. Her head dropped back against the seat as they pressed against one another, clumsy and eager, wrestling on the buttery leather that felt like a bed beneath them. His hands were nimble but they trembled as they dug through her layers of clothing to reach her skin. She gasped when his cold hands touched her warm breasts, then melted as they warmed, caressing her, pressing her farther down on the seat. She closed her eyes and felt her head swimming as he pulled up her sweater and lowered to kiss her breasts, her nipples.

With her eyes closed, she couldn't help but compare his mouth to Bud's, his taste, the way he moved. It was all happening as though in a fantasy. He lay over her, one leg between hers, with her arms around him. Bud had complained to her that she was cold, no longer interested in sex. Now she was trembling with desire, matching Lee kiss for kiss. In the heat of the moment, she heard a soft whimpering she didn't recognize escape from her throat. Her body felt foreign, like this was happening to someone else, and yet she was responding with a lust that surprised her. But when he unzipped her jeans, she blinked as though waking from a languid stupor; and when his fingers sought her wetness, she sucked in her breath, shocked at the reality of what she was doing.

"No. This isn't right."

Lee wrapped his arms tighter around her, and Carolina couldn't help but wish his firm, slender arms were Bud's broad, muscled ones. Suddenly Bud was a powerful presence in the confined space, and Carolina felt exposed. She couldn't go on.

347

This felt so wrong. She wanted Bud, not Lee.

Her body went suddenly cold and she stiffened, putting her hands against his chest. "Stop."

Lee pulled back and said in a husky voice, "We should go inside."

"No," Carolina blurted, and pushed him off. She scooted back on the seat, anxious to create distance between them. With her back against the door, she took deep breaths as she fumbled to pull down her sweater with shaky hands. "How could we do this?" she muttered, more to herself than to him. "How could *I*?"

"I thought you wanted —"

"He was your friend!" The fact that she was his wife, thus the greater sinner, floated in the air between them unsaid.

Carolina sat up in a rush, and with sudden cruelty her world started spinning off-kilter. She swallowed thickly as nausea rose up in her throat. She slapped her hand to her mouth. "Oh, God, I'm going to be sick."

"Open the door," Lee exclaimed, reaching over her in a rush to grab the handle and push the passenger door open. He didn't want her throwing up in his car.

She held on to the door handle to steady herself as she bent with her head hanging over the driveway. She felt sickened by the drink, but even more sickened by her actions. She wished she could just throw up, vomit out her shame and disgust with the alcohol and leave this whole degrading night in the gutter. But all she could manage was to sit hangdog fashion, ashamed and slumped over, while the roller coaster in her mind careened out of control and crashed.

Lee had come around the car to stand at the door helplessly. When the dizziness subsided and she could look up without the world spinning, she was relieved to see him all zipped and buttoned, respectable again. Anyone walking past would only see Carolina being helped home by an old family friend.

"Let me help you inside," he offered.

She took a deep breath of the cool air and nodded slightly, afraid to move her head too much lest she start retching again. Once again, Lee took her elbow and helped her to stand on shaky legs. He escorted her in a gentlemanly fashion along the walkway as she took mincing steps to her front door, then waited without speaking while she fumbled in her purse for her keys. She found them at last and handed them to him without looking.

She heard the click of the lock and the

creak of the door as it swung open. Lee once again took her arm, but she yanked it away.

"I can do the rest."

"But . . ."

She raised her head, feeling each degree of movement, and looked him in the eye. She hated him at that moment for not being as wretchedly sick as she was. "No."

Lee's face went still; then she saw a spark of worry in his eyes. "You won't tell Bud."

Carolina almost wept right then and there. What a fool she'd been. Instead, she released a short, pitiful laugh. "Good night, Lee."

He stepped aside to let her pass, handing her the keys.

"Oh, Lee?" she said, stopping abruptly.

Lee paused, looking at her expectantly.

"I quit."

She saw surprise, then anger, and lastly regret flicker across his face. "It's not your fault," she said. "It's my fault. I don't want you to think there's anything between us, but I can't go back to working with you. You understand, right?"

Lee released a sigh then nodded. "See you around, Carolina." He turned and walked swiftly down the gravel path and climbed into his blood-red Cadillac. The engine roared to life.

As he pulled away from the house, Carolina leaned back against the doorframe and looked up. The stars shone cold in a black sky, and she remembered reading how stars collapsed into black holes, losing their brilliant light to the vast darkness.

The moon was a pale shadow in a periwinkle sky when Carolina finally left her bathroom and could walk again without feeling the floor rise up beneath her. She'd clung to the porcelain bowl and retched till there was nothing left inside of her, then showered in water so hot it stung her tender skin. But no matter how hard she scrubbed with scented soap, she couldn't remove the feel of Lee's hands from her body or the stench of her infidelity.

She combed her hair back from her face, relishing the feel of the teeth gliding down her scalp. Then she wrapped herself in a thick terry robe, pulled socks over her feet, and, grabbing a heavy shawl, made her way downstairs. The floors creaked as she walked to the kitchen. Her stomach was still queasy and her head fuzzy. Carolina poured herself a glass of water and downed two aspirin. Then she took a box of saltines from the pantry and headed out to the back porch to sit in the wicker rocker.

Carolina rocked back and forth for hours,

holding her folded legs close and staring into the darkness. She was sober now and had to face what she had done. Through all the ups and downs of her marriage, Carolina had always believed in her vows. But tonight she'd come very close to breaking them.

Carolina rocked, going over in her mind how she could have committed this betrayal. The excuses came too easily. Yes, she'd had too much to drink. Yes, it had been so very long since she'd felt attractive or since someone desired her. She hadn't picked up some stranger in a bar, she thought, trying to validate her actions. She'd been with *Lee*. In the past few years, she'd spent more time with Lee than she had with Bud. She'd shared a camaraderie with Lee that she'd lost with Bud.

Even still, she hadn't meant for it to happen — neither of them had. It had just happened.

Bud was partly to blame, her mind argued. He'd been her husband in name only. And certainly not her lover, at least not with any regularity. He thought she was ambivalent about sex? How could she come to his bed feeling womanly and sensual when she saw her reflection as inadequate in his eyes? For six years, they'd been inseparable on the *Miss Ann*. But it was undeniable that their relationship had irreparably changed in the twenty years since Carolina was docked with Lizzy. The *Miss Carolina* had become *his* boat. In the process, Carolina had lost not only her job. She'd lost her best friend.

And now, perhaps, her husband.

Indifference cut a woman deep. Call it work, call it duty, but in reality, Bud had abandoned her. Year after year. For longer and longer periods. No matter how much he told her they needed the money, no matter what reasons he listed, all she heard him say was that her needs were not as important as his business. Their marriage didn't matter as much as his ability to captain his boat. The *Miss Carolina* mattered more to him than Carolina.

Her toes pushed against the floor, rocking her back and forth as tears flowed. She heard again Bud's words on the phone, so cold, so flat: *I'll get home when I get home.* Did he have any idea how deeply he'd hurt her? His tongue was like a knife dipped in poison that carved out her self-esteem.

Could she forgive Bud if he fooled around? She thought of the burst of passion she'd felt with Lee tonight — the thrill of the new touch, the fresh sensations, the innovative moves. God help her, she'd missed feeling that! Bud must also. Could she forgive him if he did cheat?

She exhaled heavily, knowing that, yes, she could forgive him. She might have answered differently a week earlier, but now in the aftermath of passion she'd discovered that one never fully knew what one might do until it happened.

Carolina stopped rocking and swiped the tears away angrily. She had to be honest with herself. Whatever the excuse, for whatever reason, she had allowed this transgression to occur. In truth, her biggest betrayal tonight was of herself and all she believed in. She knew she didn't love Lee. She wasn't sure she loved Bud anymore. She was fairly certain she didn't love herself. Otherwise, how could she have let this happen?

Who was she? She didn't know anymore. There was a time she'd never have let Bud — or any man — take her for granted. She'd felt a self-confidence so radiant it gave her a beauty that had nothing to do with her physical appearance. Men were drawn to her. Women admired her. Her femininity had made her feel potent.

And she'd given that power to Bud lovingly, willingly, and joyfully. She'd worked by his side with a drive and purpose that had sustained her. She'd loved being the crew on Bud's boat. She took pride in doing the books for his business. She'd tended their home, raised their daughter, supported their community, helped in their church, volunteered in the Shrimpers Association. If she fell, she picked herself up, knowing too many people depended on her.

Selflessness, sacrifice, and service — these were the time-honored virtues of womanhood. Husband and children first, then yourself. Carolina had lived by this code. She gave of herself from the moment she woke to make her husband's breakfast until whenever she finished the dinner dishes, the day's laundry, the take-home work from her job, and whatever other chore needed doing before she collapsed into bed. She hadn't thought it was possible to give too much.

Carolina stayed on the porch until the faint rays of light pierced the velvety blackness. The saltines were gone, and she shivered, chilled to the bone. She wrapped her shawl tighter around her shoulders. In the light of a new day, Carolina accepted full blame for her actions and dismissed all her weak excuses. She'd reached the bottom. She mourned the loss of that feminine power and beauty that had sustained her for so many years.

As dawn broke, flooding the sky with its

maidenly color, Carolina lifted her face to the light. She vowed to begin that day to dig deep within herself to find her inner glow again. She couldn't blame Bud alone for her unhappiness. It was up to her to rediscover her worth and to claim her own happiness. In the next few days, she'd have to decide what she would do when Bud returned home. She only knew that she couldn't remain in their marriage the way things were.

September 21, 2008
On board the Miss Ann
Carolina shivered, feeling the drop in temperature in the galley of the *Miss Ann.* She pushed back her sleeve and looked at her wristwatch, surprised that it was already half past one and her coffee was cold. A milky film floated on the top.

She made her way up on deck. The storm clouds were closer, coloring the sky a leaden gray, whipping up the wind and bringing white tips to the choppy water. She grabbed the edges of her slicker and closed it tightly as she squinted across the length of dock. The space for the *Miss Carolina* was empty.

Carolina shuddered with worry and looked beyond the creek toward the ocean. *Bud, where are you?*

Judith came to stand beside her and wrapped an arm around her shoulders. "He'll be all right."

"I know he will," she replied, knowing in her heart they were both lying.

15

September 21, 2008, 1:30 p.m.
On board the Miss Carolina

Cold, fat drops of rain fell like pellets on his skin. Bud watched the tumultuous mass race toward him like a banshee, screaming wind, and she wasn't shy to unleash her full fury. Rain whipped the boat in torrents atop cresting waves that tossed the boat. He clung to the winch with his good hand as the sea turned frothy white. With each jerk to the left or right, he felt a burst of blinding pain. Bud used his legs to steady himself against anything secure. Thunder cracked above him, boom after boom, and lightning raised the hair on his arms. He knew this would be his one chance for water, so despite the bucking boat, he leaned his head back to drink the rain, letting the cold spill sloppily into his mouth, down his throat.

Bud felt weak from loss of blood, but he held on for all his worth and trusted the

Miss Carolina to ride the waves that crashed against her sides, spewing seawater across the deck, drenching him. He coughed and spat out saltwater, feeling the sting of it in his eyes and open wound. The sky was so black and the waves so violent he couldn't see.

The storm moved quickly. The lightning dissipated and the thunder became a muffled grumbling fading out to sea. The rain slackened to a drizzle before it eventually stopped. In the wake of the storm, the clouds thinned and the sea surface appeared glassy. The sun manifested her power, piercing the gray to burnish the sky in burned orange, and when a rainbow glistened beneath the clouds, Bud was reminded of God's covenant and felt hope that he would be spared.

He'd survived the winch. He'd survived the storm. But for how long?

The tourniquet had loosened and the blood flowed more steadily again. The pain had freshened as well. He hurt bad.

He wouldn't go out like this, he thought. Pinned and helpless, more like a child than a man. If he was going to die out here, he wanted to die on his feet.

His pulse raced as he recollected stories of men who'd cut themselves free of a trap using duller knives than his. Bud had read about a climber in the mountains pinned by a rock. And a fisherman who'd cut off his hand to be free of a winch. Same as him. They'd done whatever was necessary to survive. He swallowed hard, tasting the salt. He'd never thought he'd be in the same spot. All his life, he'd taken pride in his physical power and his ability to make tough decisions. But this . . . He didn't know whether he'd actually be able to cut off his own hand. Or even if he'd survive trying. But he couldn't just lie here waiting to die. He had to try to save himself.

Was he man enough to do it?

Trapped as he was, he couldn't get to anything he'd need for the amputation. All he had was his trusty pocketknife. Hardly a scalpel, but at least it was sharp. Sweat gathered on his forehead as he went through the steps in his mind.

First, he'd have to tighten the tourniquet to pinch off the main arteries so he wouldn't bleed out after he made the cut. He'd have to cut fast, pinching the arteries. Once he was free, he could get to the pilothouse. He could radio for help. That'd be the first thing to do. Even if he passed out later, they'd have his coordinates. It would give him a fighting chance.

If he didn't pass out right away, he'd grab fishing line from the box a few feet away and tie off the arteries. Then he'd shove the boat into high gear and head straight back to the dock and medical help. Then he'd clean the wound, to avoid infection. It was too late to save the hand. Probably even the whole arm. He blanched at the thought of losing his arm. But what the hell, he thought. Better that than to die here.

Yes, he could do it, he thought. He went over it again in his mind: Cut off the hand, radio for help, get back home. He shuddered and took two deep breaths, gathering his strength. Then he reached for the knife in his rear pocket.

He didn't feel it. His pocket was empty.

Was it panic or relief that made his hand shake? he wondered. He shifted, wildly searching the deck beneath his weight. His hand smeared blood across the deck.

The knife was gone.

He blinked, trying to reason as pain hammered his temples. The knife must've fallen out in all the rocking and flailing during the storm. Desperate, he scanned the deck. There, several feet away, wedged behind a coil of rope, he spotted a flash of red metal. His hopes crashed.

He didn't know whether to laugh or cry.

"Is this the way we're going to end up?" he cried in a broken voice to the *Miss Carolina.* "Huh?" He began muttering, his mind wandering, not knowing if he was saying the words aloud. "Carolina . . . after all the years we spent together? I gave you everything I had. I kept you looking fine and sleek, painted you every spring. You're a beautiful boat. A fine, noble vessel. We had our fights, but we did okay."

He pounded the deck, scraping his knuckles. "Why like this? Goddamn it, Carolina. It ain't right."

Bud lowered his head against his damp sleeve, feeling breathless and light-headed. Disoriented.

"I loved you, Carolina. And you betrayed me."

March 12, 2001
White Gables
"I'm home!"

Bud dropped his duffel bag beside the front door. It was mostly filled with dirty laundry for Carolina to wash. He rolled his shoulders, glad to be home. Glad to be out of Florida and eager to sleep in his own bed. He'd been on the water so long he still felt the sea swells beneath him. His blue flannel shirt smelled like fish, his skin felt like

362

scales, and he desperately needed a bath.

A commotion in the front room drew his attention. He walked in to see Lizzy, in jeans and a sweater, lifting Will from the playpen.

"Hey, Lizard," he called out, using her old nickname.

Lizzy scooped Will into her arms and glowered at him, her lips in a tight line.

Red flag warning, Bud thought as his heart sank like an anchor. Josh must have beat him home and told her what he'd done. Either that, or the gossip had shot up the coast like a cannonball.

"Da-da-da-da," Will called out in a high voice.

"Least one person's glad to see me. How's my little man?"

Clutching Will close, Lizzy walked past him so fast her ponytail bounced. She angled her body to avoid bumping into him in the narrow hall.

"What'd you want me to do?" he bellowed after her.

Lizzy turned at the bottom of the stairs, her eyes rimmed red, and shouted back, "You ruined my life!"

"How did *I* ruin your life?"

She opened her mouth to answer, but couldn't find the words. Tears sprang to her eyes. Will looked at him, his big blue eyes worried.

"I hate you!" Lizzy shouted, and pounded up the stairs.

"Unbelievable." Bud cursed as he heard a door slam upstairs. That's great, he thought. Josh cheats on her, and I'm the bad guy. He ran his hands through his hair and walked down the hall to the kitchen. It was awfully quiet in the house — and Carolina hadn't even come to greet him.

Instinct spawned from years of marriage told him that he was heading for stormy weather. He wiped his hands on his jeans, wishing he'd brought her some small token — flowers, candy, or something pretty. After their last phone call, Bud knew he was in the doghouse.

Bud paused at the threshold of the kitchen, seeing his wife standing at the sink. His heart expanded in his chest. He loved the sight of Carolina in the kitchen. There was something so womanly, even sexy, about a woman standing at the sink that gave him a sense of being home and that all was right with the world. Sunlight poured in the southern windows, making her hair look like fire flowing down her shoulders. She was in stocking feet, faded jeans that hugged her rounded bottom, and a pale green sweater with the sleeves pulled back as she worked at the sink, exposing tanned forearms. Hers was no longer the figure of a girl. She had soft, mature curves that he could wrap his arms around.

He was about to walk up to her and do just that when he noticed that she was holding her back rigid and peeling potatoes with agitated movements.

"I'm home." His voice was tentative.

She didn't turn around.

"Caro —"

"I heard you the first time."

"So, that's the way it's going to be."

She didn't reply, but her hands stilled to grip the rim of the sink.

"Carolina, do we have to go through this again?" he said wearily. "I just walked in the door. I'm beat." He walked to the fridge, opened it, and stared blankly at the milk and soda. "Is it too much to ask for some cold beer?"

"You haven't been home in almost three months and I had no idea when you'd be back. Get it yourself."

Bud slammed the door, and they heard jars and bottles rattle inside.

"Nice," Carolina muttered.

Bud crossed his arms and tried hard to hold his temper. "Well, this is a helluva homecoming. Makes me wonder why I bothered."

She turned quickly, her eyes flashing. "I wonder, too."

Bud rubbed his eyes. "I'm too tired for this."

"Wait."

Bud swung his head and looked at her questioningly.

"There've been some changes."

"Changes?"

She clasped her hands, and he was surprised to see her suddenly nervous.

"Lizzy's moved back home. With Will. She's left Josh. They're getting a divorce." Carolina cast him a venomous look that spoke plainly of her thoughts about his role in all this.

Bud looked at his boots. He'd hoped it wouldn't come to that. He felt a surge of guilt for Lizzy's tears. "I told him to be a man and tell Lizzy himself. She shouldn't have to hear something like that from gossips — damn bottom-feeders. He had to do right by her. He owed her that much."

"He also said you kicked him off the boat."

"Yeah, I did."

"Wasn't that harsh? He's not just some deckhand. He's your son-in-law. The father of your grandson. Wouldn't you . . . I mean, I'd think you'd give him a second chance."

"I gave him plenty of chances and even more warnings."

"What are they going to live on?"

"If he's man enough to be a father, he's man enough to provide for his family."

There was a prolonged silence before Carolina spoke again.

"Don't you take any responsibility for the trouble they're having? You're the one who kept him away from home for so long. I told you what could happen, but you never listen!"

"Hey, I didn't put a gun to his head and tell him to sleep with those women. He did that all on his own. I don't respect that, and without respect, I don't want him on my boat. I'm done with him," he shouted back at her, fed up now. "Don't you be asking me to take him back. I won't."

Bud saw her pale face and pained expression, almost haunted, and thought for a second that maybe he had screwed up to fire Josh. Maybe he should've kept his business separate from his personal life. Now Carolina was upset and Lizzy was crying upstairs.

He ran his hand through his hair. "I didn't mean for them to get divorced," he said. "I just thought Lizzy should know. I'm her father. I couldn't watch it happen and do nothing." He met her gaze and held it, pleading for some understanding of the position he'd been put in.

Carolina's brows gathered and she averted her eyes.

"Let's talk about this tomorrow. I'm going to bed."

"Not in our room," she blurted out.

He looked at her, puzzled.

"I moved your things out of our room." Carolina drew her back straight. "Lizzy isn't the only one considering a divorce."

Bud's mouth slipped open.

Carolina lifted her chin, and he saw bright spots of pink bloom on her cheeks.

"What the hell?"

"I've been doing a lot of thinking while you've been gone," she said in a low voice that trembled with emotion. "What I have to say needs to be said now, not wait for the morning, not even for dinner. I can't go on like this," she said simply. "With our marriage. I can't go on living the way we live."

"What are you talking about? Where's this coming from? Are you so mad about Josh you'll throw our marriage out with theirs? Aren't you overreacting?"

"This has nothing to do with Josh and Lizzy. At least, not directly. Oh, let's be honest, Bud. Our marriage hasn't been that great for a long time now. We're more like roommates than husband and wife. We go through the motions just to keep up the routine. I think we stayed with it because we were comfortable. But are we happy?" Carolina swallowed and rubbed her arms. "I haven't been happy for a long time. And I don't think you have, either."

Bud gaped at her, not believing what he was hearing. "It's called *marriage.* It's not a honeymoon all the time. It's damn hard work."

"What marriage? We barely live together. The season is one thing. Going to Florida for a few weeks is another. When you started extending your trip, I didn't like it, but I was the good wife and accepted it. Then you started staying away longer every year, but I still put up with it. When you first were gone more than a month, we fought something fierce. Don't you remember? But this year . . ." She threw up her hands. "It's March, Bud!" Her voice broke and tears flowed down her face.

It was the same old argument. Bud took a long breath and said impassively, "I was working."

"You abandoned me."

Carolina wiped the tears from her face with a towel, gathering her composure.

"Sorry. I didn't mean to cry or get all emotional. Like you've said, it's a broken record. Enough. I'm done talking about it."

There was something in her voice, a strength and conviction, that put him on edge. He'd rather deal with her crying.

"So we've got problems," he said. "We'll work them out."

Her face appeared almost sad. "I wish it were so easy. We've moved beyond that point, I think. Our marriage has serious problems, and I don't know how to fix them. Bud, I think we need a break."

"A break? I thought you just said we were apart too much."

"I mean a separation."

His face hardened. "No. That's not going to happen."

"I can't go on living like this," she declared. "This isn't what I signed on for. I'm unhappy all the time. I don't like who I'm becoming. I don't like what this is doing not just to us, but to me."

Bud took a step back. Something wasn't adding up. There was something she wasn't telling him. He smelled the lie, felt it, like a foul beast hiding in the shadows. He couldn't see it, but he knew it was there.

As if Carolina sensed the shift in tension, she sniffed and wiped her nose with her towel, then leaned against the counter, crossing her arms in front of her.

Bud suddenly came to a stark realization. "Something happened," he said. "While I was away. What happened to get you so riled?"

"Your phone call," she replied, averting her eyes.

Bud didn't know guilt had a look of its own, but he saw it on Carolina's face. The blood drained from his face as an ugly suspicion took root.

"What did you do?"

Carolina paled. She turned away, but he grabbed her arm and jerked her closer. His fingers were digging into her flesh, drawing her so near that her face was inches from his own. He looked into her eyes and saw the truth. He felt himself dying. He knew what she was about to say. The bottom was about to fall out of his life. But he had to hear the words.

"Tell me."

"It's not what you think," she choked out.

"What do I think?"

"I didn't have an affair."

"What *did* you have?"

She tried to jerk her arm away, but he would not let go.

"Nothing happened."

"Don't make me break your arm. Tell me," he said, and his voice was like a low growl at her ear.

"All right!" she exploded, and met his gaze. "But first, you *let go of my arm!*" she shouted, refusing to be intimidated.

Bud glared at her, his jealousy churning, but he dropped her arm and took a step back. Instantly, the anger was defused and they both took deep breaths.

Carolina wrapped her arms around herself again in a defensive posture, but she held her shoulders straight. Despite his fury, he had to admire her courage.

She took a deep breath. "After you called, I was devastated. You basically told me I didn't matter. Our marriage didn't matter. I had to get out of the house. So I got dressed and went to the Shack for a drink."

She was leading up to something. Bud felt his back muscles tighten.

"While I was there, I had a few drinks."

"Go on."

"I ran into . . ." She licked her lips. "Lee." She glanced at him nervously.

Bud felt sucker-punched. The second he heard the name, he knew where it was leading. It couldn't have been anyone else.

"We talked. About business, real estate . . . I don't know, just stuff. And I was drinking.

I had three margaritas."

Bud knew better than anyone that Carolina wasn't much of a drinker and couldn't hold her liquor.

"Lee didn't think it was a good idea for me to drive, so he offered to take me home. I'd had too much to drink," she said again, and looked at him so he could tell she was telling the truth. "But I was also feeling so lonely and upset after our fight. He made me feel desirable again. I don't say that as an excuse, it's just a fact. I didn't mean for it to happen."

He felt sick. A crowbar could have hit him full-force in the stomach and it couldn't have felt worse.

He lowered his head so close to hers that he could see the navy rim around her pale blue irises. "What happened!" he shouted.

Her eyes widened, and for the first time he saw fear in her eyes. He hated himself for putting that there, but a feral fierceness drove him on.

"We kissed, okay?" she cried out, and tears sprang to her eyes. "We just kissed." She shook her head, causing her hair to fall over her face and mingle with the tears. "That's all."

"That's all! That's all?" Bud lifted his hand to strike his wife. He stopped short.

"Go on. Hit me. I couldn't feel worse about this if you did. Go ahead. I'm asking you to do it."

The room suddenly became small. Crowded. Bud and Carolina retreated to separate corners of the kitchen. He stared at Carolina and knew a terrible regret for ever having loved her. In that awful moment, Bud realized it didn't matter if she'd kissed the guy or had sex with him. It was still a betrayal. And with Lee Edwards, of all people! It hurt more, he thought, than if it were anyone else. Anyone else in the entire world. He felt a new rage billow up as his fists clenched at his thighs. He wanted to kill the guy.

"I'm sorry," Carolina said in a heartbroken voice. "I know what I did was so wrong. I should never have let it happen. But you let it happen, too. I begged you to come home. You refused."

"So now it's my fault?" he roared.

"Yes, it's partly your fault."

"You know what? I don't give a damn. Be with him, I don't care."

"This isn't about Lee Edwards. I don't give a damn about him. This is about us. Our marriage is broken."

"That's the first thing you've gotten right since I got home."

Her face went very still.

"You don't have to ask me to leave twice." He pushed open the screen door, slamming wood against wood, and stormed out into the night.

Bud climbed in his truck and fired the engine. He knew where he was headed, even as he knew it was a bad idea. His tires squealed as he fishtailed from the driveway, then the truck roared down the block.

It was a short drive through town and along the winding dirt road to Lee's stately home on Jeremy Creek. The sun was setting and the water reflected the blood orange color of the sky. Enormous live oaks surrounded the house, softening the harsh architectural lines with their graceful limbs. The white clapboard house was built in the southern style to blend with the historic village, but everything was new and shiny. No patched roofs, peeling paint, or shutters covered with rust. The decay was inside, he thought as he parked in the tall grass under an oak and turned off the ignition.

He didn't know the house well. This wasn't the old Gordon home that he'd spent so many idle hours at as a kid. There was no personal history here. He was glad for that. He didn't want to remember the boy he'd loved as a brother. This was a stranger's house and it suited his mood.

His heels pounded the wooden steps as he made his way up to the front door. Bud wasn't trying to surprise anyone. His sense of fair play preferred to alert Lee to his presence. He didn't want an ambush. But there would be no talk.

Bud was sweating when he reached the front door. He leaned over to look through one of the windows. In the living room, Lee was watching a sports program. The flicker of the television cast shadows on his face. Hatred pumped through Bud's heart as he reached for the door handle. It was locked. In one swift move he raised his right leg and crashed it squarely against the door. It ripped clean from the hinges in an explosion of shards of wood and glass.

Lee leaped from his leather chair, sending the beer and sandwich crashing to the floor. A cat darted from the sofa and bolted from the room. Lee's eyes were wide with shock and his arms were spread out in a fight-or-flight position. Then he saw Bud's face.

Bud watched Lee's color drain and his mouth slip open. His expression was a confession of his guilt. Lee knew why Bud was here. He'd seen the retribution in Bud's eyes.

Bud balled his fists and stepped into the room.

Lee held out his hands. "Bud, wait!"

"Damn you."

Lee ran. He made it to the dining room before Bud tackled him shoulder first, an old football move. The momentum brought Lee slamming into a large cupboard, sending his family's heirloom collection of china crashing to the floor. Bud pulled him up against the wall.

Lee ducked his head and pleaded, "Please. For God's sake, Bud . . ."

Bud's eyes narrowed and he stared coldly down at the man he'd never again call friend. Bud didn't give a damn about Lee's fancy cars or his glorified mansion. But this time he'd stolen the one thing in his world that mattered to Bud. He pulled back his fist, tightening his knuckles, taking aim.

Lee whimpered and lifted his arms to guard his face. Bud saw fear in his eyes. With a low, throaty growl Bud slammed his fist beside Lee's head into the wall. Crushed drywall flaked from his hand and forearm and a painting crashed to the floor.

Both men were breathing hard, their faces inches apart. Bud felt like he was coming out of a red fog and he could see the pathetic man slumped before him. He drew his fist from the wall and examined his bloodied knuckles. Bud was a fighter. But he was not a killer.

"I'm sorry, Bud. I . . ."

"Shut up." He leaned forward and stared into Lee's eyes. "You're dead to me. And if you so much as speak to my wife again, so help me, you'll be dead to everyone."

Rubbing his knuckles, Bud headed toward the door. A dining room chair had the misfortune of being in his way. He kicked it hard into the wall, shattering it on impact. He left the house feeling like a beaten man. As he walked through the tall grass to his truck, mosquitoes circled his head and tears streamed down his face.

October 1, 2001
The docks, McClellanville

Carolina. Will you meet me at the boat? I'd like to talk.

Bud

The sun cast a vivid, flame-kissed palette into the sea below. Carolina caught the familiar, pungent scents of the dock as she walked toward the boats. Hambone was welding in the warehouse; bright sparks burst in the air.

When Bud had left six months earlier, Carolina couldn't imagine coming for a sit-down chat with him. He'd felt betrayed. She'd felt rejected. Neither was able to come to terms with the other person's reasoning. In the subsequent months, however, both had had time to reflect. As painful as those months had been, she'd come to value her separateness again. She couldn't return to the life she'd led up to the point of her indiscretion. That one act did not define her. It was more of an awakening.

When she'd received his invitation to talk, she'd immediately agreed. To wait any longer would have made it easier for them both to envision a life without the other. It was time for them to see if they could rebuild a life together.

Carolina had dressed carefully for this visit. She'd soaked in the tub to calm her nerves, washed and brushed her hair till it shone, and donned her best jeans and a green sweater, knowing Bud liked her in that color. She'd taken special care with her makeup, applying shadow and liner, then mascara and blush. Finally, she'd splashed on the perfume he'd given her for Christmas. Before leaving the house, she'd checked the mirror, touching up her lipstick. She wanted to look her best. She hoped to please him; she was vain enough to admit that. Yet if the meeting went poorly, she'd need to feel good about herself and maintain her self-respect.

The *Miss Carolina* rested in her usual slot near the end of the dock. The late-afternoon colors reflected in the water looked like flames licking the hull. Carolina felt again the pride at seeing her name in bold red letters: *Miss Carolina.* Bud was standing with his back to her at the bow, a broad silhouette against the sunset. It was a pensive pose, and she felt again the fluttering in her stomach.

"Bud?" she called out.

He turned, caught unawares. He hurried to assist her aboard. That first touch of their hands felt electric, and she almost pulled back her hand. But he grabbed hold and hoisted her up as she swung her leg over the railing. They dropped their hands and stepped back in an awkward first moment. She let her eyes sweep over his face, catching details after their long separation. His face was deeply tanned, making his blue eyes brighter, and his dark hair, longer now, was pushed back off his face. He was still a handsome man, she thought, though a little thinner, and she was surprised — even pleased — by the flutter of attraction she felt when she looked at Bud Morrison. He wore his best tartan plaid shirt and jeans, and she smiled inwardly, knowing that he, too, was trying.

"You look nice," he said.

"Thanks. You, too." After a painfully long moment, she looked around the boat. "It's been a while since I've been aboard."

"It's pretty much the same." He looked around the boat as if to confirm the last comment.

She nodded, then clasped her hands before her, took a breath, and looked at him. He was watching her intently. "It's been a good season?"

"Pretty good. We were due."

"I'm glad."

"And you? You like teaching? Being back?"

"Yes. I'm lucky to have the job."

"They're lucky to have you."

His compliment was unexpected.

"Do you want some wine?"

"Yes," she replied, relieved. "That'd be nice. Thanks."

Everything felt unbearably strained. She hoped the wine would relax them both.

"Come, sit down."

He'd prepared a small table at the front of the boat, the way he used to when he'd take her out for a sunset dinner cruise. She was touched that he'd made the effort. He retrieved a bottle of chardonnay from the bucket of ice on the deck. She watched as he uncorked the bottle and poured the wine into two wineglasses. He'd also served a small wheel of Brie with crackers on a plate, knowing it was her favorite. He spilled a little of the wine on the table, and when he handed her a glass, to her surprise, his hand was shaking slightly.

"Thank you," she said.

He wiped his hands on his jeans, seeming self-conscious. Then he picked up his glass and raised it. His lips parted as though he was going to offer a toast, but then he simply lifted his glass to her and took a sip.

Carolina brought the wine to her lips, tasting its sweetness.

"Sit," he offered again, pulling out a chair.

Carolina slid into the folding chair. She recognized it as one they'd stored in their shed. He must've taken the chairs and table out and scrubbed the mold from the vinyl for tonight.

Bud pulled out the chair opposite her and stretched out his long legs as he eased into it. He took another sip of his wine. Carolina felt the man was stalling, looking for the right thing to say. When he lowered his glass, his eyes were troubled and his jaw worked in a silent struggle.

"I've missed you," he said simply.

"I missed you, too."

He exhaled and shook his head. "I don't know how to do this."

She laughed lightly. "I don't either. But you've made a wonderful start," she said, indicating the table, the wine, the lit lantern that was glowing in the dimming light. "It means a lot to me. It tells me you want to try." She paused, her fingers tightening around her glass. "You do, don't you? Want to try?"

"Do you?"

She nodded. "Yes."

He took a deep breath and rubbed the bridge of his nose. "After, you know, I found out — my life was crazy. I was angry all the time. I thought it was over between us."

"But now?"

He shrugged. "I went to see Father Frank. He said we owe it to our marriage to try to work it out."

Carolina was surprised to hear that Bud had gone to see Father Frank. He hardly ever went to church. She was very moved. "I went to see Father Frank, too."

"The thing is, I don't know if I can ever fully trust you again. I'm not saying I wouldn't give it a chance. But we can't act like this didn't happen, and I can't act like I'm not wounded. I can try to forgive, but I can't promise you anything."

"Bud, I know this is going to take time," she said. "You're still hurt and angry. And so am I."

"What have *you* got to be angry about?"

"Didn't you hear anything I told you?"

"At least I didn't cheat on you. I almost did a few times. A lot of guys fool around. But I was faithful."

Carolina put down her glass and rose from her seat. There was no talking to Bud when he was in this mood. "I'm going now."

He shot out his hand but held it in midair, not touching her. "Carolina, wait. I was shooting from the hip." He lowered his voice. "I don't want you to go. Let me try this again. Please?"

She fought back tears and leaned against the boat's railing. She lifted her face to the offshore breeze. "Bud, this is going to take a long time. And at the end, we may find we can't make it work."

"I know. Father Frank told me I had to admit to my part in all this. To understand why you were so unhappy. It made me realize, for the first time, that it wasn't all you."

Carolina felt hope rising. "He told me that

there was no timetable to regain your trust. Or your forgiveness."

Bud nodded his head.

"Bud, if I could go back in time and undo that night, I would. I can't. But I can work with you to rebuild our marriage. I'll work hard, I promise. But you have to meet me halfway."

"Carolina, I *want* to forgive you."

She felt her composure begin to crack. "Tell me what you want me to do."

"Come back to me," he said in a hoarse voice.

Carolina paused and pulled her hair from her face. She needed to explain her position clearly — now, before emotion swept her away.

"Bud, I want to. Very much. And I don't want to make demands now. But there are underlying problems in our marriage that we need to solve or we won't prevent them from happening again."

"What problems?"

"If you're willing to give us another shot, then we have to agree — no more off-season trips to Florida. No more long separations. They're not good for us. They'll break us."

"Carolina —"

"There are other ways to earn money in the off-season. We both know that. This is a bottom line for me, Bud. I can't go back to the life we had before. We both have to make changes."

"You know that if I can't make it, we'll lose the house."

"Then we'll lose the house. Better that than our marriage."

"But White Gables means the world to you."

"You mean more."

Bud's eyes intensified. He knew what that statement cost her.

"Bud, I have to believe in my heart of hearts that someday you'll forgive me and trust me again. I can hang on if I know that we'll move on from this. But if you don't believe you can, then we shouldn't put ourselves through this ordeal. It'll be too painful. The anger and resentment between us will fester and eat away at us. We'll end up hating each other." Her voice broke. "I don't ever want to hate you. I couldn't bear that. You don't hate me, do you, Bud?"

He shook his head, then stepped closer. Emotion swam in his eyes as he placed his hands on either side of her head and studied each feature. Lowering his head, he covered her lips with his. His mouth spoke of all the pain and longing and regret and passion that went beyond words.

This was Bud, she thought, relishing the feel of *his* arms, *his* chest, *his* smell, *his* skin. She welcomed the familiar way he covered her mouth with his, the way his calloused hands moved across her body. His kiss was possessive and raw. She felt a flame spark deep inside and turn into a swirling heat that scorched away her sins.

Bud took her hand and led her below to his cabin, undressing her and laying her naked on his bed. This was his domain. Carolina lifted her arms in surrender, feeling the crush of his weight, strong and secure. She was blanketed with memories of a lifetime.

Afterward, they lay side by side on their backs, staring at the ceiling as the boat rocked in gentle waves. Carolina heard the occasional splash of fish jumping and the muffled, monotonous thump-thump of boats as they bumped against the rubber-wheel padding on the docks. She remembered back to their first nights together, when she'd lived and worked with him on the sea. She felt hope stir in her heart, but knew that though their commitment tonight was a first step, the journey to forgiveness would be long and arduous.

Bud's skin was sweaty even though the air had turned cooler after the storm. He began to shiver and his throat was parched. He'd ripped another large swatch of fabric from his shirt to cover his head. He had to keep his body protected in any way he could. What he wouldn't give for a beer right now, he thought, and the vision of his fridge in the galley, stocked with cold ones, almost caused him to groan.

Where were they? he wondered. How long would it take them to find him? He was getting worried he was drifting off course. If someone came looking for him and he'd drifted too far, it would be like looking for a needle in a haystack.

He felt like he'd spent a lifetime already on this boat. Each minute of the day had been measured by drops of his blood. The blood was everywhere. And it was lonely out here. His only visitors were a pelican and the seagulls that sat on the rigging, staring down at him like vultures.

Bud had been alone on the sea many times in his life. He knew how long the hours and how vast the ocean could seem when one was alone in the pilothouse. He'd felt no sense of impatience. He'd chat on the radio, read, or find something to do to while away the time. But trapped, stranded without purpose — *this* was a deeper depth of loneliness than he'd ever experienced.

Bud looked down at his life's blood pooling beside him and thought of the many times Carolina had told him that she was lonely.

16

September 21, 2008, 2:00 p.m.
Coastal Seafood, McClellanville

Judith slipped the hood of her slicker over her head as the first faint drops of rain were carried in by the wind. She gazed over Carolina's shoulder with a puzzled expression. "Will you look at that? Here comes the cavalry. I wonder what's up."

Carolina turned to see Oz marching across the gravel, his large forearms pumping with exertion. He was leading the group of older men like a ragtag army.

"They're just getting out of the rain," Carolina replied.

"No, something's got them riled." Judith pointed and said incredulously, "Why is Pee Dee here?"

Carolina spotted Pee Dee lagging behind the group. She felt a chill and looked over at Judith. They shared a look of alarm.

"Come on," Judith said.

They hurried to climb from the boat and met Oz near the warehouse.

"Oz, what's going on?" Judith asked. "What's Pee Dee doing here?"

Oz paused and tried to catch his breath. "That sumbitch didn't show up this morning. Bud's out there alone. On the *Carolina*."

"Alone?" Carolina exclaimed. "With a storm out there?"

"It's that no-'count's fault my boy is out there," he said, pointing to Pee Dee. "I could kill him."

"Whoa, hold on," Judith said. "It's the captain's decision to take a boat out. You know that. Carolina, didn't you say he was due in around noon?"

She nodded. "He said he was only going out for one haul."

Judith checked her watch. "It's just two. He could be coming in now. Let's not get emotional and jump to conclusions."

As if to mock her, the wind gusted and the first wave of rain began falling.

"I don't need you to tell me what to do, missy," Oz grumbled. "We're going in to find out if anyone's heard from him. Now, get out of my way, ladies, before we get drenched."

He pushed past Judith and Carolina with an arrogant shove.

Judith's face flushed and she slanted her gaze after the old man limping toward the office. "Who the hell does he think he is, Captain Bligh?"

Carolina knew Judith couldn't abide being treated as less worthy than a man on the dock. She shifted her gaze to where Pee Dee lurked under the awning with a sad, guilty face, reminding her of a mongrel that'd been beaten by his master's hand.

"Come on," she said to Judith. "Let's find out what Oz has in mind."

Oz's booming voice was louder than the thunder of the breaking storm. When they stepped into the office of Coastal Seafood, the small space was crowded with the five captains. Oz stood at the front talking to Lee, his hands gesticulating wildly. Lee was leaning against the desk of his office manager, Gloria, a middle-aged, heavyset woman with platinum hair and a no-nonsense attitude. She didn't bother to get up, but leaned back in her chair and kept a wary eye on the group of men.

Lee was in his fifties now, but still years younger than all of the men in the room save for Pee Dee. His hair was streaked with gray, and he looked distinguished in his bright polo shirt and khaki pants. Carolina knew that it was the fact that most of the men in the room were in hock to Lee that gave him his power. His hands were on his hips, and he listened with the aura of a man accustomed to providing answers. Lee raised his hands, silencing the group. His searching eyes met Carolina's. She couldn't read his emotions.

"Carolina, you said Bud was coming in at noon?" Lee asked.

She nodded. "That's what he told me."

"That fits. He had an order to fill at one."

All eyes went to the wall clock. It was now quarter past two. She felt the tension in the room rise.

Lee looked around the room. "Anyone know what time he left port?"

Old Tom lifted his hand. He'd seen the commotion from the warehouse and followed the men into the office. He spoke in his heavy drawl. "I seen him go out sometime around five thirty. He been runnin' late on account'a he was waiting on Pee Dee."

Several men grumbled while Oz spat out profanities about Pee Dee's lineage, ending up demanding that he get the hell out of the room. Emotions rose and the room grew loud as the captains began arguing among themselves. Carolina put her hand to her forehead. She couldn't take Oz's belligerence now. The Hagg moved closer to his old friend and told Oz to settle down. Meanwhile, Pee Dee slunk unnoticed by all but Carolina from the office.

Captain Wayne Magwood made his way toward Gloria's desk, which had become a makeshift podium. He was the patriarch of an old and revered fishing family in Shem Creek. When he rapped the wood, everyone settled down to listen.

"Let's not get away from ourselves and think this through," Magwood began. "If you figure it takes an hour or more to get where you're going, right? And a drag takes two to four hours . . ." He rubbed his jaw, calculating. "Even if he only took in one haul, like he said, even working alone, way I see it, he should have made it in by now."

"Could be he had some trouble," offered Woody. "A mechanical problem."

"Or got something caught in a net," added the Hagg.

"He woulda called someone if he'd done that," said Oz, dismissing that option. "And there ain't nobody can fix a mechanical problem like my boy."

Carolina heard the emotion rumbling under those words and clenched her lips tight.

Lee moved to place a hand on Oz's shoulder. "The first thing to do is see if we can reach him or if anyone's seen him." He clapped Oz's shoulder, then headed toward the marine-band radio. "Y'all can wait here, if you like. Gloria, would you make some coffee?"

"You got anything stronger?" asked Woody, and he was met with chuckles and rejoinders, a welcome relief in the tension.

Gloria rose reluctantly and walked to the small kitchen to oblige. Lee moved to sit in front of the marine-band radio and opened channels.

"This is Lee Edwards. We're trying to locate Bud Morrison. Anybody out there seen the *Miss Carolina*?"

The radio crackled while outside the thunder rumbled closer. The men gathered around, listening in. Carolina moved to the front and sat down. She felt her chest constrict and started shaking. This was really happening. Carolina was struck with the stark realization of what her life would be like without Bud.

Answers began coming in from the boats. Captain Gay reported seeing Bud at first light. According to him, the *Miss Carolina* had passed them and moved on to points south. Lee jotted down the coordinates. A few other boats had seen him early as well, all reporting the same direction. There was talk about starting a search.

After a while, Lee turned from the radio and rose to stand beside Oz. He looked the room over. "Nobody's seen the *Miss Carolina* since dawn," he said somberly. "We can't reach Bud by radio. He's not answering."

"Could be he cut the radio off 'cause he found shrimp," said Magwood.

"Or he got delayed in the storm," offered Woody.

Lee cleared his throat. Silence fell in the room. His gaze searched out Carolina. She rose to her feet. Judith stood beside Carolina and grasped her hand.

"I think it's time we call in the Coast Guard," Lee said.

September 21, 2008
McClellanville

Word that Bud Morrison, a beloved son, was overdue spread like wildfire through McClellanville. The close-knit village responded with an alacrity that came from a century of search-and-rescue experience.

In the office of Coastal Seafood, the captains sprang into action. Time was of the essence. The men huddled over maps, piecing together the coordinates and prevailing winds to track where Bud might be. The ocean was vast. But the old captains knew this stretch of coastline better than any men alive. They pooled their knowledge to come up with a plan of action.

Once they had likely coordinates, Lee manned the radio again. It was an all-out search for the *Miss Carolina*. Men who competed with each other out at sea, who lied to their best friends and brothers as to where the shrimp might be, pulled together to search for their fellow captain. Boats already out at sea pulled in their nets. On shore, captains forgot about the expense and readied their boats to head out. Each man knew if it were him lost out there, the community would have his back.

"All tanks can be filled, no charge," Lee called out.

Carolina had been sitting ignored in the back, but she stood up at hearing this, shocked. At three thousand to five thousand dollars a boat, Carolina could do the math. She made her way through the crowded room to Lee. She hadn't spoken directly to him in a personal way for years. He was bent over the maps, listening to a current wind report. Carolina placed a tentative hand on his arm.

"Lee . . ."

He swung his head around. His brows gathered over pale, tired eyes.

"I want to thank you —"

Lee cut her off. "I owe him."

Carolina closed her mouth and dropped her hand. Lee turned back to the maps without another word.

As thunder rolled overhead and lightning flashed, Oz limped to the door, calling out, "Listen up! Everyone, listen up!" His face was unshaven, his eyes rheumy, and he tottered on his gimp leg as he waved his arms to get their attention.

"I'm taking out the *Cap'n and Bobby*," Oz shouted above the din. "I need a crew. Anybody know someone available?"

There was sudden quiet as faces turned toward the old man. Everyone in that room knew that Oz had not taken the *Cap'n and Bobby* out of dock since Bobby had disappeared. He'd cleaned it, paid dockage, and kept it as a monument to his lost son.

"I'll go," Lee called back.

Oz met his gaze. "I appreciate it, son, but we need you here to coordinate."

Other names were shouted out and pens pulled from pockets as a sea posse was quickly assembled.

Judith came to Carolina's side. She took Carolina's hands and shook them gently.

"You hang in there. We'll find him."

"I . . . I don't like to think of him alone out there," Carolina said in a taut voice.

"I ran a boat by myself for years. I did okay without any deckhand. Sometimes I think it was easier. Listen, Bud's a pro. He could run a boat in his sleep. And if something did go wrong, he'd know how to handle it." She looked closely at Carolina's drawn face. "I don't know about you, though."

"I'm fine," Carolina replied quickly, dismissing any concern for her own well-being. "It's just . . . I keep thinking, what if I don't see him again? There's so much left unsaid between us."

She looked into Judith's eyes and welcomed the understanding she found there.

Judith hugged her fiercely, then pulled back to peer into her face. "He's crazy about you. Always has been. Now, buck up, kiddo. You can't fall apart now. You need to be strong. For your family. For Bud."

17

September 21, 2008, 3:30 p.m.
McClellanville

Puddles of rainwater glistened in the late-afternoon sun. The air held the crisp freshness that often followed a quick storm. The McClellanville docks were bustling as trawlers, fishing boats, and all available seaworthy craft began heading out in search of Bud Morrison and the *Miss Carolina.*

Carolina stood on the dock and watched as a line of boats filed down Jeremy Creek. In the lead was the *Cap'n and Bobby,* taking the curve wide, followed by the *Winds of Fortune,* the *Miss Ann,* the *Village Lady,* the *Miss Georgia,* the *Betty H.,* and the *Ms. Shirley.* Her lips moved in prayer for each boat, begging God to help one of them to find Bud. To find him alive and well. That was all she prayed for, not wanting to ask too much.

After the last boat left the dock, Carolina

turned to go home. From the corner of her eye, she spotted a solitary figure standing at the far end of the dock, shoulders slumped, watching the boats head out to sea. He bent his head as his shoulders shook.

It was Pee Dee.

Carolina walked the length of the rotting dock to his side. Pee Dee stared out to sea like a half-drowned river dog looking for his master — skinny, long-nosed, sniffing the wind. His clothes were drenched and hung from his body. Rainwater streaked his angular face. She wondered if he'd been standing there throughout the storm.

"Pee Dee," she said gently.

He swiftly wiped his eyes, then shifted them to her, swollen and red-rimmed.

"Are you okay?" she asked.

He shook his head, spraying drops of water. "It's my fault he's out there alone. I never meant to be late," he cried, looking at her with a plea in his wild eyes.

"I know," she replied. Pee Dee seemed frantic, at the breaking point. "They'll find him."

"No, they won't!" he exclaimed, his voice rising to hysteria. "They don't know where to look! They'll go to all the wrong places. I'm the only one who knows his secret spot.

He never told nobody about this one. Nobody!"

"Pee Dee, do you know where Bud might be?"

"That's what I been saying, 'cept no one will listen. When I heard them say where he was last spotted and which way he was headed, I knew. I swear I know where he is."

"Then you've got to tell them! Why didn't you tell them?"

"I tried! There ain't nobody who'll listen."

Carolina's eyes darted to the curve in the creek. The last of the line of boats was disappearing around the bend. Too late. Her mind worked fast. Time was running out.

"We can radio them."

Pee Dee shook his head with remorse. "I already told 'em — told 'em all. Nobody'd take me on board. They shoved me away. Called me bad luck."

Carolina knew the local captains had followed Oz's lead and blamed Pee Dee for Bobby's death. In the end, Pee Dee had borne the guilt of the tragedy for all of them. He'd become a pariah on the docks, an outcast. Bad luck. He'd always been a drinker, but after the accident, Pee Dee had turned to hard drugs for escape. He did his work, but he couldn't hold his life together.

It was a downward spiral, sad to witness. Bud had provided him safe refuge, and Pee Dee remained slavishly loyal.

Still, Pee Dee was who he was.

"Pee Dee, if you're drunk or making this up —"

"I'm not. I swear on my life. Bud's like my brother. I got to find him." Pee Dee ran his hands through his hair, squeezing water down his back. His eyes looked wild. "If I can't get a boat, I'm gonna swim. . . ."

Carolina took his arm. "Hold on. I have an idea. Come on."

Pee Dee followed Carolina as she sprinted to the Coastal Seafood office. It was nearly empty now, though the smell of sweat and tobacco lingered. Gloria sat at her desk. Lee manned the radio. They both looked up when she entered, surprise evident on their faces.

Gloria began to stand. "Carolina, I —"

Carolina waved her off and went directly to Lee at the radio. "I need to contact Josh."

"What for?" asked Lee.

"Just get him, damn it!"

Lee's mouth thinned, but he turned and connected to Josh's channel. When he made contact, he handed her the mike.

She cleared her throat. "Josh? You there?"

"Yeah." The voice was crackling but audible. "Who's this?"

"It's Carolina. Are you coming in?"

"No. I pulled in my nets and waited out the storm. I'm joining the search. What's up?"

"Pee Dee thinks he knows where Bud might be. Nobody else is listening to him. I really think he knows. But he needs a ride."

There was a pause.

"Are you sure you can trust him?"

Carolina looked over to the door where Pee Dee stood, shifting from left foot to right, anxiously clenching his fists.

"Bud did."

There was another pause.

"Good enough for me."

Lizzy thanked Odelle, then brought the casserole to the kitchen and set it on the table beside the apple pie, the lasagna, and the boiled shrimp. Neighbors and friends had been stopping by the house for the past hour to offer food and words of encouragement since word had spread that the *Miss Carolina* was overdue. She peeked into the small family room beside the kitchen to check on Will. He was sitting on the floor beside Skipper watching television. Skipper's mother, Tressy, lifted her face when she heard Lizzy approach, eyes questioning.

"More food," Lizzy told her friend. "A casserole from your mother."

Tressy made a face. "She can't cook worth a darn. Do you want me to make you up something?"

"No thanks, I'm not hungry. It's enough that you're keeping an eye on Will."

The doorbell rang again.

Lizzy sighed. "I'll get it." She knew the support was well-meant, but right now all she wanted was to be left alone with her family.

She opened the door and was stunned to find Ben Mitchell standing nervously on the stoop, clean-shaven and smelling of cologne. He smiled expectantly at her. Then, catching her puzzled expression, his smile fell.

"Am I too early?"

Lizzy blew out a breath, recalling her dinner date with Ben for that evening. She'd completely forgotten. That breakfast conversation at the restaurant seemed a lifetime ago.

"You didn't hear?" she asked.

"Hear what?"

"My daddy. He's overdue."

Ben's features immediately sharpened. "Have they started the search?"

She nodded. "Coast Guard's out. Most every boat in McClellanville is."

A siren sounded down the road, coming closer. Then another, louder. Ben turned his head to watch the ambulance race down Pinckney Street toward the docks. Right behind it was the town fire engine, casting its macabre, twirling red light across Ben's face as it passed.

Lizzy put her hand to her chest, feeling her heart quicken. Fire and rescue were in a holding pattern for her father. Her eyes filled with tears. She couldn't believe this was happening.

Ben stepped forward to hold the door open and guide her inside.

"You shouldn't be alone. I'll stay with you."

"No, I'm okay. There's nothing you can do."

"I can keep you company. I'd like to —"

"No. Thank you. I'm with family," she said, releasing her elbow from his hand.

Her grandfather Oz had once told her that shrimpers were clannish. They had their own way of life, unique customs and traditions. They took care of their own and didn't let outsiders in. This town and these people were her family; she saw that now. And she was proud to be one of them.

"Really, Ben." She met his gaze. "You should go home."

Understanding bloomed in his eyes. He took a step back. "You take care, Lizzy. If you need me, please call." He turned and closed the door behind him.

Lizzy leaned against the door and felt a cry well up inside her.

"Daddy," she cried. She wanted her father here, safe. After her divorce from Josh, they'd made a tenuous peace. Lizzy adored her father. She wanted him back. She wanted to be "Daddy's girl" again.

She closed her eyes and recalled a favorite memory of her father. Bud had taken the family on one of his fishing trips to Florida. Lizzy was around five years old. She remembered that it was right before New Year's Eve. Bud had already taken the boat down to Florida with Pee Dee, then driven back to McClellanville in a rental car to spend New Year's with Carolina and her. When it was time to head back to the boat, he couldn't find Pee Dee. Her daddy was fit to be tied. She'd never seen him so angry. He'd come storming back into the house and told her mama, "Get your stuff, woman! We're going to Florida." He'd left his boat in dock, and every day off the water was a day he was spending money and not earning any.

Her mother started throwing clothes and

toiletries into bags. At the last minute, she drove their miniature poodle, an apricot sweetie named Lucy, to the kennel, but it being a holiday, the kennel was filled up. So they brought Lucy along. They piled in the car and drove six hours to the coast of Florida, arriving around ten o'clock that night. In retrospect, the hotel wasn't much, but it had a small swimming pool, and at age five, Lizzy thought it was luxurious.

The next morning when they boarded the *Miss Carolina,* her mother had a hissy fit about the condition of the boat. She began spouting about how, when she was the crew, they could eat off the floor, and how no child of hers was going to sleep in that pigsty of Pee Dee's. Carolina had rolled up her sleeves and scrubbed every inch of the cabins and the galley with Clorox bleach.

Lizzy was sick the first few days. She wasn't sure what was worse — the smell of Clorox or the diesel fumes. Even the dog had the dry heaves. But as her parents promised, in a few days Lizzy had her sea legs and loved being at sea.

For the next three weeks, Carolina once more was Bud's crew. Lizzy had never known her mother to be happier. They all were. Those were the best days of her life. What child wouldn't love to watch a pod of dolphins race alongside the boat, playing in the wake? Or to run stark naked along a deserted beach, arms outstretched, with Lucy barking at her heels?

But now her father was missing. Lizzy felt a hot tear slide down her cheek. There was only one man in the entire world who could call her "Daddy's girl." She might never see him again, might never be held in her father's big, strong arms, see his gentle smile.

Lizzy heard footfalls rushing down the stairs and lifted her eyes to see her mother approaching clad in the white boots and yellow rain slicker worn by deckhands. She seemed hell-bent in a hurry, but stopped when she saw Lizzy.

"Oh, honey," Carolina murmured, and gathered her daughter in her arms.

Lizzy rested her head against her mother's shoulder. "Mama, what if we don't see him again? I didn't tell him I love him."

"He knows, Lizzy. He knows." Carolina smoothed Lizzy's hair and smiled with encouragement. "We have to be positive."

"Where you going?" Lizzy followed her mother to the kitchen.

Carolina grabbed a brown bag and lifted the platter of lasagna and some biscuits into it. "To find your father."

"What? How?"

Carolina moved to the fridge and began adding bottles of water and soda to the bag. "Pee Dee thinks he knows where your daddy might be. Josh is coming in with the *Hope*. I'm meeting him at the dock."

"Josh?"

Lizzy's gaze shot to a painting that was leaning against a kitchen chair. Carolina noticed and followed her gaze.

It was a moody painting, rich with blues and blacks. A young woman sat like a shadow on the dock, pensively gazing out to sea. Far out in the blue, a shrimp boat sailed, its rigging unfolded like wings as gulls circled, mere dots on the horizon. The painting elicited a keen sense of longing.

"It's one of John's, isn't it?" Carolina said. She walked closer, lifting it higher to study it.

"Mr. Dunnan dropped it off when he heard about Daddy," said Lizzy. "He thought it might bring me comfort. He saw me sitting there this morning. I didn't know he painted me."

Carolina nodded slowly in comprehension. She stared for a long moment at the painting of the shrimper's wife and saw herself — the young wife sitting on the dock, staring with longing at her husband's boat. She set the painting on the floor.

Then she turned to face Lizzy, swiping tears from her face. "Listen to me, Lizzy. I love you, but you're letting your life pass you by. Don't sit and wait for what you want to come to you. Maybe I was a poor example for you. I don't know. But Lizzy, life is short. You never know when you'll get a second chance. So if you know what you want, you get up and grab it, hear?"

Carolina held her daughter's face and bent to kiss her cheek fervently. Turning, she grabbed the bag of food and raced out the door.

"Mama?" Lizzy called, following her to the door. Her mother didn't stop. She jumped into the car, backed out, and roared down the street, her wheels spitting gravel.

An ambulance, a fire engine, an emergency rescue vehicle, two police cruisers, and two local television-station trucks clustered around the dock. Men and women in rescue gear chatted in small groups, waiting for word. The *Hope* was already in dock when Carolina returned. She was a smaller boat, but pretty. The pilothouse sat forward, with the rigging and single winch on the aft deck. Though she was an older boat, she was freshly painted. Spots of rust were wearing through the white, as was often the case with vintage vessels. It was obvious that Josh worked hard to maintain her. The *Hope* was aptly named.

Josh was coming out of the warehouse, walking fast. He wore his yellow slicker, and his dark hair was still damp from the storm. He lifted one hand in a wave. When he reached Carolina's side, she saw his dark eyes survey her work gear with a frown.

"I've finished unloading the shrimp and we're gassed up," he said. "Pee Dee's on board. We're about to shove off."

"I'm coming with you."

He turned his head and puffed his cheeks, exhaling loudly. "Carolina —" he began, sounding patronizing. "Ma'am . . ."

"No use arguing," she replied, and stepped toward the boat.

He took her arm. "We don't know what we'll find. You don't want to be there."

Carolina swung her head around, eyes flashing. She looked pointedly at his hand on her arm, and he immediately dropped it. "Look, that's my husband out there. And my boat. I'll be damned if I'm going to be left on this dock again. So lend a hand. I'm coming aboard."

Resignation flooded his features. "Pee Dee!" he bellowed. Pee Dee hurried out of the pilothouse to the railing. "Well, what are you waiting for? Help her up!"

It was high tide, and the boat's railing rose five feet above the dock. Pee Dee took Carolina's hand while she placed her foot in Josh's clasped palms. Together they boosted her on board.

Josh unhooked the bow line from the dock cleat while Pee Dee headed for the stern.

"Josh! Wait!"

Carolina heard the voice and turned to see Lizzy running across the gravel parking lot. Her red-gold hair flailed behind her, caught by the wind.

Josh dropped the rope and took off at a sprint to meet her. He grasped her arms while she leaned into him, catching her breath.

"You're going to find my father?"

"Yes."

"Let me go with you."

"No, Lizzy. You can't come."

"But Mama —"

"She knows what she's doing out there. Lizzy, please. Don't ask me." He looked into her eyes, imploring. "Please."

Her shoulders slumped and she burst into tears.

Josh held her close and rested his cheek on her head. "I'll find him," he said in a husky voice. "I haven't been good at keeping my vows, but I swear to you, I'll bring him home. Do you believe me? Will you wait here for me?"

Lizzy leaned back in his arms so she could see his face. A thousand unspoken promises were shared in that gaze.

"Yes."

He swooped to kiss her as she rose on tiptoe and slid her arms around his neck.

Releasing her, he ran back to the *Hope* as Pee Dee jerked the stern line from the piling. Josh jumped aboard and ran to the pilothouse. A moment later, the engine roared and the water churned.

As the *Hope* pulled away from the dock, Carolina waved to her daughter. Lizzy lifted her hand and waved back. She moved her lips. Carolina thought she said "I love you," but didn't believe the words were meant for her.

18

September 21, 2008, 5:00 p.m.
On board the Hope
Josh pushed the throttle forward. The *Hope* surged ahead, slicing through the Atlantic. The splash of saltwater hit the windows like pellets. Carolina clutched his chair with white knuckles and winced each time the bow of the boat hammered into the water. Pee Dee looked nervously at Josh. They all knew the boat was being stressed.

"What makes you think he's out this far?" Josh asked Pee Dee.

Pee Dee's eyes were on the darkening horizon. "Just do."

"Yeah? Well, we're pinning a hell of a lot on your intuition here."

"He's out here. Bud, he knows secret spots. This be one of 'em. We'll find him. If you don't bust the boat first. That engine's gonna blow."

"I want to get there quick." He glanced at

Carolina, then added, "Just in case. I'm sure there's nothing wrong."

Carolina didn't reply. She knew something was desperately wrong. She couldn't put it into words, but she sensed time was of the essence. The possibilities were too numerous to think about. Bud could be injured and in need of immediate medical help. The *Miss Carolina* could have sunk and Bud was hanging on to some life jacket in the cold water, sharks circling. If he was overboard, he'd be hard to locate. Or they could already be too late. Josh knew all this. Pee Dee, too. They all knew Bud would never fail to respond to an urgent call if he could help it. No fisherman would.

"Did you work it by miles, markers, what?" Josh asked.

"Both. We only come out about a dozen times, but I know where." Pee Dee drew a cigarette from the pack, then his lighter from his pocket. "Don't you worry yourself none. I'll let you know when we're close."

Josh grew irritated. He bent over the radar, scanning for any sign of other vessels. "There's nobody out here. There's no goddamn way he'd be this far out. This isn't some seventy-foot trawler. I don't have a big fuel tank." He rolled his shoulders, anxious. "Nobody comes this far out."

416

"We do. Fishing was great."

"Bullshit." He bent back over the radar, and for a long while no one spoke. There was only the reassuring drone of the engines and the omnipresent smell of diesel in the cramped cabin. Suddenly, Josh's body tensed.

"Hold on. . . . What's this?"

Carolina and Pee Dee leaned to look over his shoulder. An electronic blip flashed on the glowing green radar screen, a small pebble in an acre of ocean.

"Told ya!" Pee Dee cried, slapping Josh on the back. "That's the spot. That's got to be him."

"Thank God," Carolina cried.

The engine didn't have anything left, but that didn't prevent Josh from pressing on the throttle. The engine screamed and the propeller roared as the *Hope* lurched.

"Come on, baby," Josh pleaded. "You can do it."

The *Miss Carolina* was still miles away. Josh immediately picked up the radio handset and switched over to the Coast Guard channel.

"This is Josh Truesdale aboard the *Hope*. We think we've spotted the *Miss Carolina*."

As Josh responded to the regimented questions as to coordinates, Pee Dee dashed out to check the engine. He didn't like the sounds it was making. Carolina paced. Her hands were clenched at her breast, and she prayed like she'd never prayed before.

Josh switched the radio to the local frequencies to report his coordinates to the other captains. If it was the *Miss Carolina,* they were likely to be the first to board. There were shouts of excitement and good-natured jokes as friends cheered the news, and in the background they heard the joyful din of blaring horns. Josh talked excitedly for a while, answering questions, as he kept his hands clenched to the wheel. When he finished, his face grew somber.

"You okay?" Carolina asked.

"We'll get there in time."

Carolina lowered her head. "I may forget to say this later," she said to Josh. "But thank you for bringing me. And Pee Dee. I needed to be here."

Josh's eyes swam with emotion. "You know, there are some days I question why I am a shrimper. I've got to be crazy, right? Every day we face these dangers and the long hours and the tough conditions — and for what? The money is lousy; I worry if I can keep my boat afloat in these hard times. Then I get calls from guys like that." He indicated with a lift of his chin the radio and the conversations he'd just had. "Every man out there hides his secret fishing spot jealously, but every man out there would risk his life for me. I know it. And Bud is the best of them. He taught me what I know about shrimping. But he also taught me how to be a man. Not some jerk who can drink and screw, but a real man — a husband and a father.

"Hell, Carolina, you know how it is. I'm young, and I know I should be thinking of doing something else to provide for my family. Something Lizzy would feel secure with. I love her something awful. I'm afraid to lose her again. But shrimping is my heritage. It's in my blood." He shook his head. "When I get back, I'm going to ask Lizzy to marry me again. After today, I don't want to wait. I want a life with her and Will. I only hope she'll say yes."

He looked at her, hoping for an answer, or at least some encouraging words. Carolina leaned back against the wall and sighed. She recalled the expression on her daughter's face as they'd left the dock. Something had changed for Lizzy today. She saw it in the way Lizzy held on to Josh, in her eyes as she watched him board the *Hope.* Still, their path wouldn't be an easy one. What couple could say theirs was?

"I can't speak for Lizzy," she replied slowly. "No decision doesn't hold some promise, and some regret. What you two have doesn't come along every day. You have to fight for it. Work hard at it. Marriage isn't easy, whether you're rich or poor. You know Bud and I have had a long ride. We've had good times and bad. There's no secret there. But I made my choice years ago. And given the choice again, I'd choose him and this life all over again. But I'll tell you this. We used to do everything together. And if I get the chance, I swear to God we'll do everything together again."

The door to the pilothouse pushed open and Pee Dee came in with a gust of wind.

"Heads up! I think I see something out there. We're getting close!"

19

September 21, 2008, 5:15 p.m.
On board the Miss Carolina

It's funny how things clear up after a storm, Bud thought as he looked out at a sky of stunning beauty. Vivid orange-pink clouds splayed like a painter's brushstrokes against a vivid sapphire sky. Great shafts of gold light pierced through to shimmer over the water.

Ah, Bobby, where are you now? he wondered. *Are you up there somewhere in the clouds? You'd like that, wouldn't you? Sitting up there with the angels, laughing at us poor devils down here. Especially me. Remember how we used to swim in the creek like Huck Finn and Tom Sawyer, trying to touch manatees? Or racing dolphins in the jon boat, and riding the backs of sea turtles? Life seemed simpler then. Freer with fewer rules. Or did I just grow old? We sure had good times together, back in the day.* He felt hot tears streaming down his cheeks. *My God, Bobby. I miss you.*

"Ah, Carolina," he said to his boat in a raspy voice. His mouth was so dry he could barely speak. "We've been through a lot together. You've heard all my stories, haven't you? And I know all of yours."

He stroked the wood, now steeped with his own blood. "You and me, we're one now, right? You carry my blood in the grain of your wood. You've been a good boat. The best. It wasn't your fault what happened. I don't blame you. We'll ride this last trip out together."

20

September 21, 2008, 6:05 p.m.
On board the Hope

Pee Dee raised his arm and pointed south. "Look there!"

Josh swung his head in that direction.

Carolina sucked in her breath. She saw what appeared to be a boat a few miles down. Even from this distance, she could make out the tall rigging that could only be a shrimp boat. She lunged for the binoculars and lifted them to her eyes. She saw the outriggers lowered, the nets hanging empty in the wind. There was the berry-red trim of the Morrison boats. And there, at the bow, were the bright red letters.

"It's the *Carolina,*" she said, her voice trembling.

Pee Dee took the binoculars. His hands shook as he brought them to his eyes. "Don't look like there's any damage done to her."

"You don't know that," Josh replied, caution in his tone. "Could be taking on water, for all we know. Damage below the waterline, blown engine, anything."

"If it were something like that, he coulda used the radio," countered Pee Dee.

Josh opened his mouth as if he might argue, then cast a quick glance at Carolina. There was still no sign of Bud. The less movement they saw on the boat, the more worried they became. There was always movement on a shrimping boat. He shot Pee Dee a warning glare to be careful of what he said in front of Carolina.

"Yeah, reckon that's right," Pee Dee muttered.

Carolina wrapped her arms around her chest. "You boys don't have to pussyfoot around me. You're not saying anything I haven't thought already. But I think he's alive. I feel it."

She saw them once again cast worried glances at each other, like maybe she was losing it. Maybe she was. Carolina thrust her arms into her slicker, eager to be alone.

"At least, I'm praying that's true," she said, then left the pilothouse.

Carolina hurried to the bow and clutched the railing, willing the boat to move faster. The *Hope* was rattling and shaking, stressed to the max as it ripped through choppy seas. Saltwater sprayed from the bow, stinging her face. She turned her head to look at the T-shaped radar beacon steadily revolving above the pilothouse. Keep on target, she thought. Excitement, fear, trepidation, hope — every conceivable emotion ran through her veins.

She turned her gaze back to the sea. Her hair whipped in the wind. Squinting, she kept her gaze riveted to the blue horizon that was slowly deepening to rose, orange, purple, and blue. Somewhere ahead in that vast sea, she had to believe that Bud was holding on. That he had faith. That he was waiting for them. Waiting for her.

"Dear God," she prayed, "Bud has to be alive. Please."

In the seven years since their reconciliation, they'd struggled to rebuild their marriage. It was hard at first. Whenever they were together, it was like walking on eggs. But they hung in there, got counseling, and slowly found solid ground again. Bud had stopped going to Florida during the off-season and instead fell back on oystering, clamming, piloting tugboats, and other odd jobs to make ends meet. Carolina had gone back to teaching at the local elementary school. Each morning they'd awakened, done their work, eaten their meals, shared the joy of their grandchild, and gradually found pleasure in each other as well.

After the first two years, Carolina had just been grateful that they were still together and hoped that, in time, they would regain that comfortable, open, say-anything closeness. Two more years passed, one much like the other, and Carolina began to fear that their marriage would never again be whole. Bud was holding back. It was so subtle that at times she thought herself mistaken. He was a good husband on the surface. But small significant gestures had ceased, things like a guiding hand at her back as she walked down the street, or her suddenly looking up in a crowded room and meeting his knowing gaze, or even just his sudden grasping of her hand with a reassuring squeeze. These seemingly inconsequential gestures had stopped — and she missed them. Terribly. With their loss came a slow decline in how often they made love, or kissed, or hugged. And when they did, the molten passion they'd once shared had dissipated to a lukewarm response.

She kept thinking, Tomorrow he will kiss me like he used to. Or the next day he'll hold my hand. Or the next.

But he didn't. Those days never came.

Carolina had tried to rationalize the cooling of their ardor to age. After all, it was happening to other couples she knew. But in her heart, she knew it was more. Bud might not even be aware of what he was doing. He wasn't a vindictive man. Still, she sensed that his holding back was a kind of punishment for her indiscretion.

Bud loved her. She knew that much was true.

But in her heart, Carolina knew that he had not forgiven her.

She gripped the railing and stared out at the vast blue for some sign — any marker at all — of Bud. She needed to find him alive. One more time, she needed to tell Bud that she loved him. She needed to ask his forgiveness once again.

21

September 21, 2008, 6:30 p.m.
On board the Miss Carolina

Bud's head was too heavy to hold upright. His eyes felt swollen and gritty. He rested his head against his arm while the boat rocked from side to side. The *Miss Carolina* was like a cradle, he thought. Rocking, rocking, back and forth . . . He felt himself drift in and out of consciousness. His vision was blurry. It was too much of a struggle to keep his lids open. He was sorely tempted to simply close his eyes and fall asleep. But he was afraid if he did, he wouldn't wake up.

So he fought to keep his focus with memories.

Not sad ones. Those sad times didn't matter anymore. The times in life he'd cried had only left him feeling regret and remorse. He had lots of good memories, too. Good times with his family and loved ones.

And Carolina.

Nothing in his life compared to his love for her. Images of their life together shone in his mind like a kaleidoscope, one brighter than the next. Bud saw again Carolina's face that first day he'd met her on the docks. Her red hair held the sun like a flame, and when he locked gazes with her, he knew she was the girl he would marry.

Carolina climbing high up on the rigging, clinging tight to the ladder, her hair flapping in the wind, a wide smile on her face as she surveyed her domain. She didn't know that he'd watched her from the deck, his chest expanding with love and pride that this exceptional woman was his bride.

Lizzy had taken to the sea like her mother, but he'd never let her run the boat or man the deck like his father had done with him from the moment he could walk. Like he would have done had Lizzy been born a male. Bud had thought keeping his daughter from shrimping was the right thing to do, that he was protecting her from harm. Now he wondered whether, had he given Lizzy a chance at sea, she might have captained her own boat, like Judith.

Another regret.

His regrets now were not for what he had done, but for what he had *not* done in his life. There had been so many opportunities to say what he felt, but he'd remained silent. So many chances to act on an impulse of kindness, but he'd stayed still. He saw now how everything he did or said — or neglected to — had cast ripples that affected so many lives.

Now it was too late. Now he lay pinned by his regrets.

You fool, he told himself, feeling his breath shorten. You're dying. You can't lie to yourself anymore. You've been blind the last seven years. Only feeling your own pain. Pawing at the ground, no better than a speared bull. You hurt Carolina. Admit it.

He sighed and closed his eyes. You didn't even kiss her goodbye this morning. You had the chance, but you held back.

Bud lowered his head, tasting the ash of his marriage in his mouth. They'd seen the counselor and made compromises. They'd jumped through hoops. But in his heart, Bud knew he'd never really forgiven Carolina. Why? he asked himself. Was it his male pride? A grudge against Lee Edwards? Did he enjoy having the upper hand with Carolina?

Yes, he thought, that was it. By punishing her, he'd maintained control over her. Carolina's spirit was wounded, and his distance had kept her in line. Wasn't this a kind of betrayal?

Forgiveness had seemed so heroic. In the end, he'd been a coward. He said that he loved her, but now he knew he hadn't begun to understand the meaning of the word. Love had the power to forgive.

What a waste of precious time! Now he might never have the chance to tell her again that he loved her. That he forgave her. And to beg her forgiveness. If he could just get back, he swore, he'd set things right with Carolina. With Lizzy. With Josh. Even with Lee. Anger was such a waste of time, especially knowing how precious time was.

"Hey, God," he said aloud, pushing his voice out, hoping to be heard. "I don't deserve to ask you anything, so I'm not asking for much. Take my hand. My arm. I don't care if I lose my boat. If it's my time, well, okay. I'm only asking — no, I'm begging. Let me live long enough to make things right with Carolina. That's all."

Bud felt his heart pounding and his vision blurred. Closing his eyes, he felt his strength ebb. Immediately, Carolina's face was illuminated in his mind. Carolina. It was always Carolina. She stood at the bow of the boat named for her, leaning back in his arms, her warmth melding into his, smelling sweet, her hair blowing in the wind, her cheeks flushed and her eyes filled with stars. Whenever he thought of Carolina, he thought of her here, on this boat. When Carolina was in his arms, they were ageless. There was no time.

His life had come full circle. Carolina was his past, his present, his hope for the future. He reached up to clutch the gold band that hung from a chain around his neck. He held it tight against his heart as he felt himself slip into oblivion.

22

September 21, 2008, 6:40 p.m.
On board the Hope

Josh slowed the engine to idle as they neared the *Miss Carolina.* Carolina stood on deck, peering across the water. There was no sign of Bud. No shout of hello. A line of gulls sat on the rigging, silent as the grave. She shuddered. It looked like a ghost ship.

"You're going to have to jump for it," Josh called to Pee Dee from the pilothouse. "I'll get you as close as I can."

Josh worked the wheel to maneuver his trawler closer to the *Miss Carolina,* careful not to scrape the boats in the rocking of the waves. Carolina licked her lips and stood at the ready, clenching the rope.

Pee Dee eyed the *Miss Carolina;* then, when the boats were close enough, he flung himself over several feet of open water, landing in a graceless heap on the deck. He scrambled to his feet, and Carolina tossed him a line, which he quickly tied to the boat. Josh cut the engine and ran from the pilot-house to pull the two boats close and tie them off.

Carolina was already at the railing, preparing to jump.

"You better wait here," he told Carolina, grabbing her arm.

"He's my husband."

Josh's brows furrowed. As captain, he was responsible for every man and woman on his vessel, and Carolina knew he was afraid for more than her safety. He was worried about what she might find aboard the *Miss Carolina*.

"Let me know what to do," he said, letting go of her arm.

Carolina kissed his cheek, then turned and leaped across the water to land on her feet aboard the *Miss Carolina*. She wobbled but spread her arms and caught her balance. Taking a breath, she exhaled and raised her head. She'd made it. She straightened and took a look around.

Pee Dee stood a few feet away, frozen to the spot. He was pale and rigid, staring fixedly. Carolina felt her blood drain and steeled herself. Then she followed Pee Dee's line of vision and saw what he saw.

"Oh, Bud. . . ."

Bud was slumped against the winch with his head on his arm. Her first thought was that he looked like he was taking a nap. The exposed skin at the back of his neck was sunburned. His shirttails stirred in the breeze, but that was the only discernible movement.

Then she saw the blood. An ungodly amount of dried and fresh blood pooled on the deck beneath his body. She blanched. No one could lose that much blood and still be alive, she thought.

Carolina stared at her husband and slipped into a surreal calm. She was good in emergencies. At the elementary school, she was always called if a child got hurt because she acted calmly, could make good decisions, and knew basic first aid. Carolina moved as though in slow motion to Bud's side.

"Bud?" she called to him.

When he didn't reply, Carolina knelt beside his body. Blood soaked through the knees of her jeans. She placed her palm on his shoulder and gently shook him.

"Bud. Bud," she called, louder this time.

She reached up to his carotid artery, the last pulse you lose before you die. His skin felt clammy, but not cold. She was stunned to feel a pulse.

"He's alive!" she shouted, tears springing to her eyes. "Pee Dee, tell Josh to radio for a medevac team. We need a rescue helicopter."

Pee Dee still stood frozen, his eyes wide and his mouth hanging open in shock.

"Go!" she barked.

Pee Dee jolted and ran to the railing, calling for Josh.

Carolina tried to move Bud into her arms, and it was then she saw that his hand was completely caught in the winch. The skin below the tourniquet was the chalky color of clay. There would be no saving his hand, maybe not the arm.

But Bud was alive! Her prayers were answered. Though he was critically hurt, possibly in shock, he was alive.

"Pee Dee! Go get blankets. Lots of them!"

Slowly, carefully, she eased his body back to rest against her chest, cradling him. She saw that his hand clutched his gold wedding band, which hung from a chain around his neck. This simple gesture brought tears to her eyes.

Bud's face was the color of porcelain, and she knew he was very near death. She brought her lips to his cheek.

"Don't you die on me," she said to him, close to his ear. "Do you hear me? It's

Carolina. I'm here, Bud. Hold on, hear? We're taking you home."

Then, to her astonishment, Bud slowly opened his eyes. She drew back, calling his name. His eyes were dilated and he seemed confused, as though he didn't recognize her. Then his lips spread in a weak smile.

"Carolina. . . ." His voice cracked. It sounded like dried wheat.

"I'm here, Bud. I'm here."

She turned to Pee Dee, who'd returned with the blankets. Together they spread them over Bud, one on top of the other. Pee Dee hovered anxiously.

"Get some water," she told him. Pee Dee hurried off, glad to have a job to do.

The sky was darkening around them, and she knew each moment worked against them. There was so little she could do to help Bud. Her gaze scanned the deck as they rocked in the ocean, and she realized in a flash how terrible it must have been for Bud to be pinned for hours, unable to help himself, unable even to call for help.

When Pee Dee returned with a cup, Carolina poured a small amount of the water into Bud's mouth. He coughed a little, but sighed when he swallowed, seeming relieved.

"They're comin', Bud. Don't worry," Pee

437

Dee said.

Bud raised his hand in a weak acknowledgment. Carolina grabbed it and held it tight. Again, he focused on her.

"Carolina . . ."

She looked into his eyes, holding his hand tight in hers. "I'm here."

"Forgive me," he said.

Carolina choked back a cry as tears flowed down her cheeks. "Forgive *me.*"

He squeezed her hand. It was a faint movement, but she felt it to her core.

"We'll try again," she said, believing the words.

Bud felt himself drifting. Pee Dee scrambled to tie down equipment and pack away loose ropes, cable, and anything else that could be dangerous when blown by the hurricane-force wind of helicopter rotor blades. Josh was shouting instructions from aboard the *Hope.*

Around him, the light was fading fast. Bud lay in his wife's arms and looked at the sunset that exploded across the horizon. Translucent purpling clouds drifted against a backdrop of spellbinding oranges, reds, and yellows.

But it was the great sun that demanded his attention. A diva, the sun was a fireball in a blazing orange-red sky. The great flaming orb took center stage, glorying in her resplendent beauty as she descended, slowly, delicately, soundlessly into the ocean. The sea welcomed her, absorbing her colors, reflecting her brilliance in its shimmering water. The sky and sea danced a duet of unsurpassed beauty and incomparable grace. It was a gift to behold. The coup de grâce before darkness fell.

In his lifetime, Bud had seen countless sunrises and sunsets. On this day, he'd journeyed from first light to last light. It was the voyage of a lifetime. And this was the most beautiful sunset he'd ever seen.

Bud closed his eyes, smiling.

23

May 2, 2009, Blessing of the Fleet
On board the Miss Carolina

The Blessing of the Fleet is an ancient ritual dating back to the Council of Nicea in AD 325, based on the belief that all people were called upon by God to be good to one another and responsible stewards of the earth. In return, God blessed them with their survival and a bountiful catch.

The Blessing of the Fleet has continued in many coastal villages. In McClellanville, the ritual has gained momentum each year, blossoming into a popular seafood festival held on the first Saturday of May. It is a day so revered that townsfolk mark it on the calendar before birthdays. For weeks prior, the docks are lined with trawlers preparing for the event. Boats are scraped, cleaned, and given a fresh coat of paint. Engines are tuned, bolts tightened, rigging checked, and nets sewn.

Every May, the town's population of 500 swells to 15,000 as tourists swarm the narrow roads, parks, and docks to buy local art, sweetgrass baskets, and crafts, and to dance, drink, and eat. And was there ever good eating — shrimp kebabs, boiled shrimp, fried shrimp, shrimp salad, Frogmore stew, crab bisque, seafood chowder, and barbecue, all served under white tents. Most of all, folks come to watch the magnificent spectacle of boats festooned with colorful streamers and pennants in the grand parade down Jeremy Creek.

Bud stood on the deck of the *Miss Carolina* and surveyed the milling crowd. The spring sun was high overhead and a stream of people and cars kept flowing in. At the dock, a long line of people jockeyed into position to climb aboard the vessels. These were prized seats, invitation only. Friends and family members who had moved away still felt the pull of the sea and returned to town for the parade. The trawlers were jammed full of revelers, young and old alike, ready to celebrate the opening of the shrimping season.

Carolina welcomed each guest aboard the *Miss Carolina* with a hug and a wide smile. Her joy could not be contained and shone from her eyes under the brim of her broad straw hat. In her jean shorts and festival T-shirt, Bud thought she looked like the twenty-two-year-old girl he'd met long ago at a dance he now found difficult to recall. He only remembered Carolina.

Bud rubbed his left elbow, where a phantom pain still sparked from time to time. In many ways, Carolina was that young gal from the dance again. Where had the years gone? he wondered. He didn't feel older. He just recognized the mileage on his face when he looked in the mirror. It was like sailing absentmindedly on a calm sea and suddenly realizing how far offshore you'd traveled.

When he'd left the hospital without his hand, he'd felt lost. Aimless. Used up. He'd even thought about selling the boat and looking for a land job. Carolina had refused to even consider selling the *Miss Carolina.* Now, she was back working on the boat that bore her name. She was his first mate, his right hand — or, as he liked to joke, now she was his right *and* left hands.

Bud knew he was a lucky man. In the seven months since his accident, they'd found their way back to that time when they were first married and worked together. It had been a long, arduous winter, and there still were tough days ahead. He wasn't naïve about that. They'd have to struggle to eke out a living. Fuel costs would always be a worry, and foreign shrimp would still be dumped in local markets. Those were the cruel facts of the industry.

Bud's gaze traveled beyond the crowd to the water glistening in a winding path through the marsh toward the great sea, and he felt a joy and contentment with life that only a man who had faced death could feel.

When the helicopter had delivered him to the hospital, he was more dead than alive. There were folks who believed his survival was nothing short of a miracle. Bud didn't see it that way. To his mind, that September day was just not his time.

He knew the hour of his death was marked in some great book in heaven, and when that day came, he'd go along without complaint. After all, he'd been given a glimpse of what was to come and the kinds of questions he'd be asked before he was allowed through those pearly gates. As tough as that day on the ocean had been, as rotten as it was that he'd lost his left arm and hand, Bud knew that God had given him a rare insight. He was blessed with knowing that each day since the accident was a gift.

Bud had never been a man of many words, and he didn't like to talk about what he'd experienced as he lay dying. Sure, he'd told stories to the guys about how he'd tied the tourniquet using his teeth and how he'd planned to cut off his hand with his pocket-knife. He was a southern male and had learned at his daddy's knee how to embellish a good tale. But he'd never told anyone except Carolina of those otherworldly experiences that some might call profound and others might call crazy.

So many scenes of his life had darted through his mind, so vivid and real that it was like living them all over again. Even now, when he looked back on past events, he saw them with greater clarity. One night after a few beers, Bud had told Pee Dee how he'd sat side by side with the spirit of his brother Bobby. Pee Dee had stared back, tears in his eyes, then shaken his head and muttered, "Well, I'll be." That was all he'd said, but Bud knew the story had brought him some comfort. Bud didn't tell him how he'd have gone to the other side with Bobby, willingly, if it weren't for Carolina.

Carolina had saved him. Not only because she'd enlisted Josh and Pee Dee to find him in the ocean. Carolina had been the line that kept him tethered to the earth when he was so near to leaving it. He'd thought he wanted to stay because he was worried about paying bills and keeping up the boat and maintaining the house. He'd thought that he was bound by his duty as a man to provide for his family. Only in hindsight did he understand that he'd been wrong to think food on the table and a roof overhead were the only measures of a man. In the end, none of those earthly concerns mattered at all. He'd learned that a man had to guide his family with as steady a hand and heart as he did his boat. To give them, at the very least, the attention and love that came so easily for his ship. That's what mattered.

On that day, he'd heard the question: *Was I loved, and did I love in return?* He knew he loved — and he hoped for the rest.

Life was short. Each sunrise could be his last. Bud only knew that he didn't want to die regretting lost opportunities for love and forgiveness. Not that it was easy. He'd lost his arm at the elbow. The seven months of recovery had been hell. He was glad to have a pulse, but the pain of surgery and recovery were brutal. Without insurance, he could have been up the creek in debt.

He'd never thought Carolina would sell White Gables.

Carolina had put the house on the market while he was in the hospital, and it had sold quickly to a wealthy couple from Georgia looking for a historic coastal property. Carolina was comforted knowing that the new owners loved the old house and would be able to afford the upgrades and rehab that it needed. She had kept a few pieces of furniture that had special meaning to her and let Lizzy choose whatever pieces she wanted, too. The rest, she'd sold at an estate sale.

Carolina said it was time to let the dead help the living.

Carolina had given some of the money to pay for Bud's prosthesis and to settle bills. Then she and Bud had bought a modest house in the village. She also gave Lizzy money for college. She'd told her daughter they'd all learned not to put off their dreams.

Bud looked down at the sleek apparatus that emerged from the cuff of his cotton shirt. The guys at the dock called him Captain Hook. He thought it childish, but knew it made them feel better. All he knew was this thing made it possible for him to get back on the ocean. One arm or two, as long as there was a breath in him, Bud would be captain of the *Miss Carolina.*

The unmistakable tones of bagpipes carried by the wind signaled the beginning of the procession for the blessing. The parish priests in flowing garments followed the bagpipes to the point of land that overlooked Jeremy Creek. Suddenly, the creek sprang to life with the sound of roaring engines. Around him, trawler after trawler churned the water as the crowd cheered. Bud fired his engine. Immediately, the smell of diesel fuel filled the small compartment and the *Miss Carolina* rocked beneath his feet. Carolina and Pee Dee leaped to untie the lines. Once she was freed, Bud guided the *Miss Carolina* away from the dock. His movements were still clumsy, but he got the job done.

Carolina came to his side at the wheel and wrapped her arms around his waist. She looked up at him, and once again, in her eyes he found his redemption.

"Look, your father's waving at you to follow him," she said, pointing toward the *Cap'n and Bobby.* Oz, ever the controller, wanted the Morrison boats to line up as a united front. Bud brought the *Miss Carolina* forward to take her place behind Oz's trawler, then handed the wheel over to Carolina and went aft to signal to the *Hope* to follow. He smiled at the sight of the berry-red Morrison trim on the small, scrappy boat. It was official, now that Josh and Lizzy were remarried. Young Will waved back at him, smiling proudly beside his father.

One by one the shrimp boats took their places in line as they slowly motored down the muddy waterway. Oz blared the horn of the *Cap'n and Bobby*. Behind him, Josh responded with a toot from the *Hope*. Bud looked at his wife, his brows raised. Carolina laughed and did the honors. The spectators lining the shore cheered as each boat honked its horn. Some vessels bore signs that read: EAT LOCAL SHRIMP! Music was blaring and folks were in a party mood. Men holding beer cans told jokes and laughed, baring burned shoulders and white bellies to the spring sun. Pretty girls wearing dark sunglasses and skimpy shirts waved, their flowing hair — red, yellow, brown — fluttering in the wind like the pennants on the rigging. Mothers with children in their arms smiled and waved American flags.

As they approached the Point, the raucous group hushed in solemn anticipation. When the *Miss Carolina* drew up before the priests, Bud took Carolina's hand. Nobody could hear the words of the priest onshore, but they understood the meaning behind the ceremony. Bud brought to mind the prayers he'd cried out to God when he was alone at sea, back when the wind had screamed and rattled the groaning riggings and the waves had crashed against the boat, swamping it with more water than he thought the vessel could carry.

Fishing was an ancient tradition, thousands of years old. What was true for the fishermen in AD 325 was still true for them today. People were more alike than they were different. They were all drops in the same great sea. Bud knew others would lead better lives if they shared his vantage point. But everyone was the captain of his own ship. That was something each person had to discover on his own time. Bud bowed his head as the *Miss Carolina* received her blessing.

Looking up, Bud gazed out at the winding creek. The shrimp boats moved in a graceful line through the muddy water, their flags and streamers flapping in the wind. One by one, they rounded the curve and disappeared, heading out to sea. Bud felt his chest swell with hope and blew his horn triumphantly. His family and friends on board cheered loudly. Bud threw back his head and laughed. As Jimmy Buffett sang in one of Bud's favorite songs, he was the son of a son of a sailor. He had his wife at his

side, his friends close by, the open sea
ahead. . . .

What more could a man want?

The employees of Thorndike Press hope you have enjoyed this Large Print book. All our Thorndike, Wheeler, and Kennebec Large Print titles are designed for easy reading, and all our books are made to last. Other Thorndike Press Large Print books are available at your library, through selected bookstores, or directly from us.

For information about titles, please call:
(800) 223-1244

or visit our Web site at:
http://gale.cengage.com/thorndike

To share your comments, please write:
Publisher
Thorndike Press
10 Water St., Suite 310
Waterville, ME 04901